DEBORAH DOBBS

The Psychotic Son

All Rights Reserved

The Psychotic Son © 2023 by Anatolian Press

This is a work of fiction. Names, characters, businesses, places, events, locales, and incidents are either the product of the author's imagination or used fictitiously. Any resemblance to actual persons, living or dead, or actual events is purely coincidental. No part of this book may be reproduced or used in any manner without the written permission of the copyright owner except for the use of quotations in a book review. For more information, email micah@anatolianpressllc.com

Cover design by Jerry Todd

Book design by Micah Campbell

Editing by Aaron Kintzle

First paperback edition June 2023
Paperback ISBN: 978-1-959396-25-3
eBook ISBN: 978-1-959396-27-7
Hardcover ISBN: 978-1-959396-26-0

Please visit us at
www.anatolianpressllc.com

For Faith ♡

1

He left the girl in a heap on the floor of the master bathroom, crying and gasping for air. In case she was tempted to call for help, he grabbed her new Nokia mobile phone and crammed it into the front pocket of his jeans. He'd wanted a piece of cutting-edge tech but never had the cash for it. Often after delivering consequences, he longed for a snack, so he exited the bedroom, locked the door, and walked down the aged staircase.

No matter the season, whenever at home, he preferred to be barefoot and shirtless. Smaller in stature than his peers, he compensated with resistance training and a sizable vocabulary. Admittedly slight, he was fit and extraordinarily strong. There was a time when he resented the mediocre height and spindly limbs he'd inherited from his mother, but over the years, he'd witnessed how his size came in handy. Smaller guys didn't arouse suspicion. Plus, he was higher in intelligence than all of his peers and most adults. He'd take wit over weight any day of the week. He descended the stairs slowly, admiring his fibrous abs with each deliberate step.

When he reached the first floor, he noticed the familiar blue glow from the television seeping into the hallway from under the guest bedroom door. He hadn't heard his mother return. Had she heard the ruckus above? His mother had moved to the first floor long ago, claiming the stairs were hard on her knees. He knew the real reason. She'd relocated to increase the distance between them and decrease the distance between her and her escape out the front door. Curiosity drew him closer, and he tested the handle.

Locked.

Twelve years his mother had been locking her bedroom door, barricading herself inside before fading to sleep. It was a futile maneuver. If he wanted her dead, and he'd considered ending her too many times to count, he didn't need to wait until dark to do it. He often dreamed of slipping into her bedroom with his Taurus 9mm, calling her name to wake her so that he could see the shock and horror on her face as he pulled the trigger. He rested his forehead against the door, closed his eyes, and listened. She was watching her new obsession, something called "Medical Detectives." She'd set up her fancy little VCR to record it every week. He sniffed around the frame. She was smoking again. Whenever she tried to quit, she became a bundle of anxiety. It was hilarious.

    He didn't know what anxiety, joy, or sadness felt like, but he knew what they looked like on the faces of others. He could mimic a number of expressions convincingly now. Sadness still needed fine tuning, and manufacturing tears proved too difficult, but most emotions he feigned were believable. Over the years, he'd learned the role context played, too. Shock, for instance, was indicated by a mouth agape and eyes wide opened. But his mother's features contorted in the same way when she was applying mascara. A similar thing had happened when his father cleaned his pistol -- lips tightened, eyes squinted, and brows narrowed. Without context, the man would've appeared angry, but he was simply focused on his task.

    His father had been cleaning his Colt 1911 pistol the last time he saw him, which was also the first time he'd observed the countenance of terror. Eyebrows high and pulled together, upper eyelids raised and lower lids tensed, nostrils flared, lips stretched toward the ears, jaw dropped open and teeth slightly exposed. It was a mesmerizing final expression on his father's face, a response to a bullet unexpectedly entering his body. The details were remarkably similar on his mother's face when she returned home to find the boy coloring in his room and her husband dead on the floor with the 1911 at his feet. He'd studied his mother's clumsy moves as she fell to her knees trying to wake up his father, as she scurried out of the room to check on his baby brother, wailing in his crib. He observed how she dropped the phone and struggled to dial the numbers on the keypad, her frenetic speech as she begged for help in between answering questions that clearly infuriated her. The baby's cries, his mother's cries. Discordant, clashing, and then harmonious.

"Please hurry," she'd sobbed and tried to follow instructions coming from the other end of the line while tending to baby Matthew.

"Help me, damn it!" she'd spat at the boy.

Without emotion, he'd collected the baby and returned to a seated position, criss-cross applesauce, with the wailing infant draped across his lap.

He'd detected a hurricane of activity in his mother and realized the immensity of the chaos that followed a simple press of a trigger. He looked down at his right index finger, bent it and straightened it. He looked back to his mother, her face wet with tears, snot streaming from her nostrils. At his age, his vocabulary was too limited to describe the sensation, but he would seek it for the rest of his days.

Back in 1984, detectives weren't inclined to interview five-year-olds. He'd made it easier for them and for himself by going mute while they worked the scene. He'd overheard a gray-haired man in a suit refer to the wound as "the money shot." The bullet had entered his father's lower left side, tore through his left lung, his heart, and his right lung, exited through his right shoulder, and facilitated a swift death. He'd heard a cop in uniform answer, "Seems like a strange angle for a suicide." He heard a few other phrases, like "*light trigger*" and "*hand-washing*," and the gray-haired man whispered, "Even if the kid did it, what the hell can we do about it?"

They'd decided to kick the can to the medical examiner. He could decide between an accident or suicide.

The police confiscated the gun, and his mother told them she didn't want it back. That's the first time he noticed a change in his mother. He'd never craved hugs and kisses, but he understood that his mother did, so he'd approached her and leaned against her leg while she talked to the men in suits. Her muscles had tightened, and her arms had remained crossed. She hadn't stroked his hair or patted his back. In fact, she'd created an excuse to put space between them.

"I have to make some calls now," she'd said with a chill in her voice. When she escorted the last detective to the door, her mother locked eyes with the man's. Their expressions looked almost the same, only the detective's eyelids were loose, not taut like his mother's. His eyes were sad. Hers, pleading.

He relied on his mother for things like food and treats, Christmas presents, art supplies, and trips to the park. His survival depended on her. Late that night, he'd crawled out of bed and tip-toed to her bedroom, planning to tell her he loved her and give her a hug. Such actions generated no warmth within him, but it was important to keep her on his side. When he'd arrived at her door, he heard her crying. He'd placed his hand on the round doorknob, yet it wouldn't turn. The crying noises stopped. He'd gripped the knob firmly and tried to force it to turn, but it wouldn't budge.

"Mom!" he'd shouted and shook the handle fiercely. "Mommy!" he'd cried out melodramatically.

Lazy footsteps, a click, and the door had opened.

"Why did you lock me out?" He glared at her with dry eyes.

"Sometimes adults need privacy." Her voice was unsteady and her face seemed empty, like the one he saw in the mirror. "What do you need, honey? You should be in bed."

He peered around her and noticed she'd pulled Matthew's bassinet closer to her bed.

Then his eyes pierced into hers. "I just wanted to tell you..." For the first time in his short life he said, "I love you." He blinked once.

She'd made the mascara face and said, "How sweet of you. I love you, too."

He'd grabbed her legs, an awkward attempt to feign affection for her. She'd patted his back, but it felt robotic.

"Good night, Mommy." He'd added a layer of sugar to his goodbye and then trotted toward his room, but stopped at the doorway and listened.

The soft thud of the door closing.

The click of the lock.

He hadn't liked the change. Locked doors and distance. The uncertainty and lack of control lit a fire of anger within him. He'd grabbed a few crayons and scribbled her a picture. Hours later, he'd slid his masterpiece under her bedroom door.

Returning to the present, he lifted his head from his mother's bedroom door and continued to the kitchen to make himself a peanut butter sandwich. White bread with four heaping tablespoons of crunchy peanut butter. He liked the way it tore at the bread when applied. He pulled off the crust and tossed the pieces into the kitchen sink. He ripped off a bite between his teeth and considered what to do with Raquel -- or was it *Rochelle?* What to do with the urine-soaked mess upstairs? He'd sneak her out the back door once his mother and Matt were asleep.

The little rich girl had put up a fight, and at the time, he hadn't been in the mood. Now, though, it sounded delightful, yet his mother's unexpected return had ruined the evening. For that, he considered putting a bullet in her brain, but he summoned the sense to know the cons outweighed the pros. For now.

He'd have his fun with another girl another night.

2

Kathleen shot the finger at her bedroom door, knowing her son lurked on the other side, as he'd been doing since he was five years old, since the night he'd slid that wretched drawing under her door. White paper littered with the colors of brick, black, and burnt sienna, crudely depicting the scene of her husband's death. Her son enjoyed probing boundaries, and she didn't have the energy to call him out tonight. She sat crossed legged on her twin bed and lowered the volume on the television, no longer needing to muffle the racket from whatever her son had been doing upstairs. Moving furniture? Rearranging that hideous collection of marionettes? She crushed out her cigarette in the ashtray and fanned the lingering smoke toward the opened window.

In four days, her son would turn seventeen and enter no-man's land. Still too young for her to wash her hands of him or kick him out of the house. He'd only completed his junior year, so the armed forces weren't an option yet, either. At seventeen, however, he would be old enough for the adult criminal justice system. Maybe now, a judge would hold him accountable for his actions, or at least protect her family and society from him.

In three hundred and sixty-nine days, she could tell him to get the hell out of their lives. She and Matthew could have the house to themselves. Four years after that, she would sell the house, buy an RV, and move to Bolivar Peninsula. Matthew would go off to a university somewhere or learn a trade. Kathleen could find work in Galveston and commute by ferry. Both of them could live their lives with no one knowing about him. The neighbors wouldn't stare or whisper when they saw her. They wouldn't feel compelled to hide their pets, raise their fences, or install motion activation devices on their outdoor lights. She could host a neighborhood barbecue and people might actually show up. Her eldest would never darken the door of her new life.

For the first several years of her son's existence, she'd felt guilty for not liking him. She'd wondered what kind of mother doesn't like her own child. It didn't seem natural, but neither did he. He recoiled from affection, never laughed or smiled until he learned that it might bring rewards. He didn't cry, either. Even as a baby, he'd cried only to alert her to hunger or a wet diaper, and the noise he'd made was more of a shriek, not so much a cry. She'd held him no less, though. She'd rocked him, sung to him, cooed and snuggled him, certain that love and attention would spark a twinkle in his eyes.

As a toddler, neither positive nor negative consequences had any effect on his behavior. The only emotion he seemed to experience was rage. Some people had suggested he had autism. As she'd learned more about autism, her heart sank deeper. Autism would have offered hope. Autism would've meant he had feelings and longed for belonging. Unlike some kids with autism, her son was keenly aware of and able to process sensory inputs. He struggled with social interactions because he simply did not care about other people. He had no regard for human life.

He easily identified emotions in others, a skill that had misled an inept school counselor to believe he had empathy. She'd explained to the well-intentioned neophyte that her son could indeed *recognize* emotions, but he did not appear to *feel* them. He could detect if someone was hurting, but he simply didn't care. In fact, her son seemed to enjoy a game of cause and effect, taking action to create disappointment, or even pain, and then observing and mimicking the response.

She'd begged for help, for an expert who could reveal some goodness in her son, awaken empathy, maybe bring some life to his dead eyes. Traditional and creative therapies had no impact. She'd heeded advice from experts and authors of books about parenting strong-willed children, and they yielded no results. He responded to nothing, and she was forced to consider that the boy was a hollow shell devoid of any real emotion other than anger. The day she came home to find her husband dead and saw the smirk on her son's face, she knew something dark and sinister dwelt within him.

Kathleen had met the spirit of the law requiring a parent to keep a child clothed, fed, sheltered, and in school. She'd financed a few of his interests, mostly art, with hopes they would unleash the light within. She put equal effort into keeping the boy away from Matthew. The younger boy had his own room, but Kathleen hadn't allowed him to sleep in it until recently, only after the new teen insisted he was too old to sleep in his mother's room and that his brother was weird but left him alone. She'd agreed only after installing a deadbolt lock on the bedroom door and obtaining Matthew's solemn oath to lock it at night and if ever he was home without her.

Although her son terrified Kathleen, she never let him see it. She'd learned to avoid reacting to him, especially when he tried to confuse her, which was often. She confronted him calmly when she caught him in a lie, which happened nearly every time he opened his mouth. He was an excellent manipulator, so she focused on staying grounded any time they interacted. The only thing that ever threw the kid off balance was questioning him about how he felt.

One time when he'd brought home a report card with straight A's, she'd praised him and asked, "How do you feel about that?"

He'd looked at her like she was speaking Swahili.

There was no living with him, anymore, only surviving.

Recently, a call from an emergency room nurse had provided a glimmer of hope. He'd taken her car in the night without permission and crashed it. The nurse had advised her to come to the hospital as soon as she could. She'd arrived, expecting to hear he'd been killed and she'd been liberated, but instead they'd delivered cruel news. All he had was a bump on the head and a few scratches. Her car, however, didn't fare so well.

Somehow, her son managed to have a girlfriend or even several simultaneously. Her son was a runt, but he made the most of his good looks. He had a knack for finding naive girls. Some of them seemed vulnerable and broken. A few came from wealthy families and were drawn to bad boys, perhaps to piss off their fathers. At least his current girlfriend appeared to be his age or perhaps his senior. Slightly dimwitted and desperate, but legal.

She suspected her son stalked Matthew's friends, so she'd stopped allowing them to come over. To avoid the appearance of being rude and refusing to host their kids, she'd explained to a few moms that she didn't allow sleepovers because she had an older teenage son at home whose friends tended to come over unannounced and age-appropriate behavior for older teens wasn't necessarily appropriate for younger ones. Some parents understood. Others thought it was odd for a mother to distrust her own son.

Under the bedroom door, she saw his shadows recede. He was finally leaving the edge of her personal space. Matthew was due home soon, so she slipped her feet into her old Birkenstock sandals, slid off the bed and used a pillow to fan the remaining scent of her vice out of the room. She smoothed her comforter and fluffed her pillows, but her bed never looked as nicely made as Matthew's. You could bounce a quarter off that boy's sheets.

Kathleen walked to the small bathroom to brush her teeth. The image in the mirror alarmed her. She looked a decade older than she should. Her collar bones protruded. The skin on her throat resembled crepe paper. One of her eyebrows had thinned down to a mere thirty hairs. The hair on her head was stringy and dull, and strands of gray were increasing in number. Her eyes, sunken and murky. She ran her fingers underneath them and checked her fingertips for smudged mascara, but the skin was clean. The darkened spots were marks of exhaustion, ever-present reminders of her miserable life.

3

Colleen Heenan parked her truck at the Alwin Police Department twenty minutes before her first shift. She'd encountered none of the obstacles or delays on her commute from Winston for which she'd allowed time. Excitement, apprehension and caffeine compensated for her lack of sleep. She scooted out of her old Chevy Silverado and smoothed the wrinkles in her slacks. She could hear Aunt Ruth in her head, *linen is supposed to wrinkle, dear.*

She'd spent too much time last night fretting over her attire, wanting to look professional but not like one of them, not like a detective. As a victim advocate, she thought she should soften her presence, and that reduced her choices. The heat limited her options even further. Today's temperature would top the nineties, and it was only June third. The truck's AC was no match for Texas summers, and she didn't want to arrive sweat-soaked and smelly. She'd finally settled on a white sleeveless cotton blouse and tan linen suit, her favorite because it allowed her skin to breathe.

She surrendered to the wrinkles and worked her jacket over her sticky skin. *It's too early to be this damn hot.* She slid the strap of her leather bag, a graduation gift, over her shoulder. On the passenger seat sat a small cardboard box she'd packed with her lunch and a few personal items. Two photos peeked over the rim -- one of her big black dog Sam with his tongue hanging out after a day at the lake, and one of her in a graduation gown, clutching a rolled-up fake diploma in one hand and holding Aunt Ruth's shoulder with the other. Aunt Ruth had framed Colleen's degree, a Master of Arts in Criminology, but she left that at home with her ego. Colleen had attended a total of one victim's assistance seminar. She remembered a few details, like *stress causes bad breath* and *death carries an unforgettably foul odor,* so she'd also packed a small makeup bag with a toothbrush, toothpaste, strong mints, tissues, and a little jar of vapor rub.

She tucked the box under her arm and closed the two-tone door with her heel. As she crossed the parking lot to the station, the strap of her bag consistently slipped toward the edge of her shoulder, and her attempts to inch it back into place made her look like she had a violent tic. Finally, she reached the entrance doors and assessed her reflection. A few feral curls had sprung from the French twist she'd half-heartedly attempted and now stuck to the sweat coating her neck. If not for that, she'd have looked like a classy old man dressed for a garden party.

She shifted the box to the other arm, freeing her hand to jerk her shoulder strap in place just before pulling open the door to the police station lobby. She silently thanked God for air conditioning and approached the reception window where a woman was talking into the phone. Colleen recognized the old fashioned up-do. It belonged to the cheerful woman she'd met when she'd interviewed for the position, only today the lady wasn't smiling.

She looked at Colleen and spoke into the phone. "I think she just walked in."

Colleen froze and tightened the grip on her box.

The lady covered the mouthpiece and asked, "Colleen Heenan, right? The victim advocate?"

"Yes, ma'am. That's right."

The woman kept her eyes on Colleen and spoke into the phone again. "I'll bring her up."

Colleen checked the clock on the wall and felt reassured. 7:45 a.m. When her eyes returned to the woman, she was gone.

The door next to the window burst open, and there she was again. "C'mon," she urged. "I'm Jeanne. We met last month."

"Right." Colleen nodded. "Jeanne." She smiled, hoping to lessen the tension.

"I'm afraid your first day on the job is going to be a doozy."

Colleen followed Jeanne through the records department and into a stairwell. The thin woman wore a light gray skirt and jacket that matched her hair. She looked older than she was, evidenced by how briskly she took the stairs. Before they'd reached the second floor, Colleen's heart was thumping furiously.

As Jeanne slapped her card against the reader, she said, "This door leads to Investigations."

She pushed open the door while saying, "We'll get you an entry card later. There's no time for that now." She held the door open for Colleen and gestured like a game show model, "Here you have CAPERS, Crimes Against Persons." Then she added, "Juvenile Crimes is beyond that wall," and pointed to a door beyond two rows of cubicles. "I'll take you to your desk, where you can drop your stuff."

"Is it always this quiet?"

"It looks like the rapture, but it's because we had a murder this morning, and everybody's in big deal mode."

"I suppose murder justifies big deal mode."

"Believe me, if the rapture happened, my ass wouldn't be here." She laughed, revealed brilliant veneer teeth, and flashed the small cross hanging from a chain around her neck.

Then her smile vanished. "We don't have murders here. Well, maybe one a year," and she took off again, charging down the carpeted path between the rows of empty cubicles.

Jeanne came to a halt at the last cubicle, across from a traditional office with a real door and walls. "This is yours. The cubicle, not the office. That's Lieutenant Martinez's, and I believe he's your direct supervisor."

"Yes, ma'am. That's what I was told." Colleen set the box on the counter posing as a desk.

"We're throwing you into the fire, hon. Call me Jeanne."

Colleen nodded, and felt her heartbeat in her throat. She inhaled deeply and exhaled slowly and pushed her tongue against the tiny gap between her front teeth.

"You ready, hon?"

"Ready as I'll ever be."

"Then let's head over to Juvenile Crimes. Sergeant Esquivel will give you details."

She followed Jeanne through the door to Juvenile Crimes and into an interview room, where Sergeant Esquivel and another detective stood, exchanging hushed words. The sergeant wore a crisp blue button-up shirt, and her biceps tested the limits of the sleeves. Two braids clung tight to her scalp and draped just past her shoulder blades, the tips resting a few inches above her narrow waist.

Hurried, Sergeant Esquivel said, "Nice to meet you, Colleen," and then, "Thank you, Jeanne."

Before Colleen could thank her, Jeanne had disappeared, along with the detective. Colleen noticed Esquivel's strong jaw and focused eyes, and she reminded her of a superhero.

The sergeant launched into a rapid-fire briefing, "Most of what we know has come from the two kids. They sit down to eat breakfast. An argument starts between the suspect and the mother. The suspect starts yelling, gets violent. He grabs a knife and stabs the mother. The girls run out of the house and next door for help."

Colleen struggled to keep up with the facts, and the images that formed in her mind didn't make it easier.

"The neighbor calls 9-1-1 and keeps the girls safe until units arrive. By then, the suspect fled. The victim died en route to the hospital, but the girls don't know that yet."

She swallowed hard and longed for water. "What do you need from me?"

"Keep the kids company. They're stepsisters, but real close. We're not telling them that their mom is dead until the grandparents and biological father arrive, the victim's parents and the victim's ex."

"You want me to keep them distracted?" Colleen struggled to arrange the pieces of the puzzle. "Any idea how long I'm supposed to do this?"

"They live a couple of hours in opposite directions from here."

Colleen's eyes darted between the sergeant and the distracting background. Men in cheap suits hurried between cubicles and spoke in hushed tones. One glanced at her as he passed, then turned to another and shrugged.

"How's the suspect related to them? The girls?"

"Stepfather to the oldest girl and biological father of the youngest."

Another detective eyed Colleen, and she adjusted the collar of her blouse.

"So, they're half-siblings, not step, right? They share the same mother?"

"Yes, I guess you're right. Half-sisters."

Colleen felt a drop of sweat trickle down the small of her back.

"How old are they?"

"Five and four. I think."

"Oh, they're tiny." Suddenly, Colleen's training in crisis intervention seemed tragically inadequate.

"Yeah."

"So, one of the girls will go with the grandparents and the other with the biological father, separated by over a hundred miles?"

"I guess so. They'll be all right. Kids are resilient."

The hell they are.

Memories sprung from their hiding places. Aunt Ruth breaking the horrible news, understanding the power of a few simple words. *Your mother died.* The betrayal, the myriad of feelings of traumatic grief.

The sergeant's voice shooed the memories back to the shadows. "I guess I shouldn't tell *you* that. You're the expert."

"I wouldn't go that far." Her brow furrowed. "What are the girls' names?"

"Shit." She shook her head. "I can't remember."

For three excruciating hours, Colleen made futile attempts to divert the girls' attention from their mother. They were hungry, so she scavenged food from the break room. They were barefoot and cold, so she found police jackets that engulfed them and provided little comfort. They were scared and bored, so she read every worn out, spineless children's book available. They played with an unimpressive LEGO set she found inside an antiquated toddler's activity table, and she wondered how a toddler's activity table belonged in the Youth Crimes Division. Every fifteen minutes, one of the girls asked, "Is my mommy ok?" and Colleen told them half-truths. "*They took her to a hospital to get help,*" and "*I know the doctors are working hard to help her,*" and the boldfaced lie, "*When I know something more, I'll tell you.*"

A few times, she stepped out to give herself a pep talk and check on the status of the family's arrival.

Finally, Sergeant Esquivel cracked open the door and asked her to step outside for a minute.

Colleen pulled her jacket off the back of the chair and joined her in the hall.

Sergeant Esquivel said, "They're here, but they need some time to let the news sink in."

"What?" The terseness in her voice startled her.

"It's a lot, and they requested some time."

Colleen swallowed her ire before pushing back. She slipped her jacket over her cool skin.

Sergeant Esquivel is a softy.

"I agree, Sergeant. It is a lot." She tugged the cuffs of her jacket sleeves. "However, those kids need to be with people they know, not a stranger." She pointed to herself. "They need to know what the hell's going on, and putting it off a minute longer is cruel."

Thirty minutes after the girls learned the truth, Colleen joined them in what was called a *soft room*. The two sisters sat on the floor, coloring. She scanned the room furnished with overstuffed chairs, a love seat, and the glow of lamps instead of overhead fluorescent lights -- a far better place to have spent the morning than the cold corner in Youth Crimes.

The older of the girls said, "I'm done." Her eyes met Colleen's, and she extended the colorful paper and said, "I made this for you."

"Thank you." Colleen admired the three flowers. One blue, one pink, one green. The girl had scrawled her name at the bottom in purple. "It's beautiful. I'm going to pin it on the wall where I work. That way, I'll see it every day, and I'll think of you."

"And say a prayer for me."

"I will do that, too."

The youngest girl looked up at Colleen with the bluest eyes she'd ever seen. "You lied to me."

The statement punched a hole in her chest. "You're right." Colleen cleared her throat, hoping the lump in it would crumble. "And I'm so sorry."

Sergeant Esquivel smoothed her sandy colored slacks and said, "Miss Colleen was doing what we told her to do. We told her to wait for the grown-ups to get here."

"It's still a lie."

Her grandmother placed a hand on the girl's shoulder and whispered, "Now. Now."

"You're right. It wasn't honest with you. I hope someday you can forgive me."

Colleen told the adults she'd help them find resources. She wished she had a card or handouts to give them. "I'll reach out to you. Maybe tomorrow? Crime Victim Compensation can help with funeral expenses. I can help you with the application."

The grandmother's chin quivered, and Colleen realized she'd been too focused on the children. The woman's daughter had been brutally murdered by a guy she probably never liked.

"Please don't feel pressured to make any decisions today. You need space to take all this in and grieve."

Another detective peeked into the soft room and called her and the sergeant into the hall.

As Colleen and the sergeant emerged, the detective motioned for them to follow him far enough from the soft room to be out of ear shot. The detective pointed at Colleen, "I called you out here in case you could use a break."

"Thank you."

Then he pointed at Esquivel, thought better of it, and stuffed his hand in his front pocket. "The suspect was found dead in a motel off of Central Expressway. Maid found him. Looks like he shot himself in the head."

Colleen walked back to her cubicle feeling detached and lifeless. Her shoes were heavy on her feet. She wanted a nap. When she sat down, she rubbed her jaw to ease the tension. Her neck and shoulders ached. She noticed the voice mail indicator was blinking red, and she had no idea how to work the phone.

"You lied to me."

Colleen was staring at the blinking message indicator and picking at her ham and cheese sandwich when her phone rang. She looked around as if she needed permission to answer, but there wasn't a soul in sight. After the third ring, she lifted the receiver, before considering how to answer.

"Hello," she said, fumbling. "Colleen Heenan speaking."

Jeanne's voice came over the line, "You haven't quit yet?"

"Not yet."

"Come down when you can. I'll get your ID card and give you a proper tour."

#

Colleen followed Jeanne around the department like a pet zombie. The tour ended at Lieutenant Martinez's office, whom she'd seen only in passing on and off through the morning. He looked as diminished as Colleen.

He thanked Jeanne for showing her around and then said to Colleen, "Come in and sit for a minute."

Martinez had a thick head of black hair and an equally thick mustache. His height mitigated the extra pounds he earned from years at a desk job. He'd rolled up the sleeves of his white dress shirt, revealing tanned, stout forearms. His loosened blue and black tie seemed pointless, a mere act of obedience to the department dress code. If Sergeant Esquivel was a German Shepherd, Lieutenant Martinez was a Mastiff. His friendly brown eyes had sizable bags under them. Otherwise, his face looked youthful in spite of decades on the job.

Colleen sunk into one of two chairs facing his desk and wondered if Martinez put everyone at ease instantly.

"So, Heenan, tell me. What do you think?"

She wasn't about to tell him how close to home the murder had hit, or how she could barely keep it together.

"I'm not sure yet, Lieutenant."

"Of what?"

"I'm not sure of what I think yet. I'm kinda numb."

He stroked his mustache and waited.

"I think I'll never shake the last few seconds. When the kid called me out for lying to her."

He cocked his head, and his dark eyebrows inched together.

"She looked me dead in the eyes. Scolded me. 'You lied to me,' she said, and she was right."

He dragged his hand over his mouth and down his chin before saying, "You shouldn't have been stuck in that position."

"Isn't that why I'm here, sir?"

"Not really. This wasn't a normal situation. You did a good job, though." He opened the bottom desk drawer, gave it a quick glance, and slammed it shut. "I miss the old days when you could keep a bottle of scotch handy and no one threw a hissy fit."

A grin wriggled its way through Colleen's paralysis.

"Kid, I've been doing this almost three decades now, and this kind of deal gets to all of us. If it doesn't stick in your gizzard, then you're probably a sociopath."

She nodded.

"Speaking of sociopaths. Did you hear what his dad said? The killer's dad?"

"He was here?"

"No, but our guys notified him about the incident and the suicide." Martinez shook his head and said, "His father said his son had done nothing but cause people grief his whole life. If given the chance, he'd hurt anyone in his path. He said he should've killed him when he had the chance.

4

Colleen stumbled into the entryway of her house, keys in hand, balancing her attaché over one shoulder and Chinese take-out over her forearm. Sam greeted her at the door. His tail wagged wildly, and he blinked furiously.

"Were you sleeping, buddy?"

His black fur still had the puppy sheen, but he'd finally grown into his paws.

She dropped her bag next to the sofa and took the meal to the kitchen. Sam exited the kitchen through the dog door and within seconds returned with the bone she'd brought home from the meat market a week earlier.

She loved her status as a property owner, especially of the house she'd called home for so many years. But the liberating feeling she experienced upon the first night of her separation had been muddied by a mixture of grief, shame, and self-doubt. Grief over a dream shattered. Self-doubt for failing to see what Aunt Ruth had seen so clearly. Shame for refusing to heed her warnings and instead, choosing to run off and marry such a deceitful man. She'd stuck around after the lies, possibly due to denial or simply needing time for the reality to sink in. She'd hung in there with Dylan for a while, but the constant revelations of his dishonesty grew too heavy to bear.

One morning when Dylan had left for work, Colleen packed her bags and ran to Aunt Ruth with her tail between her legs. She received not one *I told you so*. Instead, her aunt helped Colleen find a good attorney, and once the divorce was final, Aunt Ruth moved into her friend Martha's mansion and gifted her humble house to Colleen. Aunt Ruth and Martha started calling themselves *The Golden Girls,* even though both women were shy of sixty. Colleen wanted to call Aunt Ruth and tell her about her first day, but she didn't have the heart to stir up memories of a horrible past.

She discarded her linen suit on the bedroom floor and returned to the living room in a nightshirt the ladies had brought her from one of their excursions to Mexico. In large bright letters and fancy font, the front read *Adios* and the back read *Bitchachos!*

Colleen slid to the floor between the couch and the coffee table, turned on *TVLand* and ate her dinner out of its foam box. By the time *Cannon* started, she was horizontal on the sofa. At 10:00 p.m., the *Hill Street Blues* theme music guided her to sleep.

An hour later, the voice of a blue-eyed child woke her.

"*You lied to me.*"

5

Colleen had always thought of Alwin, Texas, as a quiet, almost idyllic town surrounded by fields of wheat, farmland, and grazing cattle. The population fell short of fifty thousand, and with a disproportionately high percentage of cops calling Alwin home, Colleen hadn't expected to have much to do. It had seemed like a great place to get her feet wet.

Violent crime in Alwin was low, which allowed her to give victims her full attention. During her first week on the job, a couple domestic violence incidents had landed on her desk, along with a few burglaries and criminal mischiefs. In recent years, the nation had seen rising rates in juvenile violent crime, but there was hope the rate had peaked and was perhaps on the downhill slide. Nevertheless, she had a surprising number of cases involving juvenile offenders. A lot of folks downplayed these crimes, but Colleen could see how the offenders' young age didn't mitigate the impact on their victims. The age of the finger pressing a trigger had no influence on the velocity of the bullet or the damage it could do. Colleen wondered what it was like for victim advocates in the bigger cities because, after five days, this small town had left her feeling drained and ready for a long vacation.

She had plans to pick up Sam and enjoy a home cooked meal at Aunt Ruth and Martha's. She'd almost made it to her truck when the mobile phone startled her to a halt. The department issued it, so if it rang, she had to answer. She dug it out of her bag, raised the antenna, and flipped it open to answer. Dispatch informed her that Officer Jones needed her back at the station.

Five minutes later, she wiped the sweat from under her eyes and shuffled through the lobby doors. A uniformed officer peered out of a conference room. "You Colleen?"

"That's me." Her voice sounded weary.

He signaled her to stop and met her just inside the lobby. He wore the department uniform, but his Sam Browne bore no pistol or the usual accoutrements.

Desk officer.

"So, you're the Colleen Heenan I keep hearing about."

"Don't believe a word they're saying." She forced a smile and inhaled deeply. "I'm assuming you're Officer Jones?"

"The one and only," he said haughtily.

"Dispatch said something about a sexual assault of a minor?"

"That's a big maybe. It's a delayed report, so we won't call in a detective." He reeked of apathy. "She's pretty emotional, so I figured that was your lane."

At least he recognized compassion wasn't his strength.

"She's in there with her mom, and she's not saying much." He pointed to a small conference room off the lobby.

"Does she have a name?"

The man patted his uniform shirt pocket and grumbled something about forgetting his whip-out book.

Colleen tucked her rebellious curls behind her ears before entering the conference room. The victim and her mother sat closely in chairs at a long table.

Jones said, "This here is Miss Heenan, the counselor I told you about."

"Victim Advocate, actually."

He cleared his throat. "Counselor. Victim Advocate." He shrugged. "Potato, Po-tah-to."

The officer played the stereotype so well it was cartoonish. Colleen looked for hidden cameras, certain this uncaring cop was playing a part in some type of initiation, a prank on the new victim advocate. When she saw the look on the mother's face, though, she knew the scenario was no joke.

"Please, call me Colleen." She extended her hand toward the woman, who gripped it confidently.

"Maxine Jackson." She wore a yellow button up shirt, softened by years of wear. Her hair was pulled back tightly into a bun. Her flawless skin, high cheekbones, strong jawline, and almond shaped eyes created a formidable ensemble of natural beauty.

The petite girl shared her mother's features, only subtler. Colleen figured she was about ten years old. The girl leaned against her mother, hugging her midsection as if she were cold, which made her appear even smaller. She peered over her glasses at Colleen.

Gently, Colleen asked her, "What would you like me to call you?"

"Trudy, please."

"I'm glad to meet you, Trudy." And to both, "I only wish it was under better circumstances."

"Me, too." The girl whispered.

"How old are you, Trudy?"

She made eye contact and answered politely, "Twelve, ma'am."

Colleen's raised eyebrows revealed her surprise.

"I'm small." She pursed her lips.

"Small but mighty," Maxine said softly and touched her cheek to Trudy's head.

Colleen chose a seat that respected the family's space yet distanced herself from the obtuse officer.

The woman addressed Officer Jones through tightened lips. "She wrote down what you asked." She nodded toward the paper on the table in front of them.

"Thank you." He replied with ill-suited cheer.

Colleen rested her elbow on the table and her chin in her hand with her fingers covering her mouth. They sat in silence as the man read the young girl's words. He remained standing, and his belly spilled over the naked duty belt.

"Trudy, are you sure about the address where this happened?"

"Yes, sir."

"How'd you know the exact address? Most kids your age don't pay that close attention."

Maxine answered, "She showed me the house, and I wrote it down."

"Ms. Jackson, you need to be careful about going over there. Let us handle things."

Maxine's nostrils flared when she responded. "I have no desire to go near that place again. I simply wanted an address because I felt confident the police would ask for it."

Officer Jones continued reviewing the report for a few long moments before speaking up again. "Was this guy a boyfriend?"

"No, sir." Trudy replied.

"Ever?"

"No." Her brow furrowed. "Never." She seemed appalled by the suggestion.

Colleen's stomach clenched, and she was thrust back in time, when she was Trudy's size, vulnerable, preyed upon. She tightened her fingers over her mouth.

"Did you *want* him to be your boyfriend?"

Colleen felt the blood rush to her face and her eyes shot to Maxine.

Maxine snapped, "What are you getting at?"

"Ma'am, these are questions I need to ask."

The hell you do, Colleen thought.

"No!" The girl choked back a sob. "He's practically a grown man."

Colleen exchanged glances with both the victim and her mother, who seemed to appreciate the fact that she was incapable of wearing a poker face.

"Look..." Officer Jones finally took a seat. Colleen hoped it meant he would soften his approach, but the sitting position seemed to enhance his level of stupidity. "I know there's a thirty percent chance that you're lying, and this type of allegation can ruin a man's life."

Maxine's jaw dropped. She turned to Colleen and asked, "What year is this?"

Colleen lifted her fingers from her lips. "1996."

Trudy's head hung lower, and Colleen saw tears fall onto her lap.

Maxine's words crawled through her teeth. "Thank you for the clarification, Colleen. I thought maybe this room here doubled as a time machine."

Colleen kept her tone in check but asked, "Officer Jones, that data? The thirty percent? Is that..." She tried to hide her disgust as she asked, "A departmental statistic?"

The officer's eyes shifted between Colleen and Maxine, as if assessing which one might pounce. "I'm simply making sure you ladies understand the gravity of the allegation."

Maxine snapped, "Are you going to ask her what she was wearing now?"

"I don't even want to be here!" Trudy sobbed. "My mom made me come here!"

Colleen couldn't look at the girl without thinking of herself, without thinking of Steven.

Maxine announced she was done. "This is why we don't report. I thought things had gotten better, but I can see I was mistaken." She rubbed Trudy's back. "Come on, sweet girl. We're leaving."

The desk jockey froze in his seat, slack jawed, with the written statement in his hand.

Maxine stood and gathered her purse. "Shame on you," she muttered toward Jones as she and Trudy walked out of the conference room. Colleen heard their footsteps, followed by the lobby door opening, then closing, and they were gone.

Jones said, "That's what I figured. A bullshit report."

Colleen stood. She wanted to catch Maxine and Trudy before they were out of the parking lot. She wanted to fall to her knees and, on behalf of the police department, apologize.

Jones asked, "You believe her don't you?"

"I have no reason not to."

"You're green. Just wait. You'll see."

"Why don't you believe her?" Somehow, Colleen managed to pose the question without an edgy tone.

"Because she just walked out of here." He motioned wildly toward the door. "She made a bad decision, and she got caught, and she didn't want her mom to be mad at her, so she lied."

"I think her reaction was pretty normal, not an indication of deceit."

"Like I said, you're green."

"What if I asked you to share with me, a stranger, the most embarrassing thing that's ever happened to you? Would you want to talk to me about it?"

He shrugged.

"Okay, let's do it. What's the worst thing that ever happened to you, like, the most humiliating thing that ever happened to you?"

"What's it to you?"

She took a few unnecessary jabs at him. "Surely, as a boy, you were bullied, maybe the last one picked for a team? Got beat up at recess or after school? Pissed your pants once or twice?"

His chapped lips parted slightly, but he said nothing. She'd hit below the belt and almost felt guilty for it. "Would you want to talk to me about it?"

"No." His lip curled.

"Why not?"

He shook his head and looked at her like she was an idiot. "I don't even know you."

"So what?" She smiled. "Tell me all of it and then, write it down, especially any degrading details so that I can hand it off to a whole lot of strangers to dissect and maybe have a few laughs."

"What the hell's your point?"

"Just the thought of doing that sucks, doesn't it? It's basically what Trudy just went through." She removed her hands from her pockets and rubbed them together. "It's chilly in here."

"What's your deal?"

She slipped the strap of her work bag over her shoulder. "Like I said, I just don't think that the kid's behavior was an indication she's lying. I think it was pretty reasonable."

"And like I said, you're green."

"I heard you the first two times." Colleen gave up. "What happens now?"

"You go home. That's what happens."

"I mean with the report or the case. What happens with that?"

"I'll write up an information report and send it up to CID, and they'll close it as unfounded."

"CID?" She knew what CID was. She wanted to get him thinking instead of feeling.

"Criminal Investigations Division."

"What does *unfounded* mean?"

"It means it's not a good case." He spoke with authority. "There's no evidence to support the alleged crime."

"Got it." She headed toward the door. "Thanks for calling, Jones."

"I won't be calling you again."

Colleen jogged into the parking lot and caught up with Maxine and Trudy as they were pulling out of a space. Maxine rolled down her window.

"I'm so sorry, Ms. Jackson. I imagine he works the desk for a reason."

"I appreciate that. I sense you get it."

"I do," she admitted. "I'll follow up with you on Monday. The report will go to an investigator." She hoped she wasn't lying.

"My expectations are low."

"I understand. I'm new here, but I haven't seen anyone else act like that. Still, I'm truly sorry.

6

Maxine looked at Trudy, who was staring out the passenger side window. "Let's get some ice cream."

"I don't want any." Her voice was too weary for someone so young.

"Well, I do." Maxine reached over and patted Trudy's hand.

"I just want to go to bed."

"It's summer, and you can sleep in tomorrow."

"Tomorrow's Saturday. It wouldn't be a school day, anyway."

Maxine took a deep breath and blew it out. "You know what I mean."

She knew ice cream wouldn't fix anything, but the whole evening had been dismal, and she was desperate for a sliver of something good. She gazed at her young daughter. *This was why I wanted a boy.*

She'd cried the moment she'd learned she was having a baby girl. She'd prayed for a boy, a boy she could raise into a gentleman, like her father. How she wished he was still alive. Instead, she would spend her life worrying about and doing her damnedest to protect her child from predators and abusers, from discrimination and minimization.

She'd tried to unleash the tomboy traits, but Trudy resisted. The little girl didn't like roughhousing, sports, or playing in the dirt. She was kind and tenderhearted, trusted too easily, and paid too little attention to her surroundings. She was introverted, so it was hard for her to make friends. Her small stature and glasses made her a prime target for mean girls. Maxine was relieved the girl had no interest in boys because she anticipated her daughter would bring home the broken ones, the wounded puppies, believing she could love them out of their shortcomings. Trudy was a lamb in a wolf's den.

Maxine had moved to Alwin to start over after her own battle was won. The adjustment was hard for Trudy, though, who felt like a misfit at her new school. Maxine had encouraged her to stand up straighter and keep her chin up. "Walk like you belong there because, my sweet girl, you do."

Maxine pulled into the Dairy Queen parking lot. Trudy's body remained tense and her eyes fixed on her lap, but she asked, "Can I have a peanut buster parfait?"

7

Aunt Ruth was washing the dishes, as she always did after dinner. Martha and Colleen sat in the living room, and Colleen had sunk into her favorite chair with Sam at her feet and a glass of cabernet in her hand. They kept the thermostat low, blaming hot flashes. A fan the size of a C-130 propeller was mounted to the ceiling. Colleen grabbed a Mexican blanket from the basket next to her chair.

Martha sat in an easy chair across from Colleen. Both had their feet propped on a massive ottoman between them.

Martha said, "You barely touched your dinner, Colleen."

"I'm exhausted."

"You didn't talk much about your first week."

"I didn't really want to. Alwin isn't the quiet place I'd expected."

Martha nodded and waited. Colleen knew she wanted her to elaborate, so she shared the details about her first day and the blue-eyed girl's final words to her.

"That had to have stirred up some emotions for you, love."

"It did." She took a sip of wine.

"That's a lot for a first day."

"It was." Colleen rolled the stem of her glass between her thumb and fingers.

"I hope your week ended better than it began."

"It didn't." She took a sip of wine and listened to make sure there was enough noise coming from the kitchen to provide a sound buffer. The water was on full blast, so Colleen continued in a hushed voice. "That's why I was running late. I invented a reason for my delay. Aunt Ruth didn't want me to go into victim advocacy. I don't want her to worry about me."

"Yes, I know. It's because she loves you, though."

"I get it. After this week, I understand why she didn't want me in this line of work."

"What happened today? Can you talk about it?"

"Yeah. I can, in general terms." Colleen sat up into a cross legged position. "A little girl was raped. At least I think she was. Her mother brought her in to report it. The officer was so…dense. He didn't believe her, and he pretty much let her know it."

"Bastard."

The colorful response made Colleen smile. "I can't argue with that. Anyway, the offender is the older brother of one of her classmates."

Martha's jaw dropped. "Another one that hit too close to home."

"Yep." Colleen finished her wine.

Martha was as close as family now, and she knew all about the neighbor boy across the street from Colleen's childhood home, her best friend's older brother.

"I didn't want to tell Aunt Ruth about that one. I'm afraid she'll start bothering me to quit."

"I don't think she'll do that."

"The case wasn't exactly like mine. The girl had been invited to a party, only there wasn't really a party. Sounded like she was duped."

Martha whispered, "How cruel."

"There was an older brother there who assaulted her."

"Poor girl."

"I guess the least *bad* part of it is that she won't have to see him again."

"Unlike you and the Steven disaster."

"Yeah." Colleen dropped her feet to the floor and leaned forward onto her elbows. "I'd always thought, or hoped, that my childhood was unique." She ran her fingers along her scalp, through her hair.

They sat in silence for several seconds before Colleen spoke again. "Truth is, I wasn't prepared."

"For what, love? The job?"

"For how ugly the world is."

8

Kathleen had an old duffel bag over her shoulder and called up the stairs to her son. "Matthew, you ready?"

She heard a muffled "*Yes, Mom!*" from behind the boy's bedroom door.

The master bedroom door flew open, and her eldest stepped into the mezzanine. "We're ready, too," he said with an English accent, an octave higher than his natural baritone. Through the balusters, Kathleen noticed one of his marionette puppets dancing at his feet. "Ready for you to bugger off, that is."

"That hurts," Kathleen replied sardonically.

Matthew emerged from his room with his backpack slung over one shoulder. The wiry boy with a mop of mahogany hair scowled when he spotted the puppet.

Kathleen was never comfortable leaving the other son alone overnight, but not because she worried about his safety. What concerned her was the state of her home upon her return and the potential for noise complaints from neighbors. Because her son enjoyed having the house to himself, he typically left little evidence of any havoc. He behaved if it provided enough benefits.

Matthew joined Kathleen at the bottom of the stairs.

"Where will you be, chickadees?" the childish voice asked.

"In Winston somewhere. I have the address in my notebook."

With a chilling tone, he addressed the marionette. "Mother is leaving without even telling us where she's going."

Damn straight, she thought.

"What if we have an emergency?" screeched the puppet. "What if we're feeling peckish?"

"You know how to call 9-1-1, and you're perfectly able to sustain your diet of peanut butter and white bread."

"Touché," the puppet answered. "Don't do anything we wouldn't do."

The remark spun a flurry of thoughts about all the decent things her eldest wouldn't do, yet she refused to respond. She was too eager to leave and give Matthew and herself a weekend of peace.

9

He studied the marionettes hanging from his ceiling, swaying slightly with the cool air pouring out of the ceiling vent. Most resembled people in his life. His mom, his faggot brother, his dead father, his despised kindergarten teacher, various idiots at school, and one that resembled him. He'd named that one *Id*. He turned onto his side and stared at the blond braids scattered across the pillow. He scanned the sheet covering her body and watched it rise and fall as her lungs took in and released air. He listened closely and thought he could hear a soft snoring noise. She was so still. He couldn't recall ever feeling peaceful, but she appeared as the state had been described in books. He smelled her head and put his mouth next to her ear and released a blood curdling scream.

She shrieked and shuddered violently and slapped her hand over her ear. Panicked, she squealed, "What's going on?" as her eyes raced around the room.

Straight faced and calm, he said, "You have to go now."

Then laughter exploded out of his mouth.

"Oh my God!" She panted and grasped at her chest. "What the hell?"

He cackled as he answered, "You should've seen your face." He sat up and said mockingly, "What's going on? What's going on?"

"That really hurt," she said, and scrunched up her face and rubbed her ear with her fingers. "You know, you can damage someone's hearing doing that." Her intonation indicated she expected an apology.

He put his hands in a prayer position, said "Sorry," and engaged in a theatric attempt to stifle his laughter.

The girl jerked herself out of bed, forced her shorts over her hips, pulled her Pearl Jam T-shirt over her head, and crammed her panties and bra into her bag. She secured her braids with a scrunchy, and worked her feet into her off-brand low tops, hopping as she fought to maintain her balance. All the while, he lay in bed and howled with laughter. One shout had triggered a hilarious chain of events.

The girl put her bag strap over her shoulder, and his tone turned paternal. "Calm down now."

She placed her hand on the doorknob.

"C'mere," he purred.

"I thought I had to go," she said with a little sass.

"I wanna get a look at you."

She hung her bag over the doorknob. Cautiously, she approached the bed.

"It's okay," he said and patted the mattress.

She sat down.

He snatched her braids into his fist and yanked her onto her back, mounted her and put his hand around her throat. He didn't squeeze. He was simply testing the waters.

Her face contorted into terror, her eyelids widened, and she shook her head furiously and pleaded, "No. No. No."

He sensed an aroma of fear and drank it in. "I'm just playing with you."

Tears spilled from the outside corners of her eyes, and he watched in fascination as they trickled into her ears.

"You're so sensitive." He kissed her forehead. "I was messing around with you, okay?"

"Okay," she whispered. "But..." She sniffed and said, "I don't like that."

"Oh, dear." He wiped her tears with the back of his fingertips. "I won't do it again," he said, although he felt certain he'd do it again.

He'd set his sights on this one a few weeks earlier. She was an attractive, albeit slow-witted, sixteen-year-old with serious abandonment issues thanks to her father. He'd easily won over her mother, who was too tired to scratch beneath the superficial charm. He'd acquired enough personal information to apply leverage when he thought he needed it. He'd once told her, "Leave me, and I'll burn your house down, with your mom and your kid brother in it." At the time, he assured her he'd done such things before, and he knew the girl believed him. Later he'd told her that he didn't mean it, that he'd said that in anger and followed it with a cliche, "*I get so emotional when I think I'll lose you. I can't control myself.*" He'd begged for her forgiveness and made a dozen empty promises. Sometimes, he vehemently denied saying such things and enjoyed witnessing her confusion. He believed the term was *gaslighting*, and it was an absolute hoot.

He kissed each temple and moved off of her. "You're gorgeous, you know."

"Thank you," she said flatly. She sat up and stood slowly, adjusted her shorts and smoothed her shirt, and produced a weak smile. "You good if I go now?"

He sensed she was still scared, which was fine, but he wanted her mood to shift. He wanted her to come back for more. "You make me want to be a better man."

Her expression told him she felt perplexed but that he'd also touched one of the many soft spots inside her. "Really," he said with a sweet tone. "I mean it."

Of course, he didn't mean it, but she ate it up.

He'd seen a gangster movie where the guys had a night of the week designated for girlfriends and a night designated for the wives. What a brilliant idea that was. He'd never think of this chick as a wife, of course, but he'd grant her a slightly higher status than that of a whore, which was what he wanted tonight.

The long-legged beauty leaned against his bedroom door frame and watched him with puppy dog eyes. "I make you want to be a better man?" Her voice was sickeningly sweet.

"You do." He winked. "I'll see you tomorrow."

He should probably have a pet name for her.

Goldie. That was good.

Before he could speak, he'd learned that making people afraid had benefits that extended beyond his amusement. Time and time again, fearful people had given him what he wanted--from skipping ahead in line, to lunch money, to test answers, to weed and beer and sex. It didn't work with everyone, of course. He'd had his ass kicked a couple of times by older kids and stronger classmates. Fear tactics didn't work with his mother, either. He'd learned that before he'd started kindergarten, yet he remembered it like it happened last week.

A few days after his father's death, during a trip to the grocery store with his mom and useless baby brother, he'd wandered off to the toy aisle. There, he'd picked up a dump truck he wanted her to buy.

His mother had said, "We're here for groceries today, not toys. You already have a treat in the cart."

That was true. She let him choose one treat every trip to the store, and this time he'd selected double stuff Oreo cookies. But he'd wanted the truck, too, so he'd ignored her and placed it in the shopping cart.

"Not today," she'd stated firmly and returned it to the shelf.

In response, he'd pulled the truck from the shelf and hurled it to the tile floor, smashing it into several pieces. Then he'd stood in front of her with arms akimbo, lowered his chin and glared at her under his hooded lids. "Did you not understand me, Mother?"

"Clearly, you did not understand *me*." Her neck flushed, and the red hue rushed upward, into her cheeks.

He raised his right hand in her direction and formed it into the shape of a pistol. "I'll get you. I'll get him, too," and motioned to baby Matthew.

Without hesitating, she eliminated the short distance between them, leaned down and grabbed the front of his shirt, wadding it inside her fist.

She jerked him toward her and sneered. "Threaten your brother again, and I'll end you." Her eyebrows formed the letter *V*, her nose wrinkled, her stare was intense, and her lips formed a square as she spoke. That wasn't the face of fear.

At the time, he'd thought her reaction was intriguing. Scaring grown-ups wasn't as easy as scaring his pre-school classmates. Also interesting was the throbbing next to her throat. He knew her heart was pounding fast. Throughout the confrontation, though, his heart beat the same as it normally did.

At the checkout, she'd paid for the damaged truck and advised the clerk not to ring up the cookies because they were put in her shopping cart by mistake. On the way home, she'd delivered a brief lecture about consequences.

He laughed at the memory. He laughed because she still couldn't sleep without locking her bedroom door.

To her credit, his mother had taught him a valuable lesson that day: he needed more tools in his toolbox. Over time he'd acquired them. He'd learned other tactics to get what he wanted, and often they required less energy than instilling fear. Some he could achieve effortlessly.

You make me want to be a better man just became one of his favorites.

10

Colleen stood barefoot on the grass with a cold Stella in her left hand. With her right, she tossed the Frisbee across her back yard, just under the low branches of the live oak trees. Sam sprinted and leaped into the air to catch it. With each return, the plastic disk became wetter with slippery drool.

The western sky reminded her of orange sherbet, but the air remained hot and thick. Entertaining Sam was a mindless activity, and her thoughts remained on work. The details of Trudy's case intertwined with her memories of Steven. Would Trudy's case go anywhere? As a victim advocate, did she have any influence over it, or would her voice go unheard? Again?

Colleen recalled how Aunt Ruth had frequently reminded her that sociologists could make good money doing market research. Market research felt like soulless work. Colleen wanted a job that required heart. But after only a week, her heart was hurting, and she was second guessing her career choice.

Sam returned with the Frisbee and acted like he was about to explode with anticipation.

"Drop it."

The Frisbee fell to the grass at the tips of her toes, and the dog's eyes darted frantically between her hands and the toy. When she reached for it, he lunged for it, too.

"Drop it!" She laughed. "I can't throw it if you're grabbing at it."

He tossed the slobbery Frisbee onto her bare feet. "Get your bare feet in the grass," Martha had said after dinner. *Earthing*, she'd called it.

Martha had also encouraged her to look for the good in the world. A happy dog was good. So was beer.

She held her palm toward Sam and said, "Wait." Then she gripped the Frisbee between her thumb and index finger. She threw it the distance of the vast yard, grimacing at the strings of drool flinging off the disk into the air.

She needed more days between now and Monday. Her first week had started and ended with gut punches. Everything in between was a blur. She wanted to clear her head, shift gears for the rest of the weekend, but she had nothing to do but think. It was too hot to do anything else.

Sam's sprint had slowed to a jog, and his lips were covered in a white froth. She grabbed the hose from the mount and opened the faucet. Sam was eager to drink. "No. No." She sprayed the water along the foundation of the house for a full minute before it had cooled enough to drink. She let the water flow into a plastic bowl, and Sam shoved his face into it. Then she hosed the drool off her feet and hands.

Colleen walked into the garage, passing the washer and dryer just before she reached the door to the kitchen. Once inside, she could still hear Sam lapping away furiously, always in threes, a sloppy waltz. She pulled a near empty bottle from the cupboard above the oven and poured herself a double over ice.

She took a sticky note from the pad she kept by the phone, scribbled a few words on it, and then stuck it to the fridge.

Buy more Jameson.

11

The rapist was seventeen now, and that called for celebration.

From the kitchen, Matthew heard his brother announce his plans. "Hey, Matty-Boy! We're gonna party tonight!"

Matthew entered the living room and scanned the faces of young men who weren't there an hour ago. "When are you leaving?" He hoped it was soon.

"Oh, we're not going anywhere. You're too young to stay home alone."

"A party here?" he asked as he maintained his distance from the tribe of thugs. He pointed toward their mother's bedroom. "What about her?"

"Kathleen picked up a night job." He lit a joint, took a long hit, and held it out to him.

He accepted the offer and said, "I know that, but she'll be pissed."

The skeleton in the recliner said, "Aren't you a little young for that?"

The rapist's eyes snapped on him. "Excuse me, Bones? Do you remember when you took your first toke?"

"Point taken." He giggled.

"Our dear mother won't be home until morning. We'll have time to clean up. Enough. Invite some of your friends over. The girls, I mean."

"I'll call some." He took a drag off the joint and immediately coughed a cloud of white smoke.

The rapist added, "That tiny chick. Call her, too."

"What tiny chick?"

"Hell if I know. She was a little thing. Meek and mild."

"Trudy." He coughed. "She only came here because you made me trick her." He held the joint out to his brother.

His brother's eyes narrowed. "Go on. Have another toke."

He took another drag.

"You tricked her, huh?"

"Tricked who?" Matthew had tried not to inhale enough to get high, but he felt lightheaded, and his thoughts fizzled before he could say them out loud.

"*Tiny Trudy,* fool. You're a giddy little boy, aren't you?"

There was something new and unsettling in his older brother's tone. He dropped his hand on Matthew's knee and squeezed it. Matthew stiffened. His brother noticed, and a hint of a smile flashed and vanished. The only time his brother looked happy was when he did stuff like this. Pranks, mind games, and now, creepy touching.

"Oh, right. Trudy." Matthew answered. "Trudy's mom is way strict. She won't be back."

"That's a damn shame. She's not the type to cause trouble. I'd like to go another round with her."

12

Earlier in the day, when Matthew's plans to sleep over at Frankie's house had fallen through, his mother said she'd call in sick to stay home. Matthew had assured his mom he'd be fine, that he'd lock his door and keep himself busy. "Besides," he'd said, "He'll go out. He always goes out."

"I'm not sure I'm comfortable with that, either," His mother had said.

"I know how to dial 9-1-1, Mom." His mom had installed a phone in his room years ago. "You worry too much. I'll be fine."

The truth was he didn't want his mom to get fired for calling in sick the first night of a second job. His mother was already exhausted and stressed out. He could tell by her sighs, and her blank stares, in everything from forgetfulness to frozen birthday dinners. But no matter how tired or stressed out his mother was, every day and night she said, "I love you," and gave Matthew a long hug and kissed his temple. And she always brought him something special from the store. Their secret, she said. She'd stopped making his lunches, but she never forgot to slip a little note in with the lunch money. They'd just spent four fun nights together house sitting. They'd played with a cool dog, watched movies, and eaten ice cream while floating around on rafts in the pool. She'd told him stories about his dad and listed the ways they were alike. He could deal with one night alone with his creepy brother and his idiot friends.

They looked like they'd melted into the living room chairs. There was the guy he knew as *Tubs*. He had bloodshot beady eyes, buried in his fat pockmarked face. The other, the skinny guy they called *Bones*, was always driving his brother around. He kicked Tubs and gave him an *are you crazy* look whenever he said something stupid. The third was about the dumbest dude Matthew had ever met, and he always looked back and forth from Tubs to Bones, and his head moved like a cat watching a ping-pong match.

Matthew looked to his brother again and said, "I'm going to go make those calls."

"Only the good-lookin' ones," Tubs called out.

He turned away and hoped another house-sitting job would come up soon.

Hearing Trudy's name had made Matthew's stomach twist and turn. Trudy was different and quiet, but she was nice. She didn't hang around people like his brother. She didn't really hang around anyone, which was probably why she'd seemed so happy when Matthew had invited her to a fake pizza party, celebrating the end of the school year. He'd invited a few others, too, but Trudy's smile had flipped a switch in his brain and turned on his conscience. He hadn't known how to un-invite the girl, to tell her to stay away, without hurting her feelings. Until now, he'd hoped nothing bad had happened to her, that maybe one of his stupid brother's friends tried to put a move on her and that was all. But now he knew his brother had done something terrible to Trudy, and he wanted to puke.

13

    Matthew stood far away from the three middle school girls who had joined the older guys. He knew it was wrong to chum the water with his former classmates, but it kept the attention off him. The first call Matthew had made was to a girl who'd beaten up at least two boys during their elementary school days. She was a latchkey kid who wore her house key around her neck, strung on a dingy shoelace. A lot of kids wore house keys around their necks, and Matthew thought it was nuts. Why would a kid advertise she was going home alone every day? This girl was pretty tough, though. Rumor had it she had beaten a pedophile almost to death with a baseball bat. She'd sounded indifferent about the party, but her cousin and a friend were listening in, and they'd gotten all excited. Three girls with one call meant he didn't have to make any more.

    A lot of girls wanted to hang around his brother and his friends, as if it raised their status to be with older guys, tough guys. His brother wasn't big and bulky, like the football players a bunch of the girls went crazy over. He was pretty short. He was okay looking. But what girls fell for was his charm. He could lay it on thick. He was like a mind reader, too. He could tell what a girl was insecure about, and if he wanted something from her, he'd compliment her on exactly that thing. One girl tried to hide curly hair by pulling it back real tight, so he gave her a compliment about how beautiful curly hair was. If a girl was a little on the chunky side, he'd talk about how he liked girls with curves, but he used words like *voluptuous*. They didn't understand that when he said, "You're so beautiful" or "I love you," his words carried no more emotion than the words he used to order a cheeseburger, if he'd ever eat one.

His brother didn't have feelings. If any of these girls took time to look into his brother's eyes for more than a couple seconds, they might see the truth. They'd know something was wrong. But he said things that made them blush and turn away giggling, or the intensity of his stare made them giddy. They couldn't hold eye contact long enough to notice that behind his dark eyes was a black hole. Everyone knows to stay away from black holes. They destroyed everything that got too close. Even the brightest light can't get out of a black hole.

Several more of his brother's friends had arrived, and a couple brought high school girls with them. Matthew faded further into the background and watched as one guy pulled his brother aside and presented him with a small clear bag containing white pills.

"Happy birthday, bro," he said as he handed the baggie to his brother, who slipped it into his front pocket.

Cheers reverberated from wall to wall when his brother announced, "It's a *Special K* night!"

The girls believed *Special K* referred to his brother's Kool-Aid recipe. When the guys jeered at their naivete, the girls assumed the Kool-Aid was spiked with alcohol.

"You'll love it," the wolves said to the sheep. "You've never had Kool-Aid this deeee-licious!"

Matthew wanted to scream at them to run and never come back. He stood by the staircase, gripping the banister while he tried to communicate telepathically. He focused hard on the message, *Don't drink it.* He made eye contact with his former classmate, and a look of suspicion fell upon the girl's face, and Matthew silently celebrated. He'd saved her.

The girl hesitated when the tray came to her. "Nah, I don't like Kool-Aid."

Maybe if she said *no*, the others would follow her lead.

Matthew caught himself nodding. He white-knuckled the banister.

But the girl's stupid cousin taunted her. She even clucked like a chicken.

And that was all it took. The desire to belong outweighed their short supply of common sense. Each one of the girls took a cup of poison. They never noticed or cared that none of the guys touched the stuff.

#

Matthew shut himself in his room and locked the door. He opened his closet and reached for the three-inch binder, labeled "Physical Science" that sat on a small bookshelf among several books that would be of no interest to his brother. He removed the empty binder from the shelf and revealed the Discman's hiding place. His best friend Frankie had given it to him last year. Matthew had found out later that Frankie had told his parents that his had been stolen at school. They'd bought him another one, on the condition it never left the house. Matthew felt bad about Frankie's antics, but Frankie said his parents were loaded and it wasn't fair that Matthew didn't have a dad to help pay for stuff.

Matthew put on the headphones and pressed the play button. Joan Osborne's voice poured out "One of Us," loud enough for him to get lost in it, but low enough to hear a knock on his door or a police siren. Then he grabbed a wad of dirty clothes from his hamper and dropped them on the floor. He retrieved a plastic bag from the bottom of the hamper. Inside was a spiral notebook and his latest book from the public library. *Without Conscience: The Disturbing World of the Psychopaths Among Us* by Robert Hare. He wished he owned the book because there were so many passages to highlight. Instead, he took notes in a spiral notebook. He'd started his list back when he checked out *Murderers Among Us*. His notes and lists were growing long enough for him to need another notebook, so he was saving his pennies.

Matthew had learned enough to know that his brother wasn't mentally ill. Maybe he was evil. That was up for debate. He definitely did evil things, and he did evil things without feeling bad at all. He had no remorse. He never felt guilty, which meant he was a psychopath. He was dangerous. He enjoyed hurting people.

That's how Matthew ended up with the white spot. Matthew was around eight years old when his brother had offered to teach him to throw a baseball, and like a fool, Matthew had agreed. Things had started off alright, and his brother had even tossed him a few encouraging words. "Nice catch," and "Good one," and stuff like that. Stuff dads might say to their kids. But then Matthew started to wonder if maybe he was doing too well. His brother started saying stuff like, "Well aren't you the shit," and "Don't get full of yourself." And then he started throwing the ball harder, not to him, but at him. Finally, Matthew had told his brother his arm was tired or something like that. He just wanted to get back to the safety of his room, where things were predictable and still. Matthew turned his back on his brother to go inside, and he felt like a brick hit him in the back of the head. He woke up on the ground, not remembering the fall.

His brother laughed and said, "I told you one more was coming."

"No, you didn't."

"Sorry, little man. It was an accident."

Matthew was a little kid then, but he knew it hadn't been an accident. His eyes welled up, and his brother said, "Don't fucking cry. Mom'll hear you and make life hell for me. You cry one tear, and I'll give you another lump to match."

The hair on the spot where the ball had hit him never grew back right. It came back white. His brother often referred to Matthew's "freak spot" as proof he sucked at baseball.

Adults were always saying stuff like *boys will be boys* and *it's natural for a teen to rebel*. Matthew's older brother didn't rebel. He hurt people. What was scarier was that he practically talked people into letting him do it.

Matthew knew his brother was going to kill one of these girls someday, if he hadn't already. Matthew knew his brother had killed Baron, their Golden Retriever, no matter how hard his mother tried to cover that up. His brother could be the next Ted Bundy, and he needed to be stopped. He also knew no one would listen to a not quite thirteen-year-old. He had to gather lots of evidence and then find someone who would listen.

Matthew sat down at his desk with his spiral notebook and opened *Without Conscience,* and started where he'd left off: *Chapter 3: Feelings and Relationships*.

He kept a dictionary on his desk. He was pretty smart, but every chapter had a word he needed to look up. *Grandiose. Glib.*

A paragraph on page forty made the hairs stand up on his arms. It talked about a psychopath who blamed his mother for his crimes, even though she hadn't done anything wrong. The psycho described her as *beautiful* and *hard-working*, words Matthew could use to describe his own mom. Then the psycho started stealing her jewelry. Things got worse from there.

He grabbed a pen that he'd nearly chewed the top off of and gripped it hard as he wrote.

Page 41. Psychopaths sometimes verbalize remorse but then contradict themselves in words or actions.

Page 43. An inmate said that his crimes had a positive effect on the victims.

Matthew added an example using his brother:

He says he taught me to always keep my eye on the ball.

As he added the period to end the sentence, a knock on the door triggered panic. He scooped up the book and the spiral notebook and tossed them into his hamper. He grabbed the dirty clothes and threw them on top. He tried to slow down his breathing and unlocked the door. Then he remembered the Discman. He ripped off the headphones and threw them into the hamper, and he shoved the CD player down the front of his pants.

He opened the door to find his brother standing there with one of the girls in his arms. She was limp, with her face turned toward his brother's chest. Matthew pulled his tee shirt down over his waistband, and his brother noticed. He noticed everything.

"Jerking off again?"

Matthew was too worried about the girl for the words to register. "What happened to her?"

"She drank too much. Lightweight."

"Too much of your *Special K*?"

"Anyway, she wouldn't stop talking about you, so I decided it's time for you to become a man."

"What?" Matthew didn't know exactly what his brother meant, but he knew it was bad, and the sleeping bear roused and stretched in his belly.

"Time to prove you're not a faggot, Matty."

Tubs appeared behind his brother and laughed that stupid laugh. "It's your turn, Matty."

Matthew's brother threw a scowl over his shoulder and said, "Fuck off, Tubs."

Matthew's heart was beating in his ears. "What do you mean by 'my turn'?"

His brother answered. "Nothing. He's drunk."

Matthew stared at his brother and the girl who didn't look so tough now with drool coming from the side of her mouth. "I think we need to call Mom."

"The fuck we do *not*."

"Or an ambulance or something."

"Grow up. She's fine. That's your fear talking."

"Yeah, I'm afraid she's gonna die, and you're going to get in trouble because you let it happen."

"Me? I'm going to get in trouble?"

Matthew stared at the two before him, but it was like he was looking at them through a toilet paper roll. He remembered the term tunnel vision, and he tried to calm down.

"Nobody forced her to drink, Matty. She just needs to sleep it off, and I don't have anywhere else to put her."

"Fine, you can put her on my bed."

His brother dropped her on the bed like she wasn't even human, like she was a bag of dirt. "And your reward for sharing your room is that you can do all you want with her until she wakes up." His brother pulled the girl's shirt up over her bra, and the house key was stuck under one of the straps. Matthew felt his groin come alive, and he hated himself for it.

"Did you rape her?"

"No, I didn't *rape* her. She got drunk, and she was hanging all over me. That's not rape."

His brother started to remove the girl's shirt.

"Don't." Matthew snapped. "I wanna do it, but give me some privacy. I don't want you watching me."

"Look at you all territorial and shit." Then he barked like a dog and left the room.

14

Kathleen closed the book. It only enhanced her stress about leaving Matthew alone with the eldest son, who'd grown stronger and somewhat smarter. His manipulation skills were increasingly effective on his peers, and he'd cultivated a thick enough layer of charm to apply them successfully on most adults. His antisocial traits had taken root long ago, which made him dangerous, yet there was nothing she could do to protect those outside her family now. She questioned how long she could continue guarding herself and Matthew. She felt certain that one day she'd read about him in the newspaper or sit in a courtroom, watching him get sentenced for murder. She felt guilty for the harm he'd caused others and for the violence he would commit in the future. How could she prevent it? She'd given countless subtle and a few blatant warnings to various girls he'd brought home, but they didn't listen. They'd looked at her like she was a crazy, unloving mom.

She'd refocused on what she could control, which was keeping her son out of her and Matthew's space, a mission that required constant, taxing attention and effort, and she wondered how many years had been taken off her life, existing the way they did. Lately, another idea had surfaced. Instead of keeping him out, could she keep him in? A few scenarios arose, but only one gained traction.

She'd been saving for months to hire someone to give the interior walls a fresh coat of paint. Painters always left the unused paint with the customer, and she considered using the leftovers to paint his window shut. One night, after enough time had passed to rule out suspicion, she could fall asleep with a cigarette burning. Her own grandfather had done that one too many times. The fire would start in her bedroom, which was directly under her son's.

No, that might take too long. He'd smell the smoke and come running down the stairs and out the front door, and at the very least, her bedroom would be destroyed.

Maybe she could obstruct his escape route.

The fire could start outside his bedroom door. He had a history of fire setting. He'd outgrown it, but it was still a believable story, certainly more believable than her falling asleep with a lit cigarette.

She pondered the details.

She could use lighter fluid to draw a pentagram outside his door and light it. He acted like the devil, so that would make sense.

No. Too dramatic, and he didn't have Satanist stuff in his room, only that collection of creepy marionettes. She could get one of those and set it on fire. She could get a bunch of those creepy puppets and douse them with gasoline. Light one that resembled her outside her own room. Now that would be something he'd do. Place them along the stairs. Light them all. That would also be cathartic for her. How she'd love to see those things go up in flames.

She didn't care if the whole house burned down as long as his corpse was in the embers and ashes.

But if *he* supposedly did this, why wouldn't he start the fire at the bottom of the stairs and just go through the front door?

Why?

Why?

To make her look guilty. Yes! To make himself look like a victim, he'd have to be trapped in his room and escape through the window. What a misfortune that the window was painted shut.

She needed to think like him. He wasn't too bright, either. Manipulative and charming, but not exceptionally intelligent.

She envisioned the scene. Fire shooting through the roof above his room while she stood in the street, looking aghast, watching her house engulfed in flames. Once summoned, firefighters would arrive quickly. They'd ask if anyone was inside. She'd have to tell them he could be in there, but three words became a mantra in her head.

Let him burn.

The door chime disrupted her fantasy, and an immense man in uniform entered the store.

"Good evening, ma'am." His voice matched his stature.

He'd caught her in the act of plotting a murder. She swallowed hard before speaking. "Hello." She took in his size. "Officer."

"Got coffee tonight?"

"Shit," she whispered. "I forgot to brew a fresh pot."

"Are you new to the store or the shift?"

"Both."

His eyes stopped on hers. "Long day?"

"Long decade."

"I understand." He nodded, and she detected sincerity.

The massive, black-haired cop with tanned skin helped her make two pots of coffee. One decaf and one regular. He poured himself one, clumsily secured a lid to the large cup, and they returned to the checkout counter.

"It's on the house," she said.

"Thank you, but I always pay."

She couldn't imagine anyone ever arguing with the man.

He spotted the book next to the register. "*Bad Men Do What Good Men Dream?*"

"You know it?"

"Can't say I do. What's it about?"

"I've just started it, but the theme seems to be that we all have a dark side, and I think he's writing about the difference between those who act on it and those who don't. It's written by a forensic psychiatrist. It has case studies and a lot of research cited."

"You a graduate student?"

"A teacher, actually." A closer look at him revealed his youth. A decade ago, he could have been one of her students. "Middle school."

"What do you teach?"

"Math."

He looked back at the book. "I see." Then he looked back to her. "This is a popular stop for beat cops on this shift." He set a dollar on the counter for the coffee, and his eyes returned to the book. "You call us if anyone bothers you."

"Thank you." She eyed his name plate. "Officer Corcoran."

"You bet," he said as he turned to leave.

After the door closed behind him, she flipped the book face down on the counter and slid it out of view.

At least three more officers came and went before her shift ended. Beyond that, foot traffic was minimal. She'd ignored the book and scrutinized her budget, determined to find more ways to cut expenses or add a little income. The mental exercise didn't distract her for long. She prayed Matthew was sleeping soundly behind a locked door, and she'd resisted the urge to call and check on him, fearing she'd wake him or rouse the monster, if he was even there. She felt like a caged animal, fierce and desperate to protect her young. She scrawled a letter of resignation, effective immediately, slipped it under the locked door of the manager's office, and counted the minutes until her replacement showed up

15

Once again, Trudy had crawled into Maxine's bed instead of her own. While her daughter slept soundly, Maxine lay awake and stared into the darkness while questioning everything.

Will the police do anything? How long will it take to arrest him?

What if the rapist retaliates? Maybe I should get a guard dog or install a security system.

Can I afford either? Can I afford not to?

Why did Trudy go there? Why did she disobey me?

At 2:00 a.m., Maxine tried reciting recipes. Usually that settled her mind, but lately it wasn't doing the trick, so she tried a different approach. She took her mind back to her dad's gym where she spent much of her time as a kid. She reviewed drills her father had taught her, like hip escapes, bridges, and sweeps. She recalled every detail of chokes, arm bars, and ankle locks. After so many years of training, the moves were still second nature.

Her recollections took a dark twist, and she envisioned the rapist in her grip. She'd never laid eyes on the monster, but she had a basic description, and her imagination filled in the blanks. She heard him crying out in pain as she hyper-extended his elbow. She felt him grow heavy under a rear naked choke as she deprived his brain of blood. But she wanted to end him as he'd tormented her daughter, by smothering him, face down in a pillow.

Trudy shifted to her other side, which pulled Maxine's attention to her current reality. Helplessness. Powerlessness. Stuck in a state of waiting. Waiting on indifferent police to do something. She knew where the rapist lived, practically a stone's throw away. She remembered the fat cop's condescending tone, telling her to stay away from his house. Would he stay away if *his* daughter had been brutalized? Would he sit on his hands?

Doing nothing felt like a betrayal. Trudy deserved better. She deserved swift justice. But by taking action, Maxine could jeopardize the case, get herself arrested, and Trudy could end up alone. She'd never do that to her. Violent fantasies were not a good coping strategy. She had to figure out a way to stay healthy and sane.

16

Matthew woke up to the sound of the girl babbling in her sleep again. He pushed himself upright. His hip and shoulder ached from lying on the floor.

"You awake now?" He asked. "Hey," he said and jiggled the bed.

"What?" She scrunched up her face. "Where am I?"

"My house. My room."

"Who?" Her words sounded heavy in her mouth.

"It's me. Matthew McDaniel. My brother brought you in here."

"Is it a school night?"

Matthew thought it was a weird question. "No, it's summer."

"Who else is here?" She rubbed palm over her face and moved her hair out of her eyes.

"I'm not sure. There were a bunch of people here. You came with two girls." Matthew wondered what had happened to them. "Your cousin, I think, and a friend. Your neighbor or somebody."

"Where'd they go?"

"I'm not sure." He leaned closer and tried to make eye contact. "Are you okay?"

She pulled his comforter over her. "I'm so cold."

Matthew thought it felt pretty warm in his room, but he heard her teeth chattering. It made her voice jerk and shake when she said, "You called me. I remember taking a drink and my cousin was clucking like a chicken."

"Yeah, I saw that." Matthew was still pissed off that this girl, who beat a pedo with a baseball bat, had caved to peer pressure. "I tried to warn you."

"Where is she?"

"I don't know. I can go look if you want."

"No, I'll go." She sat up and then careened to one side. "I feel like I'm gonna throw up."

"There's a trash can there." Matthew pointed to the small can he'd removed from his bathroom. "I put it there, just in case."

She lay down again and then she looked under the cover at herself. "Oh my God. Did we do anything?" She looked at him with eyes like saucers. "You know?"

It took him a few seconds to realize what she was asking. "No. God, no. You were passed out."

"Then where's my underwear?"

Matthew's jaw fell open.

"What did you do?" She sounded like a little kid.

"I didn't do anything except stay here and make sure you didn't croak. I wanted to call an ambulance. I've been right here on the floor the whole time."

"Sorry. I mean, thank you."

She rubbed her face on his pillow, and he remembered how she'd been drooling earlier. Even though she was pretty, he didn't want her slobber all over his pillow.

Then she said, "Your brother. He was here, right?"

"Yep. It's his party." Matthew wondered how many people were still in the house and how his mother was going to react when she got home.

"You said he brought me in here."

"Yeah. He did." Matthew wanted to ask her some questions, but he didn't know how. "Did he? Do you think my brother did something? To you?"

"I can't remember anything."

Her eyes welled up, and Matthew wished he was somewhere else, that he had a time machine and could go back and undo the damage. He was an accomplice. Again.

"You should tell someone. Tell the police."

"Tell them what? I don't remember anything."

"I dunno. Maybe we should call your mom?"

"What time is it?"

The digital clock faced the girl, so he wasn't sure. "Pretty sure it's after midnight."

"I can't call my mom. She'll kill me. I'm supposed to be sleeping over at my friend's house."

"The one that came with you?"

"Yeah."

"Where does her mom think *she* is?"

"At my house." She groaned and put her hand to her forehead. "Oh my God. What if she left me?"

Matthew was still trying to fill in the gaps. "What about your cousin? Where's she supposed to be?"

"With me, at my friend's."

"Clever, I guess."

"We do that shit all the time."

"Where were you really going to sleep, though?"

"We were going to sneak into *another* friend's house and sleep there."

The plan sounded too complicated to pull off. "Sneak in?"

"Yeah. Her dad's out of town and her mother likes to hit the sauce. Hard sleeper. My friend was going to let us crash for a few hours, and we'd slip out in the morning. Her mom would never know we were there."

"You do that shit all the time, too?"

Her breathing sounded heavy, like she couldn't get enough air. It was stuffy in his room, but he didn't want to open the door. He crawled over to a small oscillating fan on his dresser and reached up to turn it on low.

"I need to find them and get over there, I guess."

Matthew saw headlights through his window. A car had turned onto their street and was heading toward the house. "I think that's my mom. We can talk to her if you want."

"Why?"

"Tell her what happened."

"No way. She'll tell my mom, and my mom will kill me." The girl threw off the comforter, sat up and stood. She was unsteady on her feet, but determined to leave. "Besides, I don't even know what happened."

"Your mom will *kill* you?" Matthew heard that all the time and thought it was stupid.

"Yeah. I'll be grounded 'til next year."

As if on cue, Matthew's brother opened his bedroom door. "C'mon." He was giggling like a kid. "Time to skedaddle."

"To what?" the girl asked, annoyed.

"Time to get out of here, pretty girl." He winked at Matthew.

"How?"

"The front door. We time it right, and she'll never know. She comes in through the garage. Hurry up."

The girl staggered out of Matthew's bedroom with his brother, as if they were a team. Matthew heard his mother's car pull into the drive as footfalls faded as the girl and his brother headed down the stairs. He heard the garage door rising, and the front door close.

17

After her first and last night shift, Kathleen returned home to a wrecked house. Her sons were the only occupants when she arrived, but it was clear that hours, perhaps moments, ago her home had endured many others. The smell of booze and sweat lingered. There was no telling how many minors were drinking, and she expected a knock on the door any minute by an angry parent or the police.

She hoped that if her son committed a crime on his birthday, he'd be taken to the adult jail, and she had no intention of posting his bond. Maybe some time behind bars would knock some sense into him. She climbed the stairs to check on Matthew. She knocked gently, and she heard him grunt. She tried the door, but he'd thrown the lock. *Good boy.*

"It's Mom. Just checking on you. You okay?"

She heard his feet shuffle toward the door. Then the turn of the lock. The turn of the knob. "Hey, Mom," he said with a sleepy voice.

He looked like he'd grown an inch overnight. Soon he would be her height. "Are you all right?"

"Yeah, I'm fine."

"You sure?"

"Just tired, Mom. It's still dark out." One side of his mouth curled into a smile.

"I know. Go back to sleep."

"Wait." He opened his door wider and leaned against the frame. "How was work?"

"I'm not going back."

He nodded, and Kathleen sensed his relief.

"I love you, Mom."

Every few years, Matthew would do or say something that showed leaps of maturity. It could be something as simple as a new mannerism or phrase. This morning, it was the way he leaned into the door frame and the sincerity in his eyes when he'd said, "*I love you, Mom.*"

"You sure you're okay?"

"Positive."

"I love you, too, Matthew."

Kathleen looked down the hall to the master bedroom door. Her eldest had a birthday yesterday, and she'd done nothing to acknowledge it. She took slow steps in that direction until she was facing the door to the bedroom she'd surrendered to him. She raised her closed hand and considered knocking to wish him a happy birthday, but she couldn't bring herself to make contact with the door. She took a deep breath and closed her eyes. *Wish your son a happy birthday.*

She opened her eyes and gasped.

"Got ya."

Her son was standing next to her, wearing nothing but boxer shorts.

"What are you up to, mother?" He cocked his head and stared into her with eyes more suited to a goat.

"Just wanted to tell you I'm home from work. I realized I hadn't wished you a happy birthday."

"No, you hadn't, but I forgave you." He stepped into her space and put his hand on the doorknob.

Kathleen asked, "Enjoy yourself last night?"

"Sure did." He opened the door to his bedroom and stepped aside. "Would you like to come in?"

She hadn't crossed the threshold into that room for months. "I'm beat. I'm going to get some sleep."

"So am I. Are you sure you don't want to come in? Have some cuddles?"

The comment turned her mouth sour. "I'm sure."

"As you wish." He closed the door.

She returned downstairs, feeling disoriented from exhaustion. She took each step carefully, trying to avoid being distracted by the scene below. Cups on every table, overturned sofa pillows, and orange popcorn on the living room floor. How she had hoped her son had gone out to celebrate, broken the law, *any* law that would land him in jail. No such luck. She unlocked her bedroom door, stepped into her room, and glanced at the worn book on her nightstand. Hervey M. Cleckley's *The Mask of Sanity,* filled with highlighted passages and dog-eared pages. She reminded herself that her son didn't view the world the same way as normal people. He was emotionally impoverished. Jail wouldn't knock sense into him any more than it would knock stripes off a tiger.

She'd threatened to call the police a couple of times in the past, but her son had successfully manipulated her into reconsidering. The kid had a way of convincing people that doing what he wanted was good for them. Once, when she'd told him she was reporting him for stealing her car again, he reminded her that as his parent, she would have to pay the fines, go to court, attend first offender programs, counseling, and probably lose her job. He was right. She'd lost track of the times a simple value statement resulted in her returning the phone's handset to its cradle. The costs were greater than the benefits. But they weren't anymore. Today he was seventeen. He'd go to big boy jail now.

18

Trudy shuffled into the garage. The door was open, and she shielded her eyes from the shock of the morning light. "Mom, what are you doing?"

"Good morning, love." Maxine climbed down the ladder as she answered. "I'm going to start working out again."

"What's that for?" Trudy pointed to the chains hanging from the ceiling.

"That's a mount, where I'll hang this." She pointed to the canvas heavy bag propped against the wall.

Trudy's tired expression came to life. "I remember that."

"Wanna help me hang it?"

"I'll try." Trudy sounded unsure.

Mom and daughter dragged the bag from the wall, but they didn't have the strength to raise it high enough to get the S-hook over the ends of the chains hanging from the mount.

Maxine leaned over with her hands on her thighs and felt like her heart was going to break out of her chest. "I'm out of shape." She laughed in between heavy breaths. "That's enough for me. What do you think?"

Trudy nodded in agreement.

Maxine said, "Let's try again later."

Maxine collapsed the ladder and noticed the neighbor from across the street collecting the newspaper. He waved and shouted, "Good morning!" loudly enough for all the neighbors to hear.

Trudy was still in her nightgown, and Maxine directed her to go inside and get dressed.

"Morning." Maxine returned the greeting and walked onto the driveway. She noticed dark skies to the east and south. "Looks like we could get some rain today."

The man was middle-aged and fit. Maxine saw him and his wife go for a run almost every evening, but no one had ever initiated a conversation.

"Got a project going?" he asked as he pointed toward her garage.

"I do, but I've hit a snag." Maxine didn't like asking people for help, but she needed to pound on that bag. Before she could talk herself out of it, she asked, "Do you think you could lend me a hand? It'll take just a second."

"Of course." He smiled. "I'll give it a shot." He trotted across the street and met her in her driveway.

Five minutes later, her outlet and keeper of sanity hung proudly in the garage.

19

Colleen stood under an umbrella in front of the shed and sipped her third cup of coffee with hopes it would alleviate her hangover. She'd drunk too much whiskey the night before, hoping she'd fall asleep without first having to face the image of the blue-eyed girl reminding her, "*You lied to me.*" The whiskey had worked, but she was paying the price this morning.

It was an odd place for a storage shed, but it covered a more oddly placed door. Evidently, the builder had thought it was important for the homeowner to go through the garage and into the yard without having to open the main garage door, so he'd installed a standard door into the far wall. Aunt Ruth saw the addition as an invitation for serial killers, so when she'd bought the storage shed, she had the delivery guys park it against the outside of the far garage wall, over the serial killer door, forever hiding the security breach.

The shed's exterior of red paint and white frame reminded Colleen of a barn. Last night's idea wasn't so bad. Maybe she *could* convert it into usable space, sort of like a sunroom for someone who can't afford an actual sunroom. A place where she could relax, enjoy coffee and the view of the live oaks in the back yard.

She opened the door to the storage shed. It was empty except for some dirt, cobwebs and spider eggs, along with an unsettling amount of rat crap.

For this, she needed fuel beyond coffee. When Colleen was in college, chorizo and eggs had always cured a hangover, and she knew where to go to get some in Winston. She returned to the house to grab her purse and keys. Then she pulled a sticky note from a pad and scrawled a list:

>*Rent: shop vac*
>*Buy:*
>*Disinfectant/bleach*
>*Rags, scrub pads*
>*Broom, big dustpan*
>*clear sealant for floor*
>*decent garden hose*

20

His birthday weekend had been rewarding. He knew his mother didn't appreciate coming home to the mess, but she was too tired to do anything about it. In his opinion, she should've been elated he hadn't asked her to do anything for his birthday. He'd stopped doing that after the *Gremlins* fiasco when he'd turned six. He'd spent the months leading up to that day pestering her for an action figure from the movie. He'd become obsessed with Spielberg's blockbuster. So had thousands of other kids, and anything *Gremlins* related vanished from the shelves almost immediately after they were stocked.

Back then, whenever his mother had the energy to shop, he'd usually been with her, along with his little brother. She could've bought him the toy on one of their shopping trips, but timing and the element of surprise were important to her. "A matter of principle," she'd said. She'd consistently tried to go out alone to plan his special day. He'd overheard her failed attempts to get a sitter. They'd gladly watch Matthew, but none would return to take care of him, even when she offered to pay double.

She must have sacrificed her lunch breaks to buy decorations and search for a *Gremlins* toy, but she'd gotten it all wrong. When he'd opened his gift, a cute furry *Gizmo* doll, he expressed the only emotion he seemed to feel, rage. He'd wanted the red-eyed, sharp-toothed reptilian named Stripe that wreaked havoc and terrorized the town.

"*Of course,* you did," his mother had replied blandly.

He'd responded by calling her *stupid*, and he told her he "never ever" wanted her to do anything for his birthday again.

She'd replied calmly, "Now that request I can oblige."

"What does that mean?" He'd stomped one time because he hated it when she used words he didn't know.

"Happily accommodate, my dear. I will gladly *never, ever* do anything for your birthday again."

"Good," He'd said through his teeth.

That night, he'd bored screws into Gizmo's eyes and stuffed it into the coffee pot for her to find in the morning.

It hadn't produced the desired result. His mother had laughed and placed it on the kitchen windowsill, and he hated her for not being afraid.

Eleven years later, the mutilated Gizmo hung from a little noose tied around his belt loop. The thing always got a reaction. Some people laughed. Some wanted to get away from it, from him. Goldie, his wanna-be girlfriend, said it gave her the creeps. Even now, she was eying the thing. He'd allowed her to accompany him after she'd promised to never again waste his time with resistance or frivolous questions. They were riding the new DART rail system to downtown Dallas. They stood by the door of a middle car, and a couple of twenty-somethings in the nearest row were sweet on each other. As the train picked up speed, the lady held up a disposable camera and asked the rapist, "Would you mind taking our picture?"

The rapist shook his head and said, "Not my thing, lady."

Goldie started to reach for the camera, but he grabbed her arm and said, "Don't do that."

Under his breath, the lady's boyfriend mumbled, "Asshole."

The rapist cocked his head. "Hey, man. Do I know you?"

"No, punk. You don't know me."

"Oh, now I'm a punk, too?"

"Get lost, kid."

"I don't like being interrupted or taking pictures of strangers, so I'm an asshole?"

The older, bigger man began to rise from his seat, just as the brakes on the train were activated. Inertia won, and the man fell back into his seat. The rapist harnessed the laws of physics to deliver three hard blows to the man's face. Afterward, a sinister grin crawled from one ear to the other.

As if the scene had been choreographed and rehearsed to perfection, the train pulled to a stop at Mockingbird station, and the doors opened.

The rapist chuckled. "How serendipitous." He'd been waiting for the opportunity to use that word.

Like most of the riders, the wanna-be girlfriend stood frozen. He grabbed her by the arm and pulled her out of the rail car and alongside him as he strutted to the escalator while the train pulled away.

"Wait," Goldie said. "This isn't the right stop. We have to take it downtown to get to the Aquarium."

"Who said we were going there?"

"You did. You said you'd never been, and I said I'd take you for your birthday."

"I *haven't* been. I mean, I went once on a school field trip."

"But you said you'd never been."

"I haven't. Just that once. Besides, it's raining."

"The Aquarium is indoors."

"But it's not as much fun when it's raining."

He turned to face her and grabbed her hand. "Why do you look so confused?"

21

Monday morning brought Colleen a world of pain. She'd overdone it on the shed. She'd cleaned it out with a shop vac, then scoured the floors and walls with disinfectant, and then she'd painted the floor with sealant. She'd planted herbs in the small, raised gardens on either side of the shed's entrance. Finally, she'd power-washed the driveway. She was paying the price for having lived a sedentary life for too long. Every muscle ached, and she wished she'd taken a sick day.

Her arms and shoulders were so sore she could hardly lift the stack of police reports from the weekend. She scanned the cover sheet with the summary of the enclosed reports, looking for Trudy's case. She spotted an information report of a possible sexual assault of a child. The *information* qualifier indicated it might or might not get investigated. After the spectacle she'd witnessed Friday evening, she felt compelled to talk to her direct supervisor, the lieutenant over investigations, and test the boundaries of her job title.

After one week on the job, Colleen had concluded that Lieutenant Martinez was a decent guy with one foot out the door. On a white board mounted to the wall behind him, he kept a count of the days until retirement. He had an open-door policy, so Colleen left her cubicle and walked the few steps to his office. She peered inside and saw that today left 132 days. Martinez was on the phone, listening, and motioned her in.

He bobbed his head back and forth and uttered a half dozen *got its* before returning the phone receiver to its cradle.

As welcoming as he'd been, Colleen understood she was a newbie and needed to tread lightly. "I need to talk to you about a matter that might be a bit…" She searched for a word. "Delicate."

"Do you want to shut the door?"

"No, it's not *that* delicate. It's about a case, a call-out I had Friday after hours."

"Go ahead." He leaned back in his chair and let his arms fall to the sides.

Colleen reviewed the facts and noticed that Lieutenant Martinez's jaw clenched any time she mentioned Officer Jones. When she shared the comment he'd made about the thirty percent chance the girl was lying, he leaned back further, and she expected to see him tumbling backwards onto the floor.

"That stupid piece of shit!" He dragged his hands down his face and onto his neck.

Colleen stifled a smile.

The lieutenant returned to an upright position and regained his composure. "I'm sorry. I shouldn't be cussing like that."

"No need to apologize. I'm kind of relieved to hear it's not the normal way of handling things."

"Most certainly is not." His speech landed heavily on the *ts*. "I wish they'd fire that son of a bitch."

"So will the case get assigned?"

"Probably." He pulled a stack of reports off the shelf behind him and found Trudy's. He read at lightning-speed and confirmed. "Yep, this'll go to Youth Crimes, and it'll get assigned to Detective Lawler. Crimes against children."

"Is he with the Children's Advocacy Center?"

"Yeah. Good people. You know how this works?"

Colleen welcomed a refresher, so Martinez explained how the center collaborated with law enforcement. One of the center's forensic interviewers would interview Trudy. Detective Lawler would observe from another room. He'd work on a team with the advocacy center's staff, doctors from the children's hospital, and prosecutors. The center also provided free counseling services for both Trudy and her mother.

Colleen asked, "Is it okay if I let the mom know that a detective will be assigned and that the advocacy center will be involved? She left with a pretty bad taste in her mouth."

"Absolutely. She can file a formal complaint against Jones, too, if she has the inclination."

Back in her cubicle, Colleen dialed Maxine's number. On the fourth ring, a sleepy voice answered.

"Ms. Jackson?"

"Mmm-hm."

"It's Colleen Heenan. The victim advocate. I'm sorry if I woke you."

"Gimme me a second."

Colleen heard rustling and then, "Go ahead."

"I have an update for you, but I can call later if it's not a good time. If you're sleeping."

"I have a catering business. I stay up late trying new recipes. Calms my nerves."

Colleen heard a clank, followed by more rustling, and then a clearer voice said, "It's a good time. Go ahead."

She gave Maxine the updates and couldn't discern if the woman was pleased or still feeling sour. Probably a combination of both.

After the call, Colleen slowed down and reviewed the details in the report. The officer's narrative read like something a defense attorney would relish. She moved on to Trudy's written statement, and halfway through it, her throat hardened. She swallowed deliberately, attempting to force the lump down, and stopped reading. On Friday, she'd considered that the offender might be the run-of-the-mill date rapist, the guy who rapes because the opportunity arises, because he views sex as his prerogative and explains the crime away as a mere misunderstanding or blames it on drunkenness. This assault was nothing like that. It revealed signs of hatred, hints of sadism. In her statement, the girl wrote that when she cried and asked why he was doing this to her, the rapist had laughed and said, "*It's my nature.*"

Colleen struggled to keep Trudy's assault separate from her own. In her head, she'd always known it wasn't her fault, but in her heart she'd felt like she was partly to blame. She had frozen when she should've fought. She didn't tell anyone until years later because she was so scared of what he might do to her. But her head and heart aligned the moment she'd set eyes on Trudy. The girl was about the size Colleen had been, and at that moment she'd realized the futility of fighting. Her chest felt heavy as she pictured her younger self, like Trudy, so easily lured into danger and so effortlessly conquered.

22

Matthew's stomach clenched with hunger. His mom seemed lost in a trance, staring at a wall of shelves with cards showing shades of white. They had weird names like *Alabaster* and *Sea Salt*. Then, there was one called *Swiss Coffee*. He couldn't have thought of a stupider name than that for white.

Matthew said for the third time, "Mom, I'm going to look at power tools." He'd added a gentle nudge to her shoulder.

Finally, she took her eyes off the shelf. She looked at him, but she seemed detached, like a zombie. She also looked old. Her skin seemed like it was too big for her face, and she had dark pits under her eyes. Her shirt had a stain down the front. It looked like she'd spilled tartar sauce from today's cafeteria lunch. That was something kids, dads, and old people did. Not moms, and definitely not his mom. He scanned down to her toes, sticking out from under the worn tan strap of her ancient Birkenstocks. She didn't paint her toenails like the other moms did, but he didn't care about that. What bothered him was how mangled they looked. Some were too long. Others were short, but crooked, and it looked weird. The skin on her heels was cracking, too. She was starting to look like a homeless person.

"What's up?" She asked.

"Mom, it's like you're in a trance." He smiled, trying to snap her out of it.

His mother turned back to the shelf. "I don't know why it's so hard for me to choose a color. It's not like it really matters."

Matthew couldn't help but laugh at her struggle. "You're having a hard time choosing a white. Why are there so many shades of white? I don't get it."

"Too white and it blinds you. Not bright enough, and it looks stale."

"Why are you wanting to paint now? Why not wait until he's gone? He's just gonna ruin it, you know. He'll probably draw some twisted shit all over the new walls." He cussed on purpose to see if she was paying attention.

"Because it's time."

His mother didn't balk at his language.

"Time for what?" Matthew wanted to tell her it was time to eat. They didn't usually run errands after school. His stomach gurgled. It needed food.

His mother didn't look away from the thousand shades of white. "Huh?" She was still in her trancelike state.

"It's time for *what*, Mom?"

She looked at him again, and she put her hand on his cheek. "How's Frankie? You haven't seen him in a while? You should schedule time to hang out there." She paused and nodded slowly, too many times. "At his house, like you used to. A sleepover."

"Mom?"

"Yes, Matthew?" She kept her hand on his cheek.

"You said, 'it's time.' What's it time for?"

She took a deep breath and exhaled it in his face.

"I'm guessing you had the fish sandwich for lunch?"

And just like that, she snapped out of her funk and acted normal again. "It's time to eat, actually. That's what it's time for."

Matthew knew that's not what she was thinking when she'd said it the first time, but it didn't matter. She was back from whatever strange place her brain had gone to, just in the nick of time, before he passed out from starvation.

23

Colleen arrived at home feeling heavy and low on hope. She'd studied crime and criminal behavior and even taught a few college courses on the topics. But she hadn't been up close to victims before, especially one with whom she identified so intensely. She stared at the kitchen counter for a while, walked from one end of the house to the other, and then she trudged outside to the shed only to find more rat shit.

She growled as she returned to the garage for the broom and dustbin. She swept forcefully at the filth invading her sacred space and sabotaging its potential. She remembered reading somewhere that wherever there was beauty, ugly was bound to make an appearance.

Her thoughts went straight to Trudy. Colleen marched the dustbin to the metal trash can, lined with a lawn and leaf bag, and dumped the droppings into it. Then she yanked the spray bottle of diluted bleach off the shelf and returned to the shed to spray the floor. Muscles in her forearm she'd never known existed burned with every squeeze of the trigger.

The pain inflicted on Trudy's little body. She could feel it.

She used both hands to spray the disinfectant.

Unheeded cries for help. Alone in fear, confusion, betrayal and shame.

The trigger broke.

She took a few steps outside onto the grass, turned back and hurled the plastic bottle into the shed.

That was stupid. Get yourself together.

She kicked off her flip flops and paced the lawn. Sam had put distance between them and kept watch from the driveway. Under the live oaks,

Colleen gathered her composure and then returned to the shed. Watered-down bleach had splattered the walls and pooled on the floor and the air stung her eyes and sinuses. Sam came to her side, sneezed twice, and wandered off and into the garage.

After she'd finished cleaning and returned inside for the night, she grabbed a sticky note.

BUY RAT TRAPS

24

Yesterday evening, Colleen had stared at the note to herself, and she decided not to wait. She'd gone to the hardware store, bought three traps and set them up in the shed. She didn't get up early enough to check for success this morning before work, but she hoped she'd come home tonight and find carnage.

Her line rang, and the display showed Detective Lawler was calling. She placed her hand on the receiver and noticed her fingers were dry and cracking from the bleach.

She picked up the phone, and after some gratuitous, scripted niceties, Lawler said, "So, you already talked to the victim and the victim's mother." His tone was prickly.

"Yes. When I met them at the station the night they made the report."

"But you called her yesterday, too."

"I did." She pulled the phone away from her face and gave it a quizzical look. Then she spoke into it. "I called her after talking with Lieutenant Martinez, with his permission, to inform her that the case would be assigned to you." She put the phone to her ear to hear his response.

"Why'd you go to the lieutenant and not my sergeant?"

"Martinez is my direct supervisor."

She heard him sigh, and it sounded a bit dramatic.

Lawler told Colleen that he would call Maxine to schedule a forensic interview. Then he waffled between speaking vaguely about the investigative process and divulging details she knew were off limits, like the suspect's juvenile criminal history, which included an allegation of sexual assault.

Colleen was new to the job, but clearly so was Lawler, at least in the investigator's role.

He said, "We don't usually get cases involving two teens. That is, rarely do those cases go anywhere,"

"She's twelve, you know, not really a teen. He was two weeks shy of seventeen when he did this."

"I haven't read the details yet."

She couldn't resist asking, "How many of these cases have you worked?" She detected the faint but distinct scent of bleach on her fingers.

"Enough," he countered.

She grabbed a sticky note and scribbled *work gloves* on it.

The remainder of the day consisted of reading too many incidents of humans being horrible to each other. Domestic violence and sexual abuse, assaults and drunk driving were tragically commonplace. No wonder cops were so jaded.

25

Kathleen unlocked the front door, and as she and Matthew stepped inside, he asked, "Don't you want to leave that in your car or the garage or something?"

He was pointing to the red gas can in her hand.

Kathleen felt her heart rock in her chest. "Right!" She said and immediately realized her voice was too cheery. She cleared her throat and tried to speak normally. "I forgot I had it in my hand."

"You want me to do it for you?"

"Nah. I'll do it."

She started to return to her car to use the garage door opener, and she stopped and turned back to Matthew. "Hey. Did you get a hold of Frankie? About that sleep over?"

"Mom, it's only been a day. And I thought we were house-sitting this weekend? Do you *need* me to go away for some reason?"

She caught his eyes move to the gas can and then dart back to hers. "No, honey. Of course not."

"Thought maybe you had a hot date."

He was teasing, and the laugh that shot out of her mouth sounded hysterical. "God no!"

He smiled and said, "I'll call him soon."

"Whenever you want to," She said, trying to conceal her sense of urgency. "Are you packed?" she asked, pretending she hadn't forgotten about the house-sitting job.

"It'll only take me a second."

Then, he looked back at the gas can. "Mom?"

"Yeah, love."

He kept his eyes on the can and said, "I don't want you to get upset, but…"

She didn't like the way he kept eying the can. Matthew was intuitive, sometimes unnervingly so. "What is it?"

He looked back at her, and his smile was gone. "Maybe you shouldn't leave that in the garage. It might give him some ideas. You know?"

26

Colleen dropped her bags in the living room and went straight to the shed, with high hopes and Sam on her heels.

The birdseed and peanut butter were gone, but the traps were empty, and crap was everywhere.

"Damn it to hell!" She dropped to her knees, buried her face in her hands and let loose a series of expletives. Her wallowing was interrupted by strange noises that sounded like muffled coughs. She crawled a few feet toward the noise, and in the driveway she saw Sam making excited utterances in the play position - shoulders down, hips up and tail wagging -- oblivious to her angst. She looked for the source of his amusement and saw before him a gray and white cat with a dead rat in its mouth.

Pure joy coursed through her veins. She whispered, "Oh, you're a good kitty."

Sam hopped around enthusiastically. The cat couldn't have cared less.

Colleen stayed on her hands and knees. "Sam, are you going to introduce me to your most useful friend?"

The rat assassin disappeared behind a rose bush with its kill.

She climbed to her feet and jogged into the house, whispering, "Please, please, please," as she rushed to the pantry.

She pulled open the pantry door and scanned the shelves. "Yes!"

She swiped the can of tuna from the shelf and grabbed a paper plate from a stack on top of the fridge. Despite holding cats in contempt, she wanted this one to establish residency.

After placing the dinner on the driveway, she returned inside and stuck a note to the fridge.

Cat food and bowl

27

Maxine was stirring tomatillo gazpacho when she heard Trudy approaching. The sound of her feet sliding along the tile floor told Maxine the girl was already in her pajamas and bunny slippers.

"Going to bed early?"

"No. Just wanted to get comfy." She leaned against the wall by the door to the back patio and fiddled with an old Rubik's cube.

When Maxine was Trudy's age, not a weekend passed without a day at the community pool, park, or rec center, almost always followed by a sleepover. Her daughter's life felt lonely, but so did hers. Alwin was a strange place. It touted a small town feel and slathered every storefront window with posters displaying the slogan *One Town One Team*, but there wasn't any *one love* here. Their street housed families with kids Trudy's age from all over the world, yet none welcomed her. The African families at the end of the street, whose native countries warred with each other, stuck together here. They played basketball in the driveway, but Trudy was never invited to join them. She wasn't accepted by the Indian families, either, who stopped playing and stared whenever Maxine and Trudy passed by. The Mexican family across the street included a little girl Trudy's age, but the kid was kept on a very tight leash and consequently, terrified of everything. As a result, Trudy and Maxine spent weekends together. They played *Uno* and checkers. They rode bikes and cooked. Trudy even assisted her at catering events. Maxine worried the incessant togetherness might stifle the kid's growth.

The bells jingled on the outside of the back door.

"I'll get it." Trudy said, with the doorknob within her reach.

"Okay." Maxine's response was automatic, too quick. She'd taken safety for granted when in reality, no place was safe. Danger lurked around every corner.

Trudy opened the door and Maxine held her breath, looked over her shoulder, wooden spoon frozen in hand, until she saw the orange and white front paws cross the threshold, followed by a single mew, a greeting the wild neighborhood cat always delivered upon entering their home.

"Please lock the door, hon," she said as Trudy was already in the act.

Her daughter came to her side and said, "I've never been here before."

"What do you mean you've never been here before?" She chuckled. "You've been here hundreds of times."

"Not tonight I haven't. Not with you and a colorful cat and your summer soup cooking on the stove."

Maxine felt like she'd been propelled into a *Pooh and Piglet* scene, and her shoulders softened. "I stand corrected."

She put her free arm around Trudy's shoulders, kissed her head, and breathed her scent.

28

Of his few associates, the rapist was the least in both physical stature and stupidity. The disorganized group consisted of three tonight, the rapist, a half-wit, and the skeletal driver known as *Bones*. The trio cruised around Winston, killing time before heading to a party. The rapist always took the back seat so that he could keep his eyes on his companions. More than once, he had to tell the half-wit to turn the music down. The driver seemed to appreciate that, but the rapist didn't do it for his benefit. Loud music drew negative attention.

The half-wit had been tap-dancing on the rapist's nerves, which was nothing new. Now that he was seventeen, though, the stakes were higher, and every idiotic word, gesture, or maneuver ratcheted up his anger. So when De la Soul's "Me Myself and I" came on the radio, and the half-wit once again cranked up the volume, the rapist slapped him upside the head. Hard.

Bones turned down the volume.

The rapist asked the half-wit, "Do you know what ire is?"

"Ire?" the half-wit replied, still stunned by the blow. "Is that a kind of food or something?"

"No, you imbecile. It means intense anger or wrath."

The half-wit let loose a chuckle. "Wouldn't want to eat that."

"You're going to eat a bullet if you keep heating up my ire with your feeble-minded bullshit."

The half-wit cowered in his seat, rubbed his head, and mumbled, "Sorry, man."

The rapist ignored the apology. His mind had moved on to more important things. Knowing that bringing gifts to a party elevated a person's status, he told the driver, "We need beer for the guys and some of those fruity drinks for the ladies. Make it happen."

In the rearview mirror, the rapist watched the driver's eyes narrow, and his brows crept toward each other. Bones wasn't someone he wanted to piss off. Unfortunately, he needed the guy, so he said cheerfully, "You're a good man, Bones. Don't know what I'd do without you." He reached forward and patted Bones' shoulder as he'd seen men do. When he saw Bones' expression relax, he knew the gesture had worked.

Bones said, "I got you."

Then he pulled into a secluded parking lot adjacent to an independently owned convenience store known for overlooking fake IDs. Aside from that fine establishment, the strip mall was abandoned. He parked in a spot out of sight, away from any parking lot lights or security cameras, like the rapist preferred. As the group exited their vehicle, a lone young man on foot nodded as he passed by.

The rapist called to him. "Hey, man! Got a sec?"

The sun hung low, and the lone man shielded his eyes, slowed his walk, and looked over his shoulder. He stopped, leaving himself more than an arm's length of distance from the group.

"What's up?" he asked in a neutral tone.

"Can I bum a cigarette?" The rapist asked.

"Sorry. Can't help you." He locked eyes with the rapist, who saw something register in the guy. His head cocked almost imperceptibly, but the rapist caught it. Did it reveal familiarity or was the guy posturing? Either answer inspired the same response.

The rapist took three swift steps, and within seconds he had the lone man bloodied, and on his knees, staring at a pistol shoved between his teeth.

The half-wit had joined in and lost control, was frothing at the mouth and shouted, "Give us your fuckin' money!"

The rapist, whose heart rate had increased slightly and only due to having expended energy, kept the pistol in the victim's mouth and gave the half-wit a vexed look.

The half-wit looked back at him and huffed, "What?" through his spittle.

The rapist answered flatly. "I warned you." He removed the pistol from the victim's mouth and shot the half-wit in the face.

The driver's bony jaw dropped, his eyes nearly popped out of their sockets, and he threw his hands over his ears.

The lone man scurried to his feet and ran like hell.

The rapist watched the lone man sprint like his feet had taken wings. "That's how I know you."

The driver's eyes darted from the dead half-wit, back to the shooter, and to the victim on the run. Sweat beaded his brow and upper lip. He panted and repeated, "Oh shit! Oh shit! We gotta get outta here!"

The lone man flew into the traffic on Deaton Street, and tires screeched, and horns blared as he and the cars dodged each other.

Showing no sign of distress, the rapist turned to his panicked companion. His hooded eyes didn't blink but bored into the driver, and despite the deafening noise from the gunfire, he didn't raise his voice. "Bones, I should drive," he said, and extended his hand for the keys.

A clerk and two customers emerged from the convenience store, and the cool-headed shooter pointed the muzzle at them. They retreated back into the store, where they would certainly call for help if they hadn't already.

He turned back to Bones and again held out his palm for the keys.

The driver's bugged out eyes darted back and forth between the gun and his dead friend.

The rapist stated plainly, "You keep them in your right front pocket." He pointed toward the pocket in case the driver was still unable to hear or process language.

Bones dug into his front pocket, and the keys danced in his trembling hand as he passed them to his comrade. Then, he did what he was told when the shooter opened the back door.

"Lie down on the back seat and stay down. Cops will be looking for two young males, not one."

29

Officer Garrett Corcoran had completed his last phase of field training and finally had the freedom to patrol without a training officer hovering over him.

He stood inside a small pizza joint where the victim had found refuge. Corcoran could see he was young, probably an older teen. He was tall and lean and wore athletic pants and a yellow tee shirt, wet with blood. Still shaken and in shock, the kid sat slumped in a plastic chair behind the counter.

The pizza joint's owner was a large Kurdish gentleman who remained calm. He'd seen far worse than this. "He came running inside, begging for help," he'd told Corcoran.

The young man could hardly string three words together.

"He put a gun in my mouth. A gun in my mouth."

It was clear that the suspect did more than that. The guy's eye was almost swollen shut, both lips had been split, and blood had dripped from his scalp and face down his neck and onto his tattered shirt.

"He…he…he shot that guy in the face."

"What guy?"

"The guy he was with. The really mad guy."

"Where's the guy he shot?"

"My ears hurt." The kid's breathing was shallow.

"That's from gunfire. Where's the guy he shot?"

"I don't know. Probably on the ground over there." He pointed a shaky finger toward the busy street outside the pizza place.

The Kurd said, "I saw this man running from that direction," and he pointed slightly east, toward a convenience store across the road.

Corcoran spoke into the radio. "Need a unit to investigate. Possible shooting victim related to this. Approximate location is 700 block of West Deaton Street." He also requested medical assistance for the kid.

Corcoran looked at the kid and said, "Take a few deep breaths."

Dispatch responded. "Can you give further details?"

"Victim here reports that the suspect in his assault shot a fellow suspect in this offense at the scene."

Then a sergeant came over the radio. "I'm en route on that."

"The guy with the gun…" The kid paused.

"What about the guy with the gun?"

"He looked so familiar. I know him. Like, my body knew him, but my brain couldn't connect the dots."

Corcoran said, "It might come to you later. You're probably still in shock right now."

The kid's chin quivered as he spoke. "The sun was blinding me, but got a look at his eyes for just a second. I remember those eyes. Something's wrong with them."

30

Colleen stared at the computer screen and became aware of her curled lip. Aunt Ruth and Martha had been nagging her to try online dating. At best, the whole phenomenon felt soulless, but she'd promised to keep an open mind. The first dating site was *Kiss.com*, and the name alone ruled that one out. The other option was the less provocatively titled *Match.com*.

She scrolled through her saved photos that had potential to serve as her profile picture, and narrowed it down to two. Both had Sam in it. She looked better in the photo when he was a pup, but she preferred the one in which the dog looked more formidable, even if one of her eyes was half-shut. She hadn't mustered the guts yet to create an account. She stared at the screen, wondering how many psychos and serial killers lurked within the site, and she closed the window.

She checked the time and decided it was well after the appropriate hour, so she headed to the kitchen to grab a beer from the fridge with Sam on her heels.

His floppy ears perked up as much as floppy ears could, and he snapped his head toward the pet door and charged through it. That was nothing unusual. The dog did it every time he heard a car in the alleyway, a neighbor's door shut, or a leaf fall from a tree. Colleen popped the top off her beer and a sound caught her attention. She stood still and listened intently.

Baying. Sam was baying. That was a first.

She opened the kitchen door and stepped into the garage, which was opened to the back driveway and yard. Sam stood in the middle of the lawn, howling. She could hear a few other dogs doing the same. Under their cries, she heard sirens in the east, muted by distance. Then a second wave of sirens erupted and grew louder as they neared, stirring up all the neighborhood canines, and she identified the source as a fire truck and an ambulance. They'd raced from the station west of her subdivision and faded as they continued east to join the initial bunch. Two sets of emergency vehicles. A year ago, she wouldn't have thought much about sirens. Now, the sounds triggered speculation.

A car crash was probably the most likely scenario. But what if it was something else? Maybe it was a police pursuit that ended tragically for someone. Maybe they were rushing to the scene of a murder. She listened for police sirens but didn't hear any. She called Sam inside and closed the main garage door. It was probably an incident at the nursing home down the road. She slipped on a ball cap and sneakers, which sparked Sam's unmanageable enthusiasm.

"Yeah, buddy, we're going for a walk."

She took a long swig from the bottle while the dog pranced around the back living room.

"Hold on, Sam. It's a sin to waste beer."

She slammed down the remains, grabbed the leash from the hook by the front door, and off they went. The sun was nearly down, but the air was thick, pressing the residual heat against her skin. They headed east out of her neighborhood and south to Deaton Street. At the intersection, she looked east and saw the flashing lights and walked in their direction.

"We're going to do our best to pretend we're not gawkers or rubberneckers."

Sam pulled on his leash, wanting to run, so she humored him until a wet burp forced her to stop.

"No jogging for me, buddy." She felt another burp coming and braced herself for the unwanted extra.

She observed an ambulance on their side of Deaton, parked too far beyond the nursing home to involve anyone there. Several squad cars had joined it, and it appeared to be a crime scene.

"See? I bet it was a murder."

Onlookers had emerged from the nearby convenience store and several other storefronts set further off the street.

Almost directly on the other side of Deaton, in front of a take-out pizza place, was another set of flashing lights. The ambulance siren fired up and exited the parking lot, turning east onto Deaton and disappearing in the direction of Winston Regional Medical Center.

Colleen and Sam stopped at the edge of the nursing home's perimeter and then cautiously continued into the large parking lot that led to the scene. She guided Sam onto the grass, for the pavement maintained enough heat from the day to raise her concerns for his paws. A patrol car in front of the pizza place pulled out of the parking lot, turned west on Deaton Street, and made a U-Turn. The driver slowed and turned into the parking lot, passed in front of her and continued a short way before stopping again.

A tall, dark and possibly handsome uniformed officer stepped out of the vehicle. As he walked to the scene, he looked monstrous in size. She felt like a voyeur and decided it was best to move along. At that moment, the immense officer turned back in her direction and walked toward her with purpose. His approach was so intimidating and deliberate that she looked over her shoulder to see if a madman was behind her. She saw no threat, but that did little to alleviate her anxiety. Sam whined, uncertain about the events unfolding.

"Ma'am," the officer said.

"Yes, sir?" Her voice was a child's, not her own.

"How're you doing?"

She cleared the second grader from her throat. "Just fine, officer."

"Can you tell me anything about what happened here?"

I know that voice.

"No, I just walked up. Needed to take the dog for a walk."

"You live nearby?"

"About a half mile back that way." She nodded to the west.

The monster cop turned his attention to the dog. "What's his name?"

"This is Sam."

"That's easy." He chuckled. "May I?" He held up his palm.

"Sure. He's friendly."

The mammoth in uniform leaned down and let Sam sniff his hand. Then the man delighted the dog by rubbing behind his ears. There was something familiar about him. His voice. His stance. The memory refused to surface.

"He *is* friendly." He stepped back, smiling and adjusted his vest. His tanned skin glistened in the setting sun. He pulled something from his front shirt pocket. "Here's my card. If you hear or think of anything that might be relevant to this situation, please call."

She eyed the card. "Will do, Officer G. Corcoran."

Then, she remembered. Officer Corcoran taught at Winston Police Department's Citizens Police Academy.

"I went through CPA and heard you present about…" She looked up from the card, ready to share the memory, but Officer Corcoran was already marching back to the scene. She looked at Sam and finished her thought. "About officer safety."

She turned to walk home. "If I ever have to call 9-1-1, please, Lord, send that guy."

31

Untroubled, the rapist drove back to Alwin with the silent skeleton frozen in an awkward horizontal position across the back seat.

It was twilight now. He made a brief stop at Bethany Lake, unconcerned that several cars passed as he tossed the pistol into the shallow waters. Then he drove home.

There, he took two beers from the fridge and returned the keys to his driver.

"Congratulations," he said with a curled grin. "You're officially an accessory to murder."

"I am?"

"Yep." He handed him a beer and raised the can to toast. "Just in case you start feeling bad about it and experience the urge to relieve your guilty conscience, remember you'll go down with me. Best to keep quiet." His reassuring tone disguised the threat as friendly advice.

"I won't say anything."

"Bones, you wouldn't do well in prison."

He shook his head. "Hell no. I'm not going to prison." He struggled with opening his beer.

The rapist shrugged. "Makes no difference to me." He reached for his accomplice's beverage. "Let me help you with that."

The driver handed him the can. "I'm terrified of prison, living in a cage like an animal."

"I know you are." He pulled off the tab and handed it back to his frightened accomplice.

"Thanks." The driver took a long swig. He looked around as if he'd just realized where he was. "Where's your mom?"

"Kathleen's at one of her house-sitting gigs."

"That's cool for you."

"Very."

The skeleton's anxiety returned. "You worried?"

"About what?" He chugged half the contents of the can and guided his rattled companion to a chair at the kitchen table. He caught a whiff of the familiar tangy odor coming off Bones. Stress. Fear.

As Bones took a seat, he scoffed. "You're not worried about getting caught?" His hand trembled as he raised the drink to his lips.

"Can't say that I am." The rapist leaned back against the island.

Bones set his beer on the table and worked his thumb into his palm. "We don't think the same way."

The rapist chugged the rest of the beer.

The driver shifted positions twice before asking, "What made you so mad back there?"

"What makes you think I was angry?"

"I mean, you shot a guy. A friend."

"He wasn't a friend. He was more like a remora." Another word he'd had few opportunities to use.

"He was a *what*?"

"A remora. A suckerfish that latches onto a shark. Goes along for the ride."

"Oh."

"And I wasn't angry. He shouldn't have lost his shit. He'd be fine if he'd kept his fists to himself and his mouth shut." The rapist stretched, yawned loudly and then said, "The guy was a loose cannon. It's not like I didn't warn him." He moved away from the island to grab another beer. On the way to the refrigerator, he said, "I still want to make that party. It's my birthday week." He smiled and postured like The Joker. "I'm gonna celebrate it to death."

Bones dared to disagree. "Shouldn't we lay low? At least for the night?"

"Why?"

His leg bounced furiously under the table. "I thought we came here to hide out. You know, keep our heads down."

"Hiding is boring, man. We didn't come here to hide." The rapist chuckled. "We came here for beer. Why pay when we can get it for free?"

32

Independence Day arrived, and 108 degrees of heat came with it. Maxine and Trudy found a spot on the lawn in front of the stage. Emerald City would perform in an hour, and afterwards, the crowd would enjoy an elaborate fireworks display. Maxine unfolded a large, soft blanket, and Trudy helped her spread it over the grass. They plopped down together, and Maxine opened the picnic basket. She removed two handheld misters, containing more ice than water, and handed one to Trudy.

"I made your favorite."

"I know. I smelled you cooking it. Thank you, Mom."

"I packed those chips you like, too."

July Fourth celebrations were a tradition for them. Independence Day was one of the few holidays that always felt right, and Maxine was excited to attend Alwin's event. However, this year, Trudy opposed the mere *idea* of attending a public gathering. The girl had an unending list of *what-if* questions.

What if he's there?

What if his brother is there?

What if he told people from school, and they're there?

What if he tries to hurt you?

Finally, Maxine had interjected. "Maybe it would help to focus on what we can control and what we know."

"Like what?"

"Well, first of all, you're on summer break, so school isn't really a factor."

"Yeah, but people still talk."

"That's true. And there are a lot of *what-ifs* that could drive us cuckoo for Cocoa Puffs, so here is one thing we know for sure."

"What?"

"We can leave any time we want. If you feel scared or uncomfortable, we can pack up and head home."

She nodded.

"We also know that police will be there, and we can get help from them if we had to."

"Okay."

"We know we like fireworks, and it's supposed to be a great show."

"Right."

"We both like live music, and this band is really good."

"Yeah, I've heard."

"And July Fourth is *our* thing, right?"

"Right."

"Nobody should be able to steal our thing from us."

And for Trudy, that was the deciding factor. She'd been robbed of enough.

Maxine smiled and greeted people as they passed by and plopped down in the empty spaces around her and Trudy. She felt alive and normal surrounded by people with a common purpose, who seemed decent and happy, at least for tonight. As Maxine watched Trudy pick a crumb of crispy batter from a drumstick, she noticed the puffiness under her eyes, which had lost their shine. Sweat glistened on her forehead and cheeks, but still, her young skin no longer glowed. She wasn't consistently sleeping on her own yet. Most mornings, Maxine woke to find Trudy next to her. Trudy looked up from her half-eaten drumstick and released a small smile that stopped short of her eyes. Still, Trudy seemed more at ease than Maxine had anticipated.

Fifteen minutes before show time, Trudy and Maxine leaned into each other and swayed to the rhythm of an old Motown song coming through the speakers. Maxine felt normal, fully present, and hopeful, and then Trudy stiffened.

The girl tugged frantically at Maxine's arm, and tears formed in her eyes. She whimpered, "He's here."

Maxine pulled her into her chest, and Trudy buried her face under her mother's chin.

Maxine whispered, "Where, honey? Where is he?"

She shook her head fervently, as if the perpetrator could read her thoughts over the raucous music.

"Where, Trudy? I've got you. No one is going to hurt you."

She lifted her head and spoke into Maxine's ear. "By that fence near the stage." And immediately said, "Don't look."

Maxine had already looked, and the rapist's piercing gaze locked onto her and her little girl. He shook his head slowly, and Maxine knew he knew.

Trudy had talked.

33

Kathleen and Matthew were drenched in sweat and trying not to let the heat ruin the evening. Kathleen swallowed a rock that had formed when she noticed married couples and their children on proper picnic blankets or in comfortable chairs. Families played Frisbee together. Their kids ran to and from the playground. Clusters of teens checked in with their parents but otherwise strolled around independently.

She noticed only one other duo without a father, and the lady had it together. The woman and her daughter were seated on a large blanket at an angle ahead of her, allowing her to admire and envy the mom while going unnoticed. The woman brought a picnic basket packed with a variety of goodies, from homemade fried chicken to battery-operated fans that spritzed cold water.

Kathleen leaned toward Matthew and said, "I'm sorry."

"What for?"

"I should've prepared for this better. It's hot, and we're crammed onto this crummy beach towel with melted slushies and sticky hands."

"It's okay. Don't be sorry."

"I'd hug you, but it's so hot."

"Yeah, we'd stick together, and that'd be gross."

Kathleen scanned the crowd, and Matthew offered an alternative. "Wanna go?"

"Where would you want to go?"

"To the place we're house-sitting. They have a pool."

"What about the fireworks?"

He shrugged one shoulder. "You've seen one. You've seen them all."

"And the live music?"

"We've already heard a lot of music, and Emerald City isn't really my type, anyway."

"What is?"

"Joan Osborne. Sound Garden. Green Day." He wiped a mop of hair off his forehead. "Grunge."

"Grunge is still a thing?"

"I don't know. Maybe not, but I don't care. I like it."

"You sure about leaving?"

"Yeah, mom. It's fine. Let's go cool off."

As they rose to their feet and peeled the sweat soaked towel from the backs of their thighs, Kathleen noticed the little girl who had been enjoying fried chicken was now clinging to her mother. She had a more direct view of the mom, and she could see her staring ahead at something, fixated as if she'd spotted danger. Kathleen searched for the threat.

Her stomach twisted when she saw him. Her son. Staring down the mother, shaking his head slowly, menacingly. Then he raised his arm and pointed at the woman, the same way he'd pointed at her in the grocery store more than a decade ago.

Her head snapped back to the woman and the girl, who wouldn't let go of her mom. The woman was packing up with her one free hand.

"What have you done now?" Kathleen whispered.

Matthew asked, "Are you talking to me?"

"No, love. Not you."

"What's going on?"

"Nothing." Her voice was curt. "I was talking to myself. Thought I'd forgotten something."

Her eldest was too far away to reprimand, not that it would've made any difference. She didn't want to be seen with him, anyway. He'd ruined the evening for that lovely woman and her daughter, like he ruined everything. He put nothing good into the world, only pain and suffering.

She wished him harm.

She wished him dead.

Horrible thoughts swirled around her head, thoughts a mom should never have about her child. *Offspring*, she corrected herself. *He is offspring.* And she felt ashamed she'd brought him into existence.

34

The long weekend reminded Colleen of how swiftly and painfully her social circle had shrunk after her divorce. She sat on a Mexican blanket in the backyard with her meat-lovers pizza. Despite the box fan blowing in her direction, her clothes were damp with sweat. She swatted at flies and focused on the shed while Sam focused on the next piece of crust he might get.

Independence Day celebrations would continue through the weekend. Like most dogs, Sam hated fireworks, so they moved inside before the terror began. She fought the urge to climb into bed. It wasn't even dark yet. The work hours were long, the commute added at least another hour to the day, and the job was wearing her out. The schedule wasn't good for the dog, either. Sam spent long stretches of time alone, and she lacked the energy to take him for his evening walks. She knew it was unwise to leave the garage door open when she was gone, especially with the pet door visible to anyone who peered over the fence. But Sam deserved better than being cooped up inside all day, and the summer heat was too oppressive to keep him outdoors.

Colleen turned on the television, alternating between *FX* and *A&E*, with the volume loud enough to muffle the booms and crackles in the distant sky. After her second Jameson, she considered a project: installing one or two additional pet doors that would permit Sam to go from the house into the garage, through the serial killer door, into the shed and finally, into the yard. That would allow the main garage door to stay closed, thereby deterring burglars, without hindering Sam's freedom. After the third drink, she acknowledged her idea would require a substantial amount of duct tape. Otherwise, she thought the idea was pure genius.

She crawled into bed, and as she drifted to sleep, she saw the little girl with the bluest eyes.

"*You lied to me.*"

"*You lied to me.*"

35

Kathleen had looked forward to sprawling across the king-size mattress and enjoying hours of glorious sleep. But as she lay between the cool five-hundred thread-count sheets, her mind raced and refused to allow her peace. After an hour, she accepted defeat, wandered to the back patio, and sat at the pool's edge. She moved her feet back and forth in the tepid water, stared at the drain nine feet below, and contemplated her options.

The woman at the celebration had looked so familiar, but the name refused to come to her. Their kids attended the same school, at least in elementary they must have. She wanted to reach out to her, ask what her son had done. She wanted to offer help, to apologize, to tell her she was ashamed, to encourage her to call the police if she hadn't.

"Stop," she said aloud.

How bad had things become that she instantly believed in her son's guilt? She refused to give him any benefit of doubt. How long had she been that way? With no father and an emotionally unavailable mother, did her son ever have a chance? Everything she'd read about men like him listed bad mothers as a contributing factor, but they were bad mothers because they were abusive or absent, promiscuous or even incestuous. They'd murdered their sons' souls. The worst she'd done was get a little distant after her husband's death--a death she believed her son had caused. Still, she must have done something horribly wrong as a mother, yet she didn't know what it was. And whatever it was, she couldn't undo it.

"Mom."

Kathleen gasped and turned toward the voice. "Matthew." She mustered a laugh. "You scared the life out of me."

"Sorry, Mom. I can't sleep."

"Me, neither." Kathleen gently kicked her feet in the water. "Wanna sit with me?"

"Sure." Matthew joined her and lowered his feet into the pool.

They sat listening to the crickets and tree frogs, but Kathleen could sense he wanted to ask her something. She kicked at the water, creating a little splash.

"Mom?" His tone was serious.

"Matthew."

"I want to ask you something."

"Go ahead." She hoped his question would have something to do with a crush at school, or maybe for once, he'd made a bad grade. But she knew better. His tone was too somber.

"What really happened tonight? You saw something. I know you don't think you can tell me stuff, but I was there, so you might as well tell me. Otherwise, my imagination just comes up with stuff, and it makes my stomach hurt."

Kathleen watched the water swirl between her ankles as she chose her words. "Your brother was there, and I think he was acting like a jerk toward someone."

"He's more than a jerk, Mom. You know that. Don't you?"

"Yeah." She whispered.

"Like way worse."

She nodded and felt her stomach writhe, like it was trying to wring itself out.

"He's dangerous, Mom."

For twelve years, she'd sought help from doctors, school counselors, and therapists about her son's behavior. All of them combined had offered less insight than the twelve-year-old sitting next to her. All of them had also cast judgment on her, insisting the issue was parenting. The validation from Matthew was bittersweet, an overwhelming relief. She wanted to hug him and weep. Instead, she took a deep breath and scooted off the pool's edge and into the water, allowing herself to sink to the drain. Moms were supposed to hold it together. They were supposed to love their kids equally. They definitely were to refrain from badmouthing one to the other. She released a primal howl, before rising back to the surface.

Matthew was looking at her like she was nuts for taking a dip in her PJs. She returned to the edge of the pool and crossed her arms over the side. "I know…" She couldn't speak above a whisper without crying. "I know he's dangerous."

Matthew placed his hand on her shoulder. "So, what are we going to do about it?"

36

The rapist lay on his bed watching the puppets sway in the cool air pouring from the vent in the ceiling. He'd lowered the thermostat to sixty degrees. Two nights of that would make the electric bill outrageous, provided the air conditioner could keep it up. It might collapse from exhaustion.

Goldie the wanna-be girlfriend asked, "What's the deal with those things?"

"*Those things* are marionette puppets. They take skill to manipulate, but once you've learned the skill, it's easy to make them do what you want."

"Like people." She chuckled.

"Actually, people are easier to manipulate."

His thoughts turned to Trudy. *When did she talk and whom did she tell?*

If she'd talked right away to the cops, the police would've already called.

If she'd waited to tell the cops, the police were too stupid to make a case on him. *He-said, she-saids* never went anywhere. He knew that firsthand.

She probably told only her mother, but it was a good idea to motivate her to tell no one else.

He fiddled with Goldie's braids as he said, "I want to open up to you." Girls loved that crap. "I want to share something important."

On cue, she turned over to face him. "I'm listening."

He raised the pitch of his voice to sound vulnerable. "It's kind of sad. Pitiful really."

She inched herself upright, eager to take this next step, exactly as he'd predicted.

"I haven't told anyone else, but I feel like I can trust you." *That will make her feel special.* Then he feigned a little insecurity. "I can trust you, right?"

"Of course, you can." Her eyebrows came together into a raised point, and he knew she was concerned.

"Something happened before you came into my life. My kid brother..." he paused.

"Matthew, right?"

"Yeah, Matty. He likes being called *Matty*." He could sense that Goldie was pleased by this attempt to connect. "Matty had invited some friends over to celebrate the end of the school year. But my mom changed her mind and said *no* to the little party. I can't remember why."

"Bummer."

"It was for Matty. He was looking forward to it."

"Yeah, I bet he was."

"He couldn't get the message to everyone, so one kid showed up."

"Oops." She giggled. "That must have been awkward."

"I wish it stopped at awkward. Turns out, the girl had a crush on me or something. She wanted to hang around, and I was trying to be nice but, you know, keeping my distance. I didn't want to give her false hope. She's a kid, right?"

"Awe! That's sweet, though." She placed her palm on his ripped abs.

"If that had been all, it would've been sweet for sure, but she tried to get too friendly with me, and I had to shut that shit down. I didn't want the poor kid to get confused."

"How much younger was she?"

"Like, twelve or something. Matty's age."

"Oh, shit."

"Yeah, and it gets worse."

"What happened?"

"I guess she was embarrassed about being rejected, and she twisted the story around and told people I had put the moves on her."

Goldie's eyes widened and her mouth opened slightly. She was taking the bait.

"She went home all upset, and I guess she told her mom, who freaked out."

"No way."

"Oh, yes. I'm sure the kid has no idea how serious that kind of lie is, that she could ruin a man's life."

"No kidding."

"In a way, I feel sorry for her. On the other hand, making false claims like that makes it harder for the *real* victims."

A look of concern fell over Goldie's face. "She said you raped her?"

"I don't know if it was that bad, but she said something to piss off her mother. She might have called the cops. I don't know."

She gasped. "Whoa. What are you going to do?"

"I'm not worried about the cops because I didn't do anything wrong. But my reputation is important to me. I just want her to stop spreading lies, you know?"

"I get it."

"I mean, my poor mom. She's been through enough already with my dad dying, and she doesn't need some messed up kid lying about her son." For emphasis, he'd made his voice crack and rubbed his eyes. "I've basically been the man of the house my whole life, and I don't want to let her down."

"Is there anything I can do to help?"

He knew what Goldie wanted and hoped for and what she feared. She wanted love, and she hoped he was becoming the better man he pretended she inspired him to be. The better man she dreamed of, though, was a weak man, and he had no interest in devolving into that. Her most relevant fear was abandonment, particularly by another man. Her daddy issues caused her excruciating pain.

"Your brother goes to school with her, I think. Maybe he can help set the record straight when they start up again? You know, let people know I'm a good guy?"

She nuzzled against his chest. "Of course," she cooed and draped her leg over his thighs.

He relaxed his arms around her to demonstrate affection. "I know I can have a short temper, and I've done and said some things, but I'm not a bad guy. I wouldn't hurt a kid like that."

"My brother will help. Consider it done."

He convincingly expressed gratitude and then whispered three words. For him, they carried the emotional value of *I gotta pee* or *I want tacos*. But for her, they changed everything.

"I love you."

37

Colleen had spent her morning at the hardware store, where the all-male staff now greeted her by name. Most of the men appeared to be over fifty years of age, and all had been nothing less than encouraging and helpful. She wondered how her life might have been if she'd had a dad like one of them instead of the psychopath that made her an orphan.

A woodworking guy listened patiently to her elaborate plan, which she'd prefaced with the disclaimer that it had been inspired by Irish whiskey. Afterward, he gave her a hearty smile and asked if she had considered replacing the deadbolt lock on "the serial killer door" with one that didn't require a key.

He gently offered advice. "Allowing yourself the option to shut the door at night might keep critters out."

"Critters?"

"I've heard of raccoons, even snakes—"

"Got it!" She quivered. "I guess I need to hire someone."

"Nah, not you," he said. "You can do this one yourself."

Her chest warmed with confidence.

He asked, "Do you have a small screwdriver?"

"I do," she said proudly.

He explained the process, which sounded easy enough. Cutting the hole in the shed, on the other hand, wasn't so simple. For that she'd need a jigsaw, which she could rent from the store. She'd never heard of this device, but the man had insisted that "an intelligent and capable person like yourself can pull it off without a hitch." Following his advice, she purchased one pet door, a carpenter's square, work gloves, and eye protection.

By noon, she was in her garage and sweating. The jigsaw, which she found exhilarating, demanded her full attention. When she wasn't sawing and considering life without fingers, she wondered about the blue-eyed sisters and how their childhood would compare to her own. Trudy's case also swam in and out of her thoughts. So did memories of her own mess, the futile attempt to prosecute the offender, and the devastation that followed. She hoped Trudy and Maxine would avoid the regrets she had.

By 4:00 p.m., she'd finished her project, and it was beer time. She pulled a Stella from the beer fridge and grabbed the garden hose, turned on the water and let it flow for a minute before placing the nozzle against the back of her neck.

Then she went inside and made a note:

Buy nozzle with a mister setting

38

Maxine added a final tablespoon of Cajun spices into her signature boiled shrimp and red potato salad. Thankfully, today's job was a drop-off. She could deliver and leave. As she covered the disposable serving bowl with plastic wrap, she went through a mental checklist of items for the order. New clients meant new repeat business, and she wanted the job to go off without a hitch.

Before she'd made it halfway through her list, Trudy appeared and blurted, "I want to see my dad."

Maxine knew the day would come. In fact, she'd expected it to have arrived earlier, but Trudy's timing was awful. "I can't have that conversation right now, but I can—"

"I haven't seen him since he went to jail."

"Baby, I know."

"You sent him to jail, didn't you?"

Maxine felt a bolt of adrenaline shoot into her gut. "This is not a conversation I can have right now. I've got to load up and deliver this dinner. When I get back, I—"

"I'll come with you. We can talk in the car."

Maxine fought the urge to snap. "I know you've got a lot of big emotions going on right now, so I let that first interruption slide. But you did it a second time, and that's disrespectful."

"You're dodging the subject." Trudy's reply was heavy on petulance.

"*You're* going to be dodging something if you don't change your tone."

"If Dad was here, he would've handled it himself instead of going to the stupid police!"

Maxine's anger took over. Anger, a faithful protector from pain, and she felt the pain of Trudy's words down to her bones. "Your father is in prison for acting just like that snake who hurt you."

"He would've protected me!"

"You walked into that snake pit all by yourself! We wouldn't be in this mess if you'd just come home like you were supposed to!"

Trudy's jaw dropped, and her eyes flooded.

Maxine's voice boomed. "*Why* did you go over there, Trudy?"

Trudy shouted through tears. "Because I actually got invited to a party! I didn't have any friends!" She sobbed, and as she turned to run to her room, she cried out. "I just wanted some friends!"

Maxine talked to herself as she loaded the Suburban. "You gotta keep it together. It's not her fault. A little girl should be able to go to a party and not get raped. She was supposed to come home, and she made a mistake, and she was punished severely for it." She shut the hatch. "I know you're tired, you're weary, you're lonely, but you'll get through this,"

She recited *Psalms 23*, and said to herself, "Apologize."

39

Matthew was sitting on a stool at the kitchen island that was about three times as big as the one they had at home. The top was white and hard like a stone. His mother said it was marble, but the marbles he'd seen had color. This marble was boring. He slid his glass of milk from one palm to the other.

His mother was standing at the kitchen counter. It was white, too, like everything in the kitchen, except the handles on the drawers and cabinets. Those were black. Rich people liked that kind of thing, like nothing ever got dirty in their houses. He heard the toaster pop, and watched his mom pull four hot pastries out of it, trying not to burn her fingers as she dropped them onto a plate.

She poured herself another cup of coffee, set the plate of pastries in front of him, and sat down on a stool across from him. Even though he'd known how his mother would react last night, he was disappointed in her.

"We're not going to do anything," she'd said. And then she'd talked about keeping watch and calling the cops if they had something to tell them.

Maybe he hadn't been clear last night. Maybe saying *he's dangerous* wasn't enough. "Mom, I thought about what you said last night, and I need to tell you something."

She broke one of the pastries in half, revealing the raspberry filling. "Okay. Tell me." She offered him half.

He shook his head. "It's still too hot." It wouldn't have been too hot if his fingertips weren't sore from chewing his nails down to the quick last night.

She set his half on a napkin and slid it across the counter to him. Matthew saw her look at his fingers. A concerned look flashed across her eyes, but it vanished quickly, and she pretended not to notice. His mom was a terrible actress, but he was glad she let it go. Calling attention to his nervous habit only made him feel self-conscious. He picked and chewed at his fingers without thinking. He figured he'd quit doing it someday, probably the day he could finally get away from his psycho brother.

"Mom, he had a birthday party while you were gone."

"I saw the mess." She made a face like she was seeing it for the first time.

"Yeah. Sorry."

"Not your fault, hon." She put a piece of the pastry into her mouth and continued talking, which was weird. She'd always said talking with food in your mouth was rude. "I really thought he was going to go out. I never would've left you there if I'd known he was going to have a party."

"I know, Mom. It's okay."

"Have you nominated me for the Mother-of-the-Year Award yet?"

Matthew picked up his half of the pastry and blew on it, deciding how to tell his mother what else had happened. She always suggested ripping off the band-aid fast. She said it made the pain quick, so he decided to do the same here. "I think he drugged a girl and raped her. I think he's done it before."

She looked like she'd seen a ghost, or like someone in a horror movie watching a murder. "What?" Her voice sounded far away.

"He makes some kind of drink. He calls it *Special K*."

Her eyes dropped to the counter, and she picked at a paper napkin. "That's uh. That's the name of a date rape drug."

"I know."

"How do you know that? You're twelve years old. Twelve-year-olds shouldn't know that."

"I read the paper, Mom. It's on the news. Everybody knows."

"You read the paper?" She sounded broken.

"Sometimes."

"I need a minute." She rubbed the back of her neck. Then she took a gulp of her coffee. "Your brother's a rapist. That's what you're saying?"

"He says it's a Kool-Aid drink, that he's making Kool-Aid into something special." He made air quotes with his hand like Chris Farley did in a *Saturday Night Live* skit, but his mother didn't get it. He felt like a jackass for doing it, too. "He acts like he's just adding alcohol to the Kool-Aid, but I think he's adding drugs."

"You think he's drugging girls and raping them in our home?" Her voice cracked like his often did.

His mom was losing it. He'd never seen her lose it, and he needed her to get a grip. "I saw a guy give him pills, so I think he put the pills in the drink."

"Did you *see* him put the pills in the drink?"

"No, but he brought a girl to my room, and she was passed out, and when she woke up, she didn't remember anything, and..." He was talking too much. He meant to give her enough information for her to call the cops, but he went too far.

"And *what?*"

"And nothing."

"He brought a girl, passed out, to your room? Who was she?" Her words were sharp now, and they were coming at him hard. Now he was in trouble.

"I don't know." He shoved the pastry into his mouth to buy him a few seconds. He needed to think more and talk less.

"Now is not the time to clam up, Matthew. You want to do something about this? I need details."

Matthew remembered how the girl said her mother would kill her if she knew she was there. Ratting out his brother was fine, but he didn't want to rat out the girl. She'd been punished enough already. He'd chewed about a hundred times and had no choice but to swallow.

"A few girls came over. Guys, too. One slept in my bed. I don't know about the others."

"Dear God. What was I thinking when I took that night job?" She held the napkin in her fists and stared at the counter. "Was this girl there when I got home?"

"No. She left before you got home." Technically, that wasn't a lie, but his pastry threatened to claw its way back up his throat.

"And you didn't think to call me when all this was happening?"

"I told him I wanted to call you or an ambulance."

"You didn't need *permission*, Matthew, to call me. You just should've called me." She'd dropped the napkin, and her hands were shaped like she was going to choke something, and they were shaking, too. Her face was red, and she was so upset he wished he hadn't said anything. Now she was mad at him for not calling her.

"I'll call the police today, and I'll ask them." She shook out her hands and then continued. "I'll ask them if they had any calls about your brother, our house, anything about that night."

That was more than she was willing to do ten minutes ago, so Matthew considered it a win

40

At 2:12 a.m. Colleen was ripped from a sound sleep.

She'd managed a few years without a Steven nightmare. This one had been a twisted compilation, side one of Steven's greatest hits. She was a child again, arriving at her friend's house, simply wanting to play like a normal little kid. Last night's horror included that wretched grandfather clock, too. Her friend's older brother had convinced her that the dismembered body of a girl had been stuffed inside the clock, and her spirit remained trapped within it for eternity, and every night when the clock struck twelve the ghost screamed.

Even in her dream, Colleen could smell Steven's fetid breath. His diction was crisp, and he phrased things in a way that made him seem older and subsequently stronger than he really was. "*Ghosts are particularly fond of haunting children,*" he'd say with grand hand gestures. His scrawny arms and long fingers reminded her of a leafless tree she'd seen in a Halloween storybook. Then her nightmare skipped ahead to one of his many pranks. He'd held out a yellow pack of gum, which happened to be her favorite brand. She'd hesitated, and he'd ridiculed her for "*questioning the sincerity of his generosity.*" She'd tentatively accepted the offer, and politely selected the protruding stick of gum from the pack. The removal of the decoy triggered the snap of a miniature mouse trap, and the pain confirmed she should've trusted her gut. She yanked her hand away and held back tears as she clenched her aching finger.

That prank was benign compared to what he'd do to Colleen later. She hadn't dreamed about that particular horror for a long time, the night

Steven murdered a piece of her and created another *before-and-after* in Colleen's life.

Too troubled to fall back to sleep, she turned on the bedside lamp, slipped out of bed, and retrieved a box from the closet shelf. It contained only a few memories of her mother. Two photos of them together and a couple birthday cards. She also kept a few letters from Aunt Ruth, who took over as mom before Colleen had reached adolescence. She wrote to her often when Colleen was in college. The majority of the contents in the box, though, was photos of her with William. Some were taken inside the high school. Others before homecoming and senior prom. Her favorite was from a day they'd skipped school to go fishing. She spread the memories out before her on the bed, dozens of images of two kids in love, bright-eyed and smiling. The photos transported her to better days. For a bit, anyway.

She grabbed a pen and a notepad from the nightstand and wrote him a brief letter, the first since beginning her new job. Writing to him was bittersweet, and she wasn't sure she'd mail the letter, but the act of putting thoughts to paper helped her shake off the nightmare and get a couple hours of peaceful sleep.

41

Kathleen picked up the phone and dialed the non-emergency number for the Alwin Police Department. After three rings, a man answered.

"Alwin Police Department. Officer Jones speaking."

"My name is Kathleen McDaniel, and I'm not sure where to start, but I need to give you some information."

"I suggest the beginning. That's usually the best place to start."

Kathleen remembered the day in the toy aisle when her offspring threatened to kill them. "The beginning was about twelve years ago, so I won't do that."

"Is this about a cold case?"

"No, sir. I don't think so." She wondered if they would be willing to take another look at her husband's death, but she'd save that request for later.

"Well, why don't you tell me what's going on? Do you have a crime to report? A neighbor's dog that's barking all night? A suspicious person? Something like that?"

Over the line, Kathleen could hear he was a mouth breather, which didn't inspire confidence. "It's my son. My oldest. I would consider him a suspicious person."

"Can you be more specific?"

"I think he had a party. I mean, I *know* he had a party while I was gone. I think there was drinking, and—"

"When was this party?"

"Several weeks ago. It was June, actually. His seventeenth birthday."

"There's not much I can do about that now, ma'am. I hope you grounded him or something."

She almost laughed at the suggestion. "I guess I was wondering if you had any calls to the house or any reports of something having happened around that time."

"You would've been informed about that, ma'am. You definitely would've heard something by now."

"My son. My younger son Matthew thinks that something bad happened that night. Perhaps a sexual assault."

"Why does he think that?"

"He said he saw drugs, and one of the girls had passed out and didn't remember anything when she woke up."

"Ms. McDaniel, that happens every weekend. It's a sad state we live in, but it's the norm."

His breathing was irritating her. "Well, I think this girl was a minor. She was closer to Matthew's age than my older son, the one who had the party."

"Is it possible that Matthew might have been a little jealous? I mean, the girl who was close to his age might have shown interest in his older brother. Maybe this is just sibling rivalry?"

Kathleen moved the phone from one ear to the other. "No. If you knew my son, you would understand how improbable that idea is." She rubbed her fingertips over the rock that had formed at the base of her neck. "Look, my son, the oldest one, isn't *normal*. Something is wrong with him, you see."

"If I had a dollar for every time the parent of a teen told me that, I'd be living large on a beach in Mexico."

Kathleen snapped at him. "He's dangerous."

He sighed loudly into the mouthpiece. "Sounds like he needs to see a counselor or shrink maybe, but unless he's committed a crime or you have something more specific, there's not much we can do."

"Can you pass on my information to a detective? Maybe our name and address might ring a bell."

"I suppose so."

Kathleen provided the information and then asked him to repeat it back to her.

"Sorry, my pen ran out of ink. Just a second."

Kathleen rolled her lips inward to stop herself from saying something she'd regret.

She heard rustling noises and then he was back on the line. "Kathleen McDaniel, you said?"

"Yes." After a long pause, she asked, "Is that all you got?"

"Apologies. It's been one of those days. You'll have to give it to me again."

42

More than a month had passed between the time of the initial report and today's event: the forensic interview at the Children's Advocacy Center. Colleen guessed delayed reports led to even more delayed interviews. The advocacy center employed forensic interviewers, social workers, victim advocates, and children's therapists. Colleen's role seemed redundant, so she planned to sit quietly and act as an unobtrusive member of Maxine's support network.

She met Maxine and Trudy in front of the building, and after Maxine announced her identity over the intercom, the three were buzzed inside, where they were greeted by a warm but overly cheerful woman on the other side of a Plexiglas window. Maxine and Colleen provided their photo IDs and signed in as visitors. Soon, a younger but equally animated lady arrived and let them through locked double doors that opened into a large atrium. Before proceeding, she verified Maxine's status as Trudy's mom and then asked Colleen, "Are you related to the family?"

"No, I'm a victim advocate with Alwin PD."

Maxine interjected assertively but politely, "I asked her to be here."

"Oh, of course." She sang and put her attention on Trudy. "My name's Elena, and I'll be the one talking to you today if that's okay." And then to the trio, she said, "But first, please follow me."

Elena led them through the atrium and past an art station and play area for younger kids. Rays of sun spilled through the skylights. Small sofas, bean bag chairs, and rugs added rainbow colors to the white tiled floor. They arrived at a private room, its worn couch and plastic chairs a stark contrast to the bright path that led there. Maxine and Trudy took the couch. Colleen took a seat in one of the unsteady chairs.

Elena exuded warmth and compassion, and Colleen noticed Trudy relax into her mom. After some additional rapport building, Elena asked if Trudy was willing to talk to her privately, and she agreed. The two left Maxine and Colleen alone in the room.

"Thank you for being here," Maxine said.

"You're welcome. I'm glad I could come."

Maxine cleared her throat. "We saw him at the July Fourth celebration." Before she could continue, a much younger woman entered the room.

This one announced she was a family advocate, and Colleen suspected she was a graduate student doing an internship. She went through an extensive questionnaire with Maxine and recited a script, which included a lengthy description of services offered by the center. "We offer therapy for you and your daughter for no charge. We have art therapy, music therapy and groups." Then the advocate opened a fire hose of information that couldn't possibly be absorbed. She explained crime victims' rights. "For instance, you have the right to be informed about hearings." Next came Crime Victims' Compensation. "You might be able to receive reimbursement for lost wages if you miss work to cooperate with prosecution efforts." And finally, she talked about the investigative process. The spiel took a good fifteen minutes.

When the advocate finally excused herself, Maxine let out a long, tired sigh and said, "I don't remember five percent of what she just said."

"An intermission would've been useful."

"Couldn't she have provided the CliffsNotes version?"

"It's all in that packet." Colleen reassured her. "We can review it again later if you want." Then, Colleen tried to pick up where they'd left off. "You said you saw him?"

Maxine stared at the floor and nodded. "We did."

"Did he follow you or threaten you?"

"He pointed at us, like it clicked, like he knew Trudy had told me what he did."

"Did he follow you or approach you?"

"No." She looked up at Colleen. "We left, and he didn't bother us."

"Did you let the detective know about this?"

A sour smile emerged. "We were in a public place. He didn't follow us or anything. What's the detective going to do?"

Two quick knocks on the door startled them. It opened, and a man with a legal pad entered the sterile room. He wore khaki pants that were an inch too long and a light blue dress shirt. Maxine said under her breath, "Sweet Jesus, another one?"

The man smiled at Maxine and greeted her warmly. "I'm Detective Lawler. It's good to meet you in person."

Maxine's greeting was halfhearted. "Hello, detective. I wasn't sure you'd be here."

Lawler's confidence appeared shaken. "Actually, my office is here. I work here and visit the station about once a week."

Maxine nodded with approval. "Interesting."

"It's a good concept. We take a team approach to every case."

Lawler's eyes moved to Colleen. "How are you related to the family?"

It was a nicer way to ask *who are you and what are you doing here?*

"I'm not family. I'm Colleen, the victim advocate."

It took a couple seconds for Lawler's brain to process the data, and once he did, his expression shifted from pleasant to neutral.

More firmly than before, Maxine stated, "I asked her to be here."

Maxine's comment prompted him to turn his attention back to her. "I observed the interview from another room, and Trudy did great. She was consistent, and I think we have a good case here."

"Where's Trudy now?" For the first time since they'd arrived, Maxine seemed nervous.

Lawler spoke with a reassuring tone. "Trudy is with the interviewer in a break room. She's in good spirits. When I passed by, they were exchanging knock-knock jokes. I just wanted a word in private."

Maxine exhaled forcefully. "Okay."

Lawler's ability to ignore Colleen was impressive, and she bit back a smile. He continued to address Maxine as if they were the only two people in the room. "Trudy seems very afraid of the suspect. Has he tried to make contact with either of you?"

Colleen shot Maxine an encouraging look.

"We saw him at the Independence Day celebration, and he pointed at us. It shook Trudy up pretty bad."

"Did he make any threats or follow you?"

"He was at a distance, just shaking his head and pointing at us."

"Nothing direct or verbal?"

"No." She passed a told-you-so look to Colleen and asked, "What's else can you tell me, detective? What's next?"

"Because he was a juvenile at the time of the offense, we have to give him the opportunity to come in and talk to us voluntarily."

"Why?" Maxine asked with a frown. "He's not a juvenile now."

"Well, he was at the time, so we'll give him a chance to talk to us. In the meantime, I'd like to schedule a forensic medical exam if you'll agree to that."

Because of the delay, the medical exam wouldn't be as invasive as the full forensic exam, also known as a rape kit. Colleen had learned the details about the various forensic exams at a victims' assistance conference, and, while useful to an investigation, for a little girl who'd already endured rape, even the watered-down exam sounded cruel.

Maxine asserted, "I want him held accountable for his actions, so go ahead and schedule it."

After Lawler exited the room, Maxine chuckled and asked, "What's his beef with you? You turn him down for a date or something?"

"Nothing like that." Colleen clicked her tongue. "My position is still kind of new. We're going through an adjustment phase I guess."

The door opened and interrupted again, and Trudy walked in with the interviewer, Elena. Colleen had feared the girl would return tearful, or at least unnerved, but she wore a smile.

"Trudy did great," Elena said. "She had some yogurt. I hope that's okay."

Trudy took a seat on the couch and snuggled against her mother. "The people here are nice."

Elena remained standing and asked, "Are you ready to go now?"

Trudy perked up and asked, "We're done?"

"Yep," Elena chirped. "All done."

Elena escorted Trudy, Maxine, and Colleen out the way they'd come in. Once outside, Colleen noticed Maxine's chin was quivering. The woman pulled Trudy to her and made a playful growling noise. Colleen knew she didn't want Trudy to see her upset. Maxine mouthed *Thank you* to Colleen and took a deep breath and shook off the urge to weep.

"Of course." Colleen nodded. "I'll touch base with you later today or tomorrow. That okay?"

"Perfect," her robust voice had returned, and she gave Trudy a quick kiss on the head, and said, "Let's go get some ice cream."

"Is ice cream for you or for me this time?"

"Today, I think it's for me, baby girl."

43

Sleepy kids. Energetic kids. Kids reuniting after a summer apart. And kids like Trudy, arriving alone and intimidated.

Maxine and Trudy sat in the carpool line, staring at the school entrance, creeping closer to it every few seconds.

"I don't want to go in there."

"I know you don't."

"What if everyone knows?"

"I know you're scared. But you have to go to school."

"He has a brother, Mom."

"Doesn't his brother go to school somewhere else now?"

"What if he doesn't?"

"Honey, I checked. I called to make sure you wouldn't have any classes with him." She patted Trudy's knee. "I think his mom's a teacher, and he's going to school with her."

"What if he has friends here, and they come after me? Or *you*?"

"Please, Trudy." Maxine heard exasperation in her voice and took a deep breath before finishing. "Try to think of what *is* instead of what *if*."

Neither of them had slept well in weeks. Maxine was juggling her business and a traumatized kid, and the case was always hovering over them, like a dark circling cloud threatening to drop a funnel onto their world. The case seemed to consume Trudy. To her, the rapist was the most powerful and influential monster that ever existed.

"He's a criminal, Trudy, and he's young. He's not a Mafioso member. He has no special powers. He's just a person who did a horrible thing to you."

Tears fell down her daughter's cheeks.

"And you didn't deserve it, baby girl. It wasn't your fault. But we are responsible for your healing, and the world won't wait. The law says you must attend school. Your education is that important."

Maxine handed Trudy a tissue, and the girl wiped her face and blew her nose enough for Maxine to hand her another. But her eyes returned to her lap.

"Look at me, Trudy."

Trudy sniffed and complied.

"Sit up straight and take a deep breath."

Trudy inhaled, but not sufficiently.

"Take a big ol' deep breath." She demonstrated, and Trudy begrudgingly followed the example. "And blow that shit out."

Trudy's jaw dropped and a smile emerged.

"Yeah, that's right. I said *shit*. By shit, I mean fear and anxiety and all that…shit."

After three rounds of breathing, they had only two cars left in front of them.

Maxine took Trudy's hand and said, "You've done hard things before. You can do this."

The girl pushed her glasses up the bridge of her nose and nodded, without confidence.

"You walk in like you belong there." She caressed her daughter's cheek. "Because you do."

"Okay." Trudy spoke just above a whisper.

"If you don't *feel* it, then fake it. You're a survivor. You are stronger than you know."

"Okay." Her voice gained strength.

"You're a light in this world, and light is powerful. One little candle flame can drive the darkness out of a room. Remember that."

"Okay, Mom. I got it." The smile reappeared as the Suburban reached the head of the line. Trudy hopped out and grabbed her backpack. Maxine watched as she walked toward the school entrance and a sob leaped up her throat.

44

Kathleen and Matthew made it on time to school, a safe haven, a refuge. Her offspring was skilled at sabotaging their morning routine. She'd learned to keep toothpaste, a toothbrush, a hairbrush and toilet paper in a box hidden under the floorboards in her closet. These were things her son would steal from Matthew in the middle of the night. Some adults chalked up his actions to typical mischief or sibling rivalry. They'd laugh and say, "He sounds like a normal boy."

This morning, his antics had been relatively benign. He'd simply announced he was "*opting out of school today.*" His surprise was palpable when Kathleen had shrugged it off. While she needed to avoid the public shaming and fines that resulted from truancy court, a couple of absences wouldn't result in a court summons. This morning, she wanted to enjoy the first day back to school without any drama. Within a week, she'd have to apply pressure to get him to school. Her prediction was that he'd try to drop out. She could almost hear the collective sigh of relief from the entire staff at Alwin High School upon learning that news. If only he could. He was still too young to make that decision.

She tried to push those thoughts out of her mind and soak in her surroundings. At school, life felt normal, and she would bask in that feeling until 4:00 p.m. Here, she was a math teacher with a son who was an honors student, who would enjoy going to football games with friends, school assemblies, and maybe a crush or two. She would enjoy comradery with teachers and several hours that, for the most part, were predictable.

The only thing Kathleen didn't enjoy about returning to school was the cafeteria food. For the first few years of elementary school, she'd packed their lunches, and it always felt like an act of self-care. Her offspring had ruined that, though. Sometimes, if they left early enough, Kathleen would stop by a grocer's deli and have sandwiches made special for her and Matthew. Rarely, though, did they get out of the house with enough time for that.

The last lunch she'd made almost sent her to the hospital. The disaster had been set in motion late one Thursday evening. She'd felt so drained that the easy task of preparing lunches seemed like an insurmountable feat, but then the oldest had offered to help. Three words, *I'll help you*, had boosted her morale and provided the second wind that usually eluded her.

"That means a lot. Thank you," she'd said without revealing the shock she'd felt from the offer. At the time, she'd wondered if he was extending an olive branch. She certainly wouldn't reject it. She'd hoped it was a step in a new, positive direction.

On the kitchen island, she'd placed a bag of soft honey wheat bread, a jar of creamy peanut butter, and a jar of grape jelly for her and Matthew's lunches. Because the only thing her older son would eat for lunch was crunchy peanut butter on white bread, she'd set out those items, too.

"How 'bout I make the sandwiches," he'd suggested, "and you do the rest?"

"Sounds good."

She'd put chips in sandwich bags for both her and Matthew and added two cookies for him. As her son pulled a gallon of milk from the fridge, she noticed he was putting extra care into making the sandwiches, as if it was the first time he'd ever done it. He fixed them for himself all the time, yet making lunch for another was indeed a novel experience. Suddenly, she'd felt hope. That feeling had been absent for so long its return nearly overwhelmed her.

She'd poured milk into two thermoses for Matthew and herself. Something about milk in her lunch comforted her. Perhaps it reminded her of the years when someone took care of her needs and fulfilled so many of her wants. What she would give for a day from her childhood—waking up to a hot breakfast, grabbing a lunch packed with love, walking to school with her friends, *having* friends, then returning home at the end of the day to the smell of dinner cooking, warm hugs, safety, and stability.

She'd secured the tops onto the thermoses, and assembled the items in the two lunch totes. She'd eyed the cookies in Matthew's lunch and added one for herself.

The eldest slid each sandwich into a plastic bag and placed them tenderly on top of the chips and cookies and said, "There. PB and J à la *moi*."

"Nicely done," she said, and patted him on the back.

He gave her a vacant look. "Thank you, mother."

That day at lunchtime, she'd joined the usual group in the teacher's lounge and smiled again when she'd opened her tote and saw the sandwich. She unwrapped it, took a bite, heard a crunch between her molars, followed by sharp pain and the taste of metal and salt. She jumped up from her chair and let the chunks of sandwich fall into her cupped hand and tried to hide the blood and saliva oozing from her mouth as she stumbled to the sink. She snatched several paper towels from the dispenser, laid them on the counter, and the contents from her hand dripped onto them. Then she stood still, mouth agape, fearing more sharp objects but afraid to explore with her tongue. Gently she closed her lips and slowly pushed air into her mouth, creating space between her teeth and cheeks and tongue. The pain was intense, but she couldn't feel any additional stabbing, so she carefully used her finger to remove the remaining food and threats from her mouth.

And then she remembered.

"Matthew," she'd cried as she bolted out of the teacher's lounge and sprinted down the hall to the cafeteria, where she spotted her little boy smiling at a table with his classmates, with sandwich in hand before his lips. She shouted his name, startling and silencing every kid in the cafeteria. They stared at their teacher, with crazed eyes and blood on her chin and chest, breaking all the lunchroom conduct rules. Shouting, running, disturbing others, going to a table that wasn't assigned to her.

She'd closed the distance between her and her boy, but yelled nonetheless, "Don't eat that!"

Confusion and fear spilled over his face. "B-but it's *mine*."

"I know, honey." Her voice sounded frantic and hysterical, and she knew she needed to calm down.

She noticed the sandwich was half eaten and squatted down beside Matthew. "Open your mouth," she demanded.

"Why are you bleeding, Mom? What happened?" Matthew's eyes were wide and wet.

"Open your mouth."

He did as he was told. She stared into her son's mouth, and saw no evidence of injury.

"You're scaring me," her boy's voice was thin.

"He put…," she'd stuttered, "There was something…," she'd panted. She'd noticed her son's chin trembling and tried to offer comfort. "It's okay. I'm okay."

"But why are you bleeding?" Matthew had touched his fingers against her bottom lip and displayed them in front of her. "See?"

She hated the memory as much as she'd hated the moment. Today's menu included meatloaf. Hundreds of slices of meatloaf with that red stripe across the top they called *sauce*, served on a plastic plate with clear plastic wrap over each and every one. Cafeteria lunches lacked love and flavor, but they also lacked shards of glass.

45

Colleen's drive consisted of hard brakes, rapid accelerations, and expletives. She'd forgotten about the countless number of school zones between her home and the station. She'd whipped into the parking lot at 8:00 a.m. on the dot and hoped the lieutenant wouldn't notice she was a couple minutes late to her desk.

She grabbed her lunch and work bag and jogged to the front doors, cursing the heat. When she entered the police station lobby, an older couple was huddled together on one of the bench seats in the small sitting area. Jeanne summoned her with a wave.

"They're waiting to talk to a detective. You might want to meet them. They had a house fire last night."

"Arson?"

"Think so."

Colleen walked toward the haggard couple and lowered herself into a chair across from the husband and wife.

"I'm Colleen Heenan. I'm the department's victim advocate. I'm here to offer support and help you find resources if you need them."

Simultaneously, almost inaudibly they replied, "Nice to meet you."

The edges of the woman's eyelids were reddened from crying. Her husband's looked about the same, but his also revealed anger. Colleen didn't want to ask any questions about the fire. Her questions would pertain only to their welfare and needs. She was about to ask them if they had a place to stay when the woman foiled her plan.

"It was our daughter who set the fire."

Shit.

"We know it was her."

The husband countered. "It could've been her, but we don't know that for certain."

The woman had fire in her eyes, and she flashed them at her husband. "Well, I do." She turned back to Colleen and said, "He's always wanted to think better of her than she is. He still holds out hope."

The man nodded as if accepting defeat.

"Have you told anyone else this? The police or firefighters?"

"Oh, yes. That's why we're here." She spoke as if she'd been here many times before.

"I see." The urgency waned. "Do you know where your daughter is now?"

The woman's bloodshot eyes held contact with Colleen's. "Probably laughing it up somewhere."

The man ran his hands over his thinning gray hair.

Despite her anger, the woman's voice was perfect for reading bedtime stories. "Our parenting wasn't unblemished, but we gave her love and everything she needed and more. She wanted for nothing." She dabbed her eyes with an overused tissue. "I don't know what happened. She's always been a little…" she searched for the word. "…off."

"Angry," her husband said. "She wallows in rage."

"We used to call her *the princess of darkness*. Not when she was in the house, of course. We aren't cruel. It's just, a little gallows humor goes a long way with coping."

"I understand." Colleen understood the humor but didn't understand the family dynamic. Without a briefing, she was piecing together bits of information. The couple had a troubled daughter, messed up enough to set the house on fire.

"How old is she?"

He answered, "Thirty-four."

Colleen spotted a box of tissues and placed it within their reach. "Do you have somewhere to stay?"

"We're debating," the man said.

The woman elaborated. "I don't want to burden our son, and we can afford one of those hotel suites. You know the kind with a sitting area, and a little kitchen."

The man grunted.

Her face soured. "We absolutely can afford it. It's not The Four Seasons."

The arson investigator entered through a secured door. His gait displayed confidence and his salt and pepper hair suggested experience. He acknowledged the couple by name and introduced himself. Then he asked Colleen, "How are you related to the family?"

"I'm not, actually. I'm the PD's victim advocate.

"Right. Got it." Colleen could see the wheels turning in his mind. "Well, thank you. I'll take it from here."

"You're a lovely girl." The woman's voice caught in her throat. "I'd be so proud if you were my daughter. I hope your mom appreciates what a lovely young woman you are."

Colleen's response leaked out before she could stop it. The woman's vulnerability and kindness had disarmed her. "She passed away long ago, but thank you. That's kind of you. I'll be here if you need me."

Passed away. She'd never diluted the truth that much, but she didn't want to tell the poor lady her father had murdered her mother before offing himself.

"Let me give you my contact info." Colleen fumbled with her work bag to find her stash of business cards.

The woman turned to the investigator. "May she stay, please? I find her presence quite comforting."

He appeared to be taken off guard. In fairness, a victim advocate was a novel concept, and they'd never crossed paths before.

"I guess so. I don't see why not."

The four rode an elevator to the second floor. Until then, Colleen had thought it was a freight elevator and off-limits. From there, they followed the investigator to a small interview room, where the couple shared the history of problems with their daughter and their many attempts to alleviate her aggressive behavior with various tactics and treatments. Counselors, psychiatrists, even a wilderness camp after they'd reached their wits' end. Nothing had made an impact on the girl. From an early age, she had been detached and cold, and manipulative with an insatiable desire for power. She'd been diagnosed with various disorders, engaged in some juvenile delinquency, and as she aged, she grew clever enough to avoid getting caught.

"She's quite cunning," the father had said.

"Practically ingenious," the mother added. "I don't confuse easily, but my daughter can have me completely muddled."

"She can be gracious and doting when it suits her," the gentleman continued. "That's the most difficult part for me. She's so elegant and even enthralling."

The woman's eyes saddened, "And then something or someone flips her switch."

Colleen's memories of her father tugged at her.

A lone sob escaped out of the woman, snapping Colleen's attention back to where it belonged. "We can't take any more of this. We need help."

The investigator saw the opening but trod lightly. "Arson is a felony. Because the fire appears to have been set intentionally, and it was done while you were in the house during a time when it was logical to believe you were sleeping and possibly defenseless, the act may be classified as a first-degree felony."

The father responded. "You're wanting to know if we'll press charges?"

"The state actually presses charges, not the victim, and as the investigator I will continue investigating and file the case."

"You're wondering if we'll cooperate." The woman said.

"Yes, ma'am. That was going to be my question."

"I will," she answered without hesitation. "Absolutely."

The investigator nodded twice and said, "As difficult as this can be, from everything you've shared with me, the criminal justice system might be the best way to keep you and the community safe from your daughter."

The father appeared to struggle with the idea. "Until now," he said, "it's been nickel-and-dime stuff. It adds up, but it hasn't been this destructive before."

"That's not entirely accurate, darling. She assaulted you. We had to take out a protective order against her."

"She did, but that was a while ago, and she didn't *hurt* me."

"That wasn't even a year ago."

Colleen could hear the bitterness in the woman's voice.

"She could have killed us last night!" The woman took a deep breath through flared nostrils and continued with a calmer tone. "Her entire life we've been killing ourselves for her. We burned through savings, canceled vacations, chucked our retirement dreams trying to help her out of her misery. All futile efforts, to boot." She turned to Colleen. "She couldn't keep a job. She worked as a vet tech once, and she came home and told us about a cat waking up in the middle of surgery. She mimicked the yowling the cat made, like the animal was in agony."

Colleen grimaced.

"Oh, but she thought it was hilarious. It was *appalling*. Thank God, they fired her."

The investigator nodded compassionately, and Colleen got the feeling he wanted to let the woman talk.

The wife asked her husband, "How many times has she told us, flat out told us, she'd burn down the house with us in it?"

He stared at his hands, folded in his lap. "A few. A few times." He looked away and worked his jaw.

The investigator asked, "When was the last time she threatened to do that?"

"Saturday," he answered.

The woman's jaw dropped. "Saturday?"

"Yeah." He cleared his throat. "She showed up and asked for money, and I'd told her we couldn't do that, anymore."

"Where was I?"

"Honey, I don't remember. Grocery shopping or something."

"I grocery shop on Tuesdays."

"Like I said, I don't know where you were."

"Why didn't you tell me?"

"Because I didn't want to upset you, and she's always saying horrible things when she doesn't get her way. Always has."

The woman looked at the investigator. "Since she was about twelve, we've known she was dangerous, and we tried and tried to help her correct course." Then she turned back to her husband and drew her line in the sand. "It's time to get your priorities straight. You choose. Are you going to enable her or protect us?"

"I'm not ready to accept she's some kind of sociopath or psychopath or whatever it's called."

"Maybe she's not, dear, but there's something irreparably wrong with her."

"You're making her out to be a female Ted Bundy or Richard Ramirez."

"No, I'm not, but the world is filled with Bundys, and people like him, who have no regard for human life, and they all have parents." She continued with a stream of consciousness. "Granted, Ted Bundy had a bizarre childhood, but not all parents of disturbed people are bad parents. Not all disturbed people had horrible childhoods." And it was like a light bulb turned on over her head. Tenderly, she placed her hand on her husband's knee. "Is that what concerns you? If you admit how bad she is, people will think we were terrible parents?"

The man discreetly wiped at tears under his eyes. Colleen wanted to comfort him but sensed the couple had had decades of conflict and grief over their daughter, and while the man undoubtedly acted out of love, he'd enabled her horrible behavior.

The woman then looked at the investigator. "We need peace. Regardless of what he decides, you'll have my full cooperation."

As the investigator gathered information, which included written statements and their dates of birth, Colleen noticed how the couple looked many years beyond their actual ages. Life with their daughter had drawn deep lines on their faces, darkness under their eyes, and heavy shoulders. Colleen thought of her late father's parents, whom she'd never met. Were they beat down like this? Did his death give them relief? It released her from a childhood of violence and terror, but he'd robbed her of so much. The system had never helped them, but surely after a murder, he would've been held accountable. Sometimes, she dreamed he was alive and in prison, and she was staring him down through the glass partition, unafraid, telling him how much better life was without him. She couldn't imagine ever wanting reconciliation. But she had deserved a reckoning. He went out on his own terms, though, and he'd stolen that from her, too.

46

The rapist stood in the kitchen with the phone to his ear, playing with the cord, with his eyes locked on the dumb driver, whom he'd talked into cutting class with him.

He spoke with a chipper tone. "Sure, detective. I'll tell her. I'm happy to help. See you then." He returned the phone to the receiver on the wall.

The driver's eyes bugged out of his skull.

The rapist laughed loudly. "What's wrong with *you*, slack jaw?"

"You're going to talk to the cops?"

"A detective. Maybe." He shrugged. "If I don't have anything better to do."

Beads of sweat formed on the driver's bony brow.

A hollow grin crawled across the rapist's face as his skinny driver swallowed hard.

The rapist snickered. "Don't you worry, Bones. It's not about M-U-R-D-E-R."

"What's it about then?"

"I don't know, but if it was about *that*, they wouldn't be calling me. They'd scoop our asses up." He chuckled and walked into the living room as if he was handcuffed.

The skinny man didn't seem too bright, which could present a problem if he was interviewed alone. However, no matter what, the rapist's plan was to deny, deny, deny. If Bones slipped up or confessed, he'd take one hundred percent of the fall. For now, they needed to keep things simple.

"Listen to me. They got nothing. We weren't there. Right?"

"Right." Bones ambled into the living room. "So, where were we?"

"Here, numb nuts!"

He fell into the couch, observing the driver's expression: a blank stare, brow furrowed slightly, bottom teeth gnawing on his upper lip. *Pensive.* He practiced the look while the driver worked over his pea brain.

Finally, Bones asked, "What department?"

"What department?" He fished a joint from his pocket and lit it.

"What department was the detective with? The one who just called."

"Alwin. Why?"

"Weren't we in Winston when you shot him?"

"No, we were *here* when *somebody else* shot a guy in Winston."

"Okay, then." He stretched his jaw. "The *killing* we had nothing to do with happened in Winston, so any detective investigating that would be from Winston."

"I know that." The rapist lied.

"Yeah." His voice was thin. "I figured you did."

"It's probably about my skipping school or something." He offered Bones a hit.

He grabbed the joint between his trembling fingers and took a long toke. After he exhaled, he asked, "Was the detective from the juvenile division?"

The rapist sensed his associate was not merely curious, but was questioning his intelligence and leadership. He hadn't listened closely enough to know if the detective had mentioned the division.

"He was in fact," he lied again and reached for the joint.

"I heard you say, 'I'll tell her.' Was he asking for your mom?"

The rapist preferred it when Bones was the dumb one. "Yeah, that's how I know it's about some truancy bullshit." He took a long lazy drag and leaned back into the couch, and waited for the weed to quiet his mind and abate his anger. He wanted to rip Bones' throat out, but he needed a driver.

"That's pretty damn fast. I mean, it's the first day of school."

"I don't fuckin' know, Bones. Maybe they have a campaign going or something."

He knew damn well it wasn't about the guy he shot or skipping school. It had to be that kid Trudy. Another little bitch causing trouble.

47

Colleen returned to her desk, feeling uneasy about the fact that so many dangerous people ran free to wreak havoc. Her cases were starting to pile up, too, and she worried about keeping them straight. She'd forgotten to talk to the couple about Crime Victims Compensation. She whispered, 'CVC. CVC. CVC," as she marched to her cubicle. It was the only way she would remember. *CVC. CVC. CVC.* She would scribble out a reminder the minute she sat down in her chair, which was only a few steps away.

"You're late!"

The voice came from Martinez's office.

She turned on her heels and walked the five steps to his office door. "I was downstairs with the couple whose daughter, *allegedly*, set their house on fire last night."

"Arson? That's not our department. That's the fire department, and you don't work for them."

Colleen felt herself frown.

Martinez's tone became reassuring. "Don't worry about it, but you won't see that report, and don't follow up on it."

"Did I mess up?" She smoothed the wrinkles on her skirt. "I walked into the lobby and Jeanne directed me to them."

"She's a softie. It's okay. Forget about it." He waved her away.

When Colleen returned to her cubicle, her phone rang, and she checked the display before answering.

"Hello, Lawler."

"I figured you'd be calling me soon, so I'm saving you the trouble. I scheduled an interview with the suspect."

"Well, thanks, Detective. I appreciate that."

"No problem."

She seized the opportunity to gather information. "Do you have a minute for a couple of questions?"

"Sure."

"Does he know this is about Trudy? She's pretty scared of this guy."

"He doesn't know anything. I just asked to sit down with him, and to have his mom call me."

Colleen wondered if Lawler put effort into sounding aloof or if it just came naturally. "He doesn't know what it's about?"

"Not to my knowledge."

"He didn't ask?"

"Nope."

"Is that weird? I mean, if the cops wanted to meet me about something, I'd want to know why." Then she remembered Lawler was new at this and probably hadn't made a lot of those calls.

"It could mean a lot of things, but I don't think he has any idea why I want to talk to him."

"Can I let Maxine know you have the interview scheduled, or do you prefer to do that?"

"I got it," he said with an edge to his voice. "Any more questions?"

"No, sir," she sang.

48

Matthew's stomach tightened as soon as the school was in the rear-view mirror, along with the bright sun.

His mother asked, "So how was your first day?"

He'd been relieved to be back in school. There, he felt normal. It wasn't really *normal* to grow up without a dad, and people would find that out eventually. But he could pretend he didn't have a brother, or he could pretend his brother wasn't a psycho. Some kids worried about bullies in junior high, but the worst of them were amateurs compared to his brother. He'd relished every minute away from him. He hoped the cops picked his brother up for skipping the first day of school. He thought there should be extra punishment for skipping the first day.

The best thing about this year, though, was speech class. He'd never been so excited about a class before, but Ms. Houston was everyone's favorite. Ms. Houston had given out something called a syllabus that listed all the assignments and tests for the semester. The students knew what to expect, and Matthew always liked knowing what to expect. He could even get ahead if he wanted to. He looked forward to shutting himself in his room and preparing his outlines and proposals.

"Matthew? You okay?"

"Yeah. Sorry. I was thinking about a speech project."

"Did you like Ms. Houston?"

"Yeah. She's pretty cool." He laughed softly and said, "She has a real loud voice."

Matthew wasn't in the mood to talk. He was too focused on the dread of going home. He loved his mom, but sometimes he wished he could live somewhere else, like at Frankie's. But he didn't want to leave his mom alone with his brother, either. He stared at his sneakers and picked at the skin by his thumbnail. His mother placed her hand over his.

"Tell me about Ms. Houston, or the class, or whatever. Just something."

His mom turned the car north, and Matthew prayed for lots of traffic.

He pulled the green folder from his backpack. "We have to give three speeches this semester: an informative, an explanatory, and a persuasive."

"Do you know what they have to be about?"

"We can decide our own thing or choose from a list of topics she gave us. Just a sec." He slid a sheet of paper out of the folder. "I got a list of things here. My hero or heroine. Favorite vacation spot. Favorite food." He skimmed down the list and continued. "What I would do if I were the president, which sounds like a topic for third graders."

"Why's that?" His mom asked as they came to a stop at a red light.

"I dunno. It's stupid. Who cares what a seventh grader would do if he was president?"

His mom laughed a little, the way she did when she agreed but knew she shouldn't admit it.

"Like Derek Houser. Do I really want to hear what a guy who eats boogers would do if he was the president?"

His mother looked at him and gave up. "You make a good point."

Someone behind them honked the horn, and they noticed the light had turned green. She waved at the driver behind them and accelerated harder than she usually did.

"Here's some more." Matthew read off a few more items from the list, and then he reached one that ruined the mood. "How to get along with your sisters and brothers."

They went through four intersections before either of them spoke again.

Finally, his mom broke the silence. "Wanna grab a burger before we go home?"

Matthew's heart flooded with relief. "Yeah. Thank you, Mom."

He realized she didn't want to go home either.

49

Fake fall had arrived. It happened every year at the right time for autumn, but it didn't stick around. Within a week or two, the highs would climb back into the nineties.

Kathleen set a single bag of groceries on the counter, and placed a small flower arrangement beside them.

"BLTs are heavenly," she said to Matthew. "You're gonna love it."

She couldn't remember the last time she and Matthew had done anything together outside of school. Unless they were house sitting, her youngest spent most weekends, and even some school nights, with Frankie, and she couldn't blame him. In fact, she felt at peace knowing her youngest slept elsewhere, not under the same roof as his unpredictable brother, who usually arrived home long after she'd fallen asleep. But the physical distance influenced an emotional distance, and sometimes she felt like she was losing him.

Matthew dropped his backpack into a chair at the dinner table and returned with a spring in his step to Kathleen's side. She watched him remove the items from the bag: a head of iceberg lettuce, a gorgeous red tomato, soft wheat bread, travel-sized mayonnaise, and a package of bacon. Kathleen removed a cookie sheet from the cupboard and covered it with foil. She watched Matthew working to open the package of bacon, and grinned at his expression. When focused, he made the same face he'd made since he was a toddler. She felt reconnected to him now. An almost electric energy flowed between them, and the worry of losing him dissolved. The house felt untroubled and brighter and the air cleaner. A feeling settled in, *happiness* if she dared to be so bold. It had been absent for so long that its return overwhelmed her. She breathed it into her lungs to absorb it into her blood and to press it upon her memory.

"Mom, what is it?"

"This is nice. That's all."

"I know what you mean."

Then Matthew's eyes stopped smiling.

The oldest and his hostility traipsed into the kitchen, and with their arrival, the light faded, the air thickened, and the ambiance soured. He wore nothing but cut off jean shorts, like something out of the 1970s. He leaned back against the pantry door.

Kathleen rubbed Matthew's back, offering condolences. "I didn't expect you to be home."

Matthew ignored his brother and began placing bacon strips on the foil in even rows.

"I thought it would be nice to have dinner as a family," the oldest said.

"You did, huh?" Kathleen swallowed the rage that rose every time he spoke in that sickening, paternalistic tone. She was certain it was his way of reminding her he'd robbed the family of its father. "Then go put on a shirt."

He ignored the order. "We never eat together. That doesn't seem normal."

He talked as much with his hands as his mouth, a habit that annoyed her. It smacked of insincerity.

Her youngest huffed, and she gave the boy a silent admonition. One offhand remark, even a sigh, could ignite a middle-of-the night rampage of narcissistic rage. Matthew would have to share her quarters tonight.

She asked her oldest cheerfully, "So, were you planning to cook for the family?"

This time, a genuine smile spread over his face. "Have you forgotten the last time I made you a meal?"

She refused to take the bait. "We're making BLTs. Want one?"

"You know I don't, Kathleen."

She shrugged. "Suit yourself."

Matthew asked, "What temperature?"

"Put the tray in and set it to four-hundred degrees."

"For how long?"

"Check on them in fifteen minutes."

The oldest retrieved a near-empty jar of crunchy peanut butter and what was left of the loaf of white bread from the pantry and tossed it onto the counter opposite her.

She played along and attempted what she imagined was normal conversation with a high school senior. "Have you thought about what you want to do after you graduate?"

He plopped four pieces of bread onto the countertop. "I want to get into business."

"Have you applied to any universities?" She cut the tomato into thin, even slices.

"Not gonna waste my time with college. I'm going to be an entrepreneur."

She grabbed the head of lettuce, whacked the stem against the counter, and handed it off to Matthew to wash. "An entrepreneur. Ambitious. What industry are you pursuing?"

"Well, first, I'm going to run for city council, so I can get my name out there."

Kathleen closed her eyes to keep them from rolling out of their sockets. "Interesting. I had no idea you were interested in politics."

He spun the lid off the peanut butter jar. "I've always been interested. I mean, it's stupid, but it's a great way to network and find investors."

"What are they going to invest in?"

"A coffee house, like that one in that lame-ass show everybody likes."

She could feel him staring at her, but she kept slicing. "Are you talking about *Friends*?"

"Yeah, that one."

"Ah. I see."

"Pretty sure that's the route I'm going."

There was nothing left to slice, so she put the knife down and met her offspring's eyes. "Have you researched the requirements for getting onto the council?"

"I'll figure it out. It can't be that hard."

"So, you're going to get elected to city council and then figure out what to do from there?"

"It's a coffee shop, Kathleen. It's not rocket science."

"Have you considered taking any business courses at the community college? Accounting might come in handy."

"Community college is for losers and imbeciles." He thrust a knife into the jar of crunchy peanut butter.

"Really?" She felt the side of her face tug at the corner of her mouth, and she couldn't stop a contorted half-smile from sliding across the right side of her face.

"Yeah. Really." He slapped peanut butter onto the bread and dragged the knife across it, tearing the bread in the process.

"Think you'll ever be interested in eating something other than peanut butter sandwiches?"

"I have discriminating taste."

"Is that what you're calling it?" Her contempt slipped out with the statement.

"What do *you* call it?"

"Actually," she said, laughing. "I'd call it imbecilic."

Matthew shot her a worried glance. He looked at the knife on the cutting board and then back at Kathleen. The oven timer went off and broke the tension.

The oldest carried his sandwiches to the table and pulled out a chair.

Kathleen was serious now. "You can sit there after you've put on a shirt."

She hoped he'd lose interest, protest and leave. Instead, he said, "As you wish, Kathleen." Then he sauntered to the stairs and ascended, taking two steps at a time.

Matthew had taken two small plates from the cupboard and placed them on the island. He whispered, "Maybe he won't come back."

Matthew followed Kathleen's moves and assembled a BLT with extra mayonnaise.

The oldest returned wearing a rock band T-shirt that was a size too small.

They took their seats at the long table for six. The oldest sat at one end, Kathleen at the other, with Matthew at her left.

As her offspring meticulously removed the crust from his bread, he delivered a monologue about his grandiose plans, born out of his inflated sense of importance and influence. True to form, he crammed half a sandwich at a time into his mouth. Years ago, Kathleen would have expressed concern about his choking. She would've coached him on displaying good table manners. Now, as disgusting as his eating habits were, at least he finished quickly and brought the uneasy interaction to an end.

He made smacking noises and then said, "This was enriching. We shall do it more often."

He pushed his chair away from the table and returned to the kitchen. He tossed the pieces of crust into the trash can under the sink. As he turned from the sink to leave, he flipped the cooling cookie sheet off of the stove, splattering bacon grease onto the cabinets and the kitchen floor.

"What the hell?" Matthew shouted, rewarding him with his outrage.

"What?" her offspring asked, pretending to be offended.

Kathleen looked at Matthew, shook her head, and whispered, "Don't." Fighting the urge to shout, she said, "You need to clean that up, son."

"Why? It was an accident."

"You knocked it off the stove top. On purpose."

"No, I didn't."

"Clean it up."

"Do you want me to be late for work? I got a job, you know, to help with things around the house, but if you'd rather I clean this up, that's cool."

"I have confidence you can accomplish both." There was no way he had a job.

He pulled the foil from the cookie sheet, dripping more grease onto the floor. Then, he wadded it up and put it in the trash can.

"Oh, hey. I forgot to tell you. If a detective calls, just ignore it."

"Ignore it?"

He made a lackluster attempt at wiping the floor. "Yeah. It's nothing. Just a misunderstanding."

Deep in her belly, hope aroused, like a cat stretching after a long nap. Her offspring walked briskly out of the house and slammed the front door.

Kathleen trotted to the door and opened it. "Wait a minute!"

Her offspring had barely made it off the front porch. He turned to face her and raised an eyebrow. "Excuse me?"

"Don't play that haughty attitude with me now. Tell me about this detective."

"Let's see. He sounded single and insecure. Maybe you two could, you know…" He rubbed his palms over his chest and down to his crotch.

"What does he *want?*"

"Beats me, lady. I haven't done anything wrong."

He'd done plenty wrong, and she hoped he'd finally gotten caught, especially now that he was an adult in the legal system. "Does this have anything to do with that woman you were staring down at the Fourth of July celebration?"

"What the hell are you talking about?"

"I saw you."

"No, you didn't because I wasn't there."

"Bullshit."

"You're losing it, Kathleen."

"Did you get the detective's name, or the department's name, or anything useful?" Kathleen hoped her call to Alwin PD months ago had finally gotten somewhere.

"He's from the Alwin Police Department, and he's in the juvenile crimes unit or whatever. Think his name's Lawless or something like that. Ironic, isn't it?"

"Juvenile department? You sure?"

"Pretty sure."

Damn.

Juvenile crimes meant another slap on the wrist for him and possibly more effort and money from her, a thought that made her sinuses burn, so she shut the door.

Matthew had abandoned a half-eaten sandwich to clean up the mess in the kitchen. Kathleen saw him wipe his eyes on his shirt sleeve.

"I'm sorry honey." She rubbed her son's back. "Are you okay?"

He recoiled from her touch, and Kathleen felt a jolt in her solar plexus. Matthew had never pulled away from her before.

"I don't want to talk about it."

"Okay." She smoothed her own hair and tugged at the tail of her blouse to help her resist the urge to hug her son. "You don't have to talk about it."

"He ruins everything," he said. "All he does is hurt people."

Kathleen couldn't argue.

Matthew placed the grease-soaked paper towels into the trash bin. "He belongs in jail."

Matthew was right.

"He's evil, and I hope the cops kill him."

She cleared her throat to avoid agreeing. Matthew returned to the table for the rest of his sandwich. "I like it, Mom. BLTs are really good." Before Kathleen could respond, he asked, "May I eat in my room, please?"

Kathleen agreed, but there was no way she'd let him sleep upstairs tonight.

50

Matthew's uneaten sandwich sat on his nightstand, and he rocked and shouted into a pillow. If the cops were calling because of something his brother did when he was a juvenile, it had to be about Trudy. He hadn't told his mom about that one. He wanted to tell her what happened but didn't know what to say or what his mom could even do. Matthew hadn't *seen* anything. He wasn't even in the house. Was he supposed to tell his mom that he had a feeling that his brother did something to Trudy, but he wasn't sure what it was?

But he was sure.

And if he told his mom, then what?

He knew the word *accomplice*. He'd heard his brother say it a lot. Matthew could get into trouble for helping, and that would break his mother's heart. It meant he was just as bad as his brother.

A foul taste overtook him, like he had a mouthful of coins and lemon juice. He dashed to the bathroom and threw up.

51

Kathleen woke to Matthew's voice. "Mom, wake up. Do you smell that?"

Something's burning. Plastic?

"Is he trying to cook?" Matthew asked, but Kathleen was still trying to regain her wits.

She hadn't heard the oldest return. She pushed herself upright and breathed deeply, trying to identify the odor.

She flipped back the covers and staggered to the bedroom door with Matthew on her heels. She stopped him and placed her palm on the door. "It's not hot." She opened the door and charged toward the kitchen with Matthew trailing behind her.

The trash can that belonged under the sink now stood in a space between the island and the counter, with flames raging inside it.

Water. Water. It's too big for water. Fire extinguisher!

Kathleen grabbed the fire extinguisher from the pantry and fiddled with the pin. Her fingers were shaking. "Damnit!" She looked back at the flames, giant tongues licking at the air, hungry for the ceiling. She cursed at the extinguisher, not noticing that Matthew had grabbed a bag of flour from the pantry shelf. It was one of the few items in the pantry other than bread and peanut butter.

Before Kathleen could stop him from approaching the fire, he'd ripped open the bag and dumped all the contents onto the flames, which calmed the blaze. Finally, Kathleen freed the pin and snuffed out the remaining flames.

Panting, she asked Matthew, "Where'd you learn that?"

"I saw it on TV." He fanned the smoke.

Kathleen opened the window over the sink. "We have a smoke alarm. Why didn't it go off?"

Matthew stared at the deformed plastic trash bin as if it would reignite. "Maybe the battery's dead."

Kathleen dragged a chair from the dining table to the kitchen and climbed onto it to check the detector. The battery wasn't dead. It was missing.

52

 Maxine peeked into the oven as she swayed to *Buena Vista*. The single slice of French country bread was toasted perfectly, so she pulled the cookie sheet out from under the broiler. She rubbed a garlic clove around the crust, centered it on a plate, and topped it with chopped Caesar salad. She honored the original recipe for the dressing but audaciously modified the presentation. She slid a wedge of Parmesan against a grater about a foot above the salad and hummed while the snowfall of buttery cheese floated down onto the delicious creation. She topped it with a sprinkle of sea salt and freshly ground black pepper. She was admiring the beautiful display when the phone stormed into her happy place.

 Caller ID showed that someone from Trudy's school was calling.

 Maxine had noticed a change in Trudy since the medical exam. Hearing the words, *injury due to forced penetration,* validated Trudy's account of the incident, particularly considering the amount of time that had passed between the assault and the exam. Maxine's heart broke upon hearing the doctor's report because she realized how badly Trudy had suffered in silence. The doctor had said from a medical perspective, she felt confident it strengthened the case. Maxine only hoped the conclusion would help put the rapist away for at least a few years.

 Trudy, however, felt deformed, and she pulled herself deeper into her shell.

 Maxine answered the phone and heard the school counselor's voice on the other end of the line. The woman sounded young enough to be one of the students. "Ms. Jackson."

"Please, call me Maxine." Maxine could feel her breath quickening.

"First of all, Trudy is okay. Please don't worry. She's not in any trouble. I just wanted to let you know a few things."

The school counselor explained that Trudy had been discovered spending lunchtime not in the cafeteria with her classmates, but in a stall in the girl's bathroom.

"I invited her to have lunch in my office any time she wanted to."

Maxine removed her hand from over her mouth. "That's kind of you."

"She's been spending her lunch period in my office for about a week. I hope that's all right."

"Of course." Maxine felt the words catch in her throat. "That's perfectly all right."

"She's welcome to continue that routine for as long as she wants. I simply wanted you to be aware of it in case she comes home and mentions it to you."

Maxine pictured Trudy in a filthy bathroom, sitting on a commode, with her lunch on her lap. She wanted to rush to the school and scoop her little girl into her arms.

"Ms. Jackson?"

"Yes."

"You make Trudy the most wonderful lunches. That's a sign of deep love for her. You're a good mom. She's going to be okay."

53

Several days had passed since her offspring's attempt to burn down the house. Had he read her mind? Had he noticed the paint? The gas can? Kathleen tried to distract herself by giving the kitchen a deep clean. She'd just started on the backsplash when she heard the key turn the deadbolt on the front door. Her chest grew hot with anger.

She tossed the sponge into the sink and faced him. "Where've you been?"

"None of your business."

"Actually, it is my business for…" She checked her watch. "…about another nine months."

He responded with the usual scoff. "Good one." He shuffled his feet as he walked to the kitchen.

"He's expecting you. The detective. His name is Lawler, by the way."

Her son glared at her, intending to intimidate her, but she could see he was trying to buy time, concocting a lie.

"I see the wheels turning in your head. Don't bother. He called to remind you of your appointment."

"I told you not to talk to him."

"You don't tell me who I can talk to."

Before she could move, protect herself, or protest, searing pain shot into her cheekbone. The force of his right cross dropped her to the floor. Then he pounced, slammed her head against the tile and gripped her throat with both hands. Ignoring the inferno of pain in her face, she kicked and writhed and tried to dig her heels into the floor and thrust him off with her hips, but her shoes wouldn't grip the tile.

"Shut the fuck up!" he hissed, and spit flew from his mouth onto her face.

She clawed at his hands, desperate for air. Terror made the pain irrelevant. She knew she had only seconds of life remaining.

At the end of a black tunnel, her son's dead eyes stared into hers. And the tunnel closed.

54

Kathleen heard Matthew say her name and their address. "It's my mom." His voice cracked and he whimpered. "She's hurt. Please hurry."

Her head was throbbing, and she persuaded herself to open her eyes, if only to reassure the frightened boy. She pushed herself into an upright position and used the cabinets for support.

"She's sitting up." Matthew was panting and crying. "She's alive." He dropped to his knees next to Kathleen and answered a string of *yes*, *no*, and *okay* into the cordless phone. Then, "I hear the sirens," followed by a quiet "Thank you."

Paramedics arrived first. As the small pale woman examined Kathleen, she didn't pay much attention to her comments about her vitals. Kathleen whispered *yes* or *no* to her questions, watched her tighten the blood pressure cuff over her upper arm.

But then she heard the lady say to her partner, "Petechiae in both eyes."

The unfamiliar word triggered Kathleen's anxiety. "What's that?" Her gravelly voice alarmed her.

The paramedic spoke softly. "Petechiae. Strangulation can cause the blood vessels in the skin to rupture above the area of constriction."

Strangulation.

The realization jolted every nerve, as if she'd fallen into icy water. She fought back tears, which caused greater pain in her throat, and waited for a detailed explanation.

"Pressure builds in the capillaries, and when the vessels rupture, small red dots appear. Those dots or splotches are petechiae. You have that in your eyes. The whites of your eyes."

A wave of panic washed over her. "Is my eyesight damaged? Does it go away?" She tried to hide her fear for Matthew's sake, who stood out of the way, wearing a terrified expression.

"It should clear up on its own in a few days, and it shouldn't have any impact on your vision." The woman had a calming presence, and Kathleen felt her bottom lip tremble.

The second paramedic said, "We'd like to transport you to the hospital."

"No, that's not necessary." She had mediocre health coverage, and she envisioned her mailbox stuffed with overdue medical bills.

He implored her to reconsider. "What your son did is incredibly dangerous. He could've killed you."

Her thoughts raced to Matthew, and what her death would've meant for him. An orphan whose only sibling murdered both his parents.

The first paramedic gently squeezed her hand. "The police are almost here."

55

Some victims called Colleen daily, hoping for updates or a piece of good news. Some left multiple voice mail messages in the middle of the night, followed by calls the following morning during which they would vent or cry or, less often, express rage. Maxine, however, had contacted Colleen infrequently and only when she felt she had good reason. Her last call was for reassurance that the interview with the perpetrator had been scheduled. She admitted she was on edge that the suspect wouldn't show, or if he did, he'd retaliate after he figured out that Trudy was the accuser.

When Colleen had contacted Lawler to confirm the interview was still on the calendar, his reply had been peppered with frustration. "She knows she can call me directly, right?"

"She knows."

Today, two hours after the scheduled interview, Maxine called Colleen and said the wait was killing her.

"Did he show?" she wanted to know.

"I haven't heard from him yet. I assume these interviews take time. I just don't know how long." Colleen considered the guy might have confessed, and Lawler was booking him.

"I'll give the detective a call, and I'll let you know what, if anything, I find out."

Colleen called the detective, and to her surprise, he answered.

"I know what you're going to ask, so I'll just tell you. His ride fell through."

Colleen looked at the ceiling and tucked her bottom lip between her teeth. She inhaled sharply. "You believe that?"

"He doesn't have a car, so yeah."

Still staring at the ceiling, she asked, "Are you going to arrest him?"

"Because he's a juvenile--"

"*Was*, barely."

"Because it's a juvenile case, we can't be too aggressive."

"The *victim* is a juvenile, and her mom is concerned about their safety."

He replied with silence.

Colleen continued. "Have you considered the idea that he might run?"

"He has no car and nowhere to go.

56

Colleen drove home engaged in an imaginary conversation with Detective Lawler.

"He has nowhere to go, you say?"

She mimicked his attitude. "He doesn't have a car."

"Has that stopped him from going anywhere else, Lawler? Did it stop him from going to that July Fourth Celebration thing and scaring the shit out of Trudy?"

She exaggerated Lawler's canned responses. "He's a juvenile, Colleen. We have to treat him like an itty biddy baby. Can't go too hard on him."

"I dunno. He went pretty hard on a little girl."

She'd reached a red light, and she felt someone staring at her. She turned to look at the passenger in the car to her left. The guy quickly looked away.

Colleen finished the argument in her head and then considered backing out of a commitment. She'd promised to meet Aunt Ruth and Martha at Nathan's Cafe for dinner. It was a special place, and Nathan was a good man.

Colleen hadn't seen Nathan or enjoyed a meal there since she'd started the job. Nathan had become a close friend, and she felt guilty about disappearing on him. But as she neared her house, all she wanted to do was melt into the couch, and maybe, if she had the strength, crawl into her bed for the rest of the night.

#

Aunt Ruth smiled when she saw Colleen sitting at their favorite table. "I was afraid you were going to cancel on us." She blew Colleen a kiss.

Colleen threw a kiss back at her as she stood from her chair. "Not a chance."

Martha gave her a sideways glance.

"Okay, I considered it."

Martha came around the table to hug her. "Let me guess. You got here early because you knew if you sat down at home, you wouldn't get back up again to go out."

"Exactly. Seven? Why y'all eat so late?"

Aunt Ruth shook her head. "You sound like an old woman."

"I feel like an old woman." She plopped down into her chair.

Nathan arrived with a tray of snacks. He had a small staff of servers, but he always handled their table. It gave him a chance to catch up.

He looked at Colleen and then back to Aunt Ruth. "Is that who I think it is? I'm not sure because it's been so very long."

"Stop it." Colleen pursed her lips. "It hasn't been that long."

"Oh, but indeed it has, my dear friend."

"I'm sorry. I'll do better."

"You look different." He waved his hand in a circle framing her face.

"It's a new style, Nate. It's called heavy-laden. It's a trend."

"Is it now?"

"I see you're not concerned about fashion. You look fabulous, as always."

He did. Nathan was tall and lean and wore a beautiful, tightly trimmed black beard. His hazel eyes were mesmerizing. In addition to having movie-star good looks, he was witty and kind. Despite Aunt Ruth and Martha's hopes, there was no spark between Nathan and Colleen. They'd cultivated a precious friendship and, like two siblings with their parents, they kept secrets from Aunt Ruth and Martha. Nathan had spent most of his life in Texas, but he wanted to marry someone who shared his family's culture and religion. Christian Pakistani women were a rare find.

After the last customers left, Nathan took a seat with the women.

Martha said, "Can you believe it's been three years, Nathan?"

"It's crazy how fast time goes by."

Aunt Ruth said, "Colleen had just decided to go to graduate school."

Aunt Ruth and Martha loved to remember the story of how their friendship was born at the cafe. Both had been dining alone, and it was a slow night, back when the restaurant was new, and word had yet to get out. Martha was a widow, with more money than she knew what to do with. Aunt Ruth had never married, and she said she'd reached the age where she had no desire to. Both wanted to travel and enjoy life, and they discovered they traveled well together. They became inseparable, and some people thought they were sisters.

\#

After dinner, Colleen stuck around to help Nathan close the cafe.

Nathan sat in the booth he always used when doing his bookkeeping. He organized sales receipts, counted cash, typed into his adding machine, and made notes in his ledger. Colleen meandered back into the kitchen, found the bag of Navrattan mix and poured some into a bowl.

She heard Nathan shout. "You're like a freaking raccoon!"

Colleen returned from the kitchen. "You have ears like a dog." She emptied a handful of the snack mix into her mouth.

"I have ears like a moth."

"A moth?"

His eyes remained on his work. "Don't talk with food in your mouth. It's rude." He raised his pencil and pointed it in her direction and said, "The greater wax moth is said to have the best hearing of all the animals in the kingdom."

"I'm not rummaging through the garbage or anything gross like that." She slid onto the bench across from him.

He typed something into the adding machine and hit the button that triggered the machine to print a subtotal. "Yes, but I hid it from you, and you found it, like a raccoon."

"It's because you put crack in this stuff."

Without looking up from his work he said, "I assure you I do *not*."

She put her elbow on the table and rested her head in her hand. "Also, it's *the animal kingdom*, not *animals in the kingdom*."

He continued organizing receipts and slips of paper with orders scribbled on them. "It's *the kingdom* if I want it to be the kingdom."

"If you say so."

"God says so. It's His kingdom."

Colleen saw a hint of a smile appear.

He paired the last receipt with an order and added them to a pile. Colleen didn't understand his system, but she recognized when he'd finished. He placed the cash into a bank bag, secured the orders to the adding machine tape with a giant paper clip, and closed the ledger.

Nate looked at her and rested his forearms on the table. "Enough talk of animals. Tell me what has been keeping you away."

Colleen gave him a synopsis of her job with vague information about the cases.

"How many bottles of Jameson have you emptied since you started?"

"I dunno."

"Then that's too many."

"You sound like Martha."

"We care about you." He reached across the table and gave her hand a gentle squeeze.

She relaxed at the human touch. Aside from hugs from Aunt Ruth and Martha, she hadn't been touched in ages. Not even a tap on the shoulder. "Have y'all been talking behind my back?"

"You're never here, so yeah. We can't talk to you, so we talk behind your back."

"Fair enough."

He mirrored her posture, and he looked like a model posing for the perfect shot. He held eye contact with her until she blinked several times and looked away, unable to cope with the intimacy.

His smile stretched from ear to ear. "You've never won a staring contest, have you?"

"Probably not." She leaned forward and said, "Your teeth are perfect. They're so white and shiny."

"That's because I don't drink coffee or red wine."

"Weirdo."

"I hope you don't lose yourself in this work. I don't have a lot of friends, you know."

She stretched her arm across the table and laid her head down. "Let's go see a movie or something, like we used to. You're closed on Sunday. Let's go."

"Hm. Maybe."

"C'mon. We'll see whatever you want."

Without hesitating, Nathan said, "*The Rich Man's Wife*. I want to see that."

"I heard it sucks." She hadn't heard anything about the movie, but Nathan had never been able to hide his love for the leading actress.

"*Nothing* with Halle Berry can suck. It's impossible."

"Okay." She rubbed her face against her bicep and let out a loud yawn.

"It's a date." He knocked on the table.

Colleen laughed onto her arm. "Don't say that in front of Ruth and Martha."

He ruffled her curly hair. "They'll start making wedding plans."

She slapped his hand away and whined. "Stop!"

"I love you, grumpy."

"I love you, too, weirdo."

57

Hanging out with Nathan had helped Colleen forget about the lousy week she'd had. But all day her thoughts zig-zagged between her home projects, tedious chores and her cases at work. It didn't seem fair to check out and enjoy time off when she knew Maxine was on high alert and angry. Colleen couldn't do anything about it, and that was maddening.

Colleen shook out her hands and resisted her mind's attempts to keep her thoughts on work. She stood inside the empty shed, admiring the pet door and contemplating insulation and drywall. That would require money, a learning curve, tools, and a lot of time. And no amount of insulation would successfully combat the Texas heat. To do that, she'd need an air conditioning unit, which was taking things too far. She considered painting the walls white, but why put lipstick on a pig?

The rattle of cicadas, which seemed to be hanging around extra-long this year, drowned out the songs of the birds and the rustling behind her.

"Who is this for?" she asked herself.

She answered herself. "Me and the dog."

"What are you going to do in this thing?"

"Drink coffee. Maybe read."

"Then all you need is a place to sit and a small table."

She turned around to exit the shed and froze.

He sat on the grass directly in front of her, scrutinizing her. She avoided making eye contact with him for fear he would perceive it as a challenge and then attack. Neither of them moved, but unlike hers, his posture was relaxed and indifferent. She expected him to speak, perhaps to mock her for talking to herself.

Then she saw it. His latest conquest. At the edge of his white paws lay a dead rat.

"I think I love you, cat."

He stared at her with unadulterated apathy. Then, he picked up the dead rat between his teeth, tossed it into the air and chased it. Colleen appreciated the kill, but the way he batted the carcass around for entertainment was disconcerting.

"You need a name." She was certain the feline understood her, even if he ignored her, pretending to be immersed in his sinister game.

She contemplated names. *Psycho. Killer. Matador. Hunter. Muerte.*

She'd always been a dog person, and despite feeling somewhat spooked by the cat, it had claimed her, probably because she was feeding him, essentially compensating him for killing unwanted vermin.

"That's it." She whispered.

Before turning in for the night, she stuck a note to the fridge:

Throw rug for the shed

Cat bed for Sicario

58

Maxine had a catering gig, and she was not comfortable leaving Trudy home alone, not after the suspect no-showed the interview.

Trudy emerged from her bedroom wearing the catering company's sweatshirt.

"Trudy, please put on one of the t-shirts, like the one I'm wearing."

"But I'm comfortable in this."

There wasn't time to negotiate. "I asked you nicely. I won't again."

About five minutes later, Maxine's patience had thinned, and Trudy stepped out of her room wearing the company t-shirt over her sweatshirt.

"No, ma'am. Just the shirt."

"But, Mom—"

Maxine snapped her fingers. "We need to go. Fix it." She winced at the sound of her venomous tone. Lately she'd been irritable and short-tempered. She was living on high alert and sleep deprived.

Trudy appeared the third time wearing the company shirt, and she walked with her arms folded across her torso.

"Thank you." The edge in Maxine's tone vanished. "Now I need help loading the truck, hon." She pointed at a crate on the kitchen table containing an organized assortment of cups, plates, cutlery, and napkins and returned to wrapping the last platter of her signature shrimp souffle rolls.

She reached the back of her Suburban as Trudy was lowering the crate into the hatch and noticed red marks on Trudy's left forearm. Maxine placed the platter on ice inside, shut the back and said, "Let me see your arm, honey."

Trudy's expression was empty, and her body stiffened.

"Show me."

Trudy held out her right forearm.

"No, the other one."

She complied and revealed a fury of superficial cuts.

"Who did that to you?"

"I don't want to say."

"I don't care if you don't wanna say. Tell me who did that to you."

Trudy's eyes filled with tears, and she whispered, "I did."

59

Trudy's head rested on Maxine's chest, her body enveloped in her mother's strong arms. The sun had long set, but they could sleep late tomorrow.

"Trudy, please help me understand." She kissed her head. "Do you want to kill yourself?"

"Sometimes I want to die, but I don't want to kill myself. Just not wake up."

"Why are you cutting yourself?"

"It helps." She spoke lazily. "It's like I have so much in me. I can't take it, and I can't get it out, but when I cut, it helps. It gets it out."

"We have to find another way for you to get it out, Trudy."

"There isn't another way, not without me getting into trouble."

"What do you mean?"

Her voice was monotoned. "If you knew what was going on in my head, you wouldn't like me."

Maxine rubbed her back. "I don't believe that. I love you, Trudy. More than anyone or anything in the world. Nothing can interfere with that."

"You'll still love me, but you might not like me anymore." Trudy's body felt heavier against Maxine. She was fading into sleep.

Maxine suspected Trudy had fantasies similar to hers. Dreams of revenge. She wondered if, like Maxine, Trudy daydreamed about hurting or killing the rapist.

She whispered to her, knowing the girl was asleep. "Whatever you're thinking, no matter how ugly, I'll understand, and I'll like you and love you no less for it."

60

Inside the parked vehicle, staring at the Alwin police station, feeling godlike, the rapist could think of nothing less edifying than an interview with that inane detective. Furthermore, he wasn't in the mood to get arrested, in case that's what the pig had in mind.

He told the skeleton, "I'm going to absent myself. Let's go."

"Home?"

"Not today." Then he howled with laughter.

He felt confident his mother wouldn't be talking to the police anymore. Still, he preferred to avoid the drama that surely awaited.

"Where do we go then?"

"Road trip!" he cheered.

"Dude, I need gas money for that."

"I got you," and morphing into a bad Stevie Wonder impersonation, he sang, "Don't you worry 'bout a thing," which, as always, brought a smile to his driver's face, which also meant he'd do what the rapist wanted.

He pulled cash out of his right front pocket. Fifty bucks he'd taken from his mother's purse.

They headed south toward Winston, and the rapist informed the driver he needed a favor.

As they left Winston city limits and crossed into Garland, the driver asked, "So you want me to get my sister to mess up that Trudy kid?"

"No need to get medieval, Bones. Just mess with her head for now, enough to shut her up if she's talking or thinking about talking."

"Nobody gets hurt?"

The bag of bones required reassurance. "Only a little fear of getting hurt. That's all."

"I'll talk to my sister. She'll want to know why, though."

The rapist knew the driver's little sister had a thing for him, and she'd do it solely to please him, but he wasn't going to let Bones know that.

"Because that little twat is going to rat her out. That's why. Your sister has been with us, smoking and shit, and Tiny Trudy was there."

"How do you know?"

The rapist detected skepticism in the skeleton's voice. "Bones, I just do." That should've been enough, but he upped the ante, "Isn't your sister a cheerleader or something?"

"Yeah, she is."

"She'll get kicked off the squad for smoking weed."

"That'll motivate her, but what would Trudy get out of it? Ratting her out?"

"Beats me. Something's off with the little girl. I'd feel sorry for her if she wasn't trying to mess up my life. *Our* lives."

The driver looked confused, so the rapist said, "You were there, too, man. Tiny's talking will have a domino effect. You're an accomplice, man."

#

The rapist called his associates by their hometowns. After picking up Mesquite, a like-minded guy who was useful because his dad was out of the picture, and his mom was usually too drunk to get in their way, they'd headed west to collect Arlington.

Arlington was twenty-one, but his enormity and features, including a thick dark beard made him look closer to thirty. Why he hung out with people so much younger than him was a mystery. He wasn't a highly intelligent person, but he wasn't mindless like a lot of people who ran with younger crowds. The rapist suspected Arlington didn't have many options. Pock marks peered over the border of his beard. He smiled often, which unveiled some jacked up teeth, and he was overweight. Perhaps he'd been rejected by his peers, who were hitting the clubs and trying to get laid. His younger companions benefitted from his age and stature, and they never let him pay for anything. Arlington could run up a bar tab, but having a twenty-one-year-old acquaintance was worth every penny.

When Arlington dropped into the back seat, the car listed. The rapist greeted him and said, "I like your shirt, man." He thought the shirt was nasty, but he needed the guy to feel good today.

Arlington smiled big revealing the train wreck in his mouth. "My mom got it for me. I dig it."

The rapist smiled as he pictured his own mother's eyes bulging out of her head as he strangled her. Then, he got back to his scheming. "Arlington, I need a favor."

"Tell me." Arlington's voice was deep and raspy, like he'd been chain-smoking for a century.

"I need you to get me a Taurus .38." He dug into his left front pocket and said, "With this."

He revealed his mother's wedding ring set.

"Daaang," Arlington crooned. "Why a Taurus, man? You should get yourself a Glock or something."

"Because a Taurus is like me. A bull." The rapist spoke with a Mexican accent. "Not to be messed with, you see."

The driver said, "I think it's *toro*."

"Bones, there's no pistol named *toro*."

"No, I mean bull. In Spanish, *toro* means bull."

"I'm not talking about Spanish. I'm talking about the stars."

"Well, you were speaking with an accent, so." Bones shut his mouth and seemed to shake off the thought.

The rapist assumed he remembered what happened to the last member of the group that pissed him off.

Arlington directed Bones to a pawn shop where the rapist hocked one of his mother's few tangible reminders of the marriage he'd cut short. After that, they gassed up and drove east again, cruised downtown Dallas, and walked the streets of Deep Ellum. There, they met up with one of Arlington's contacts, who sold him the pistol.

#

After the night at Deep Ellum, the rapist spent the next three days squatting in Mesquite smoking weed, couch surfing, joy riding, and terrorizing people. His entourage returned to Winston late one evening and crashed a party. When they were told it was time to leave, the rapist shot up the ceiling.

As they drove away from that incident, Bones had said, "Maybe we ought to stay out of Winston for a while."

"Have you not noticed?"

"Noticed what?"

"I don't get caught. You know why?"

"Luck?"

"Nothing to do with luck." The rapist spoke his truth. "First, I'm smarter than the cops. Second, we move fast. We skedaddle before the cops are even close. Third, people deserve what they get. There's no injustice in anything I do. Human nature, man. It's rough."

"Seems that way." When Bones wasn't checking his speed, he kept his eyes on the road.

The rapist said, "The fittest cull out the weak. That's the way it's always been."

It was a speech he'd given many times. His associates never challenged his theories. They listened like disciples, and the rapist lolled in his elevated status among them. If they kept it up, he'd include them in his business ventures. The coffee shop would be a good, legit business, but maybe he'd enjoy more money with a side gig under the radar, and that's where these guys might be useful.

"I tell you the truth, my friends. The future is bright."

61

Colleen returned from her lunch break to find a daunting stack of reports. She'd only seen a few last week, and they were all minor offenses from the juvenile crimes division. Sergeant Esquivel had been out one week for training, and Lieutenant Martinez was supposed to have assigned cases. Evidently, it hadn't been a priority. Now, Colleen had at least a dozen CAPERS reports to review. She scanned the incident types to organize them by urgency. She had no problem deciding which one to review first: an attempted murder. The date it was reported was two weeks earlier. The victim's last name was McDaniel, the same as the suspect in Trudy's rape. She flipped the pages and ruled out coincidence. As she read the narrative, a sickening feeling stirred in her belly.

She pounded the number on the keypad to get Lawler. He answered after the first ring.

"Can you believe it? Your boy tried to kill his mother."

"My boy?"

"The perp in Trudy's case. He beat and strangled his mom and left her for dead." She dialed back the melodrama. "At least, it seems that way. She was unconscious, and he took off."

She heard a faint clearing of his throat.

"She and her son also think he tried to burn the house down."

Colleen waited for Lawler to say something.

After several seconds of silence, she said, "No one told you."

"No. That case would go to a different unit."

"Y'all don't communicate with each other?"

"Not that quickly." He sounded annoyed. "When did that happen?"

"Two, maybe two-and-a-half weeks ago."

"Who's it assigned to?"

She squinted at the name scribbled on the cover page. "Sutton?"

He spoke just above a whisper. "He's on vacation this week."

Lawler went silent for a few breaths. Then he sighed, only it sounded more like a growl. "I bet that's why the kid didn't show up again."

Kid? How about killer?

Colleen wanted to drop a load of expletives on him. If only Lawler had made the arrest after the first no-show, how different things would be now. She figured he had the same thoughts swirling around his brain. She rested her head in her hand and spoke into the receiver. "I guess, considering this turn of events, there's no telling where he is."

Detective Lawler didn't respond. He'd messed up. Treating the suspect like a child set this mess in motion. Still, pity tugged at her. Lawler had to be kicking himself.

"You okay?" Colleen asked.

"Yeah, I'm okay."

"Have you told Maxine yet? That he no-showed a second time?"

"No, I haven't," Lawler said quietly.

"Wasn't that interview scheduled a while back?"

"It was scheduled right around the time that report was made. The attempted murder. A few days before, maybe."

Colleen waited for him to explain the delay.

"I went to a training school and then took a few days off."

"I'm surprised she didn't call me."

"I told her I preferred that she contact me or the advocacy center about matters related to the investigation and to reach out to you for other stuff."

"Like what other stuff?"

"Resources, I guess. Emotional support."

"So, when are you going to tell her?"

He paused and then said, "She seems to prefer talking to you."

"This should probably come from you." Colleen wasn't about to do his dirty work. "I'm sure she'll have questions I can't answer, and I have a meeting across town to get to."

"Right. I'll handle it."

"Good luck."

A hint of guilt pestered her on the way to the meeting. She'd felt compelled to call Maxine prior to leaving, but it was best to let the detective handle it. She would contact her as soon as she returned. She also had a moral conflict. The guy who hurt Trudy had tried to kill his own mother and was on the loose. In her heart, she believed Maxine had the right to know, but the development wasn't public information. She was facing her first conflict of interest. The suspect's mother was also a victim, and she had to reach out to her this afternoon. There was no other advocate at the department to take that case, and Colleen felt like she was about to carry on an affair. Things were getting messy.

#

Once a month, a coalition of local victim advocates met, supposedly to network and support each other. At first, the group had sounded great to Colleen, but at her first meeting she'd witnessed how risky it was to share if one was struggling to sleep, was drinking too much, or losing interest in hobbies or friends. The support the coalition members offered was meant to help victims, not the advocates. If an advocate alluded to having a hard time with a case or feeling the impact of the work, she heard the message swiftly: she wasn't cut out for the job.

It was perfectly fine, however, to trash cops and prosecutors. Therefore, Colleen shared her frustration with units failing to communicate, the tense dynamic between her and Lawler, and the way the investigation was going overall. She asked for guidance since it was, after all, her first job as a victim advocate and the case was complicated. She struggled to be concise with the general outline of the situation, a sexual assault case involving a minor perp and a minor victim and a case with the same perp, now an adult, attempting to murder his mother.

One advocate spoke up. She was a salty woman, the victim advocate for Winston PD. Colleen thoroughly enjoyed her because she could retire any time she desired and as a result, she'd said more than once, "I'm completely out of fucks." When one victim advocate jumped down another's throat for daring to express frustration with a victim, the salty older woman brought the invective to a screeching halt. The woman's skin and facial structure resembled that of a Native American. She wore a cotton plaid shirt and a jean jacket, despite the lingering heat. Her long gray hair was gathered into a leather hair slide secured with a wooden stick.

She listened to Colleen's concerns and then replied with a raspy voice. "Get with me afterward. It's a sticky situation, and we should talk about that. Also, your perp sounds familiar."

The meeting dragged on as the coalition discussed hosting an event, a divisive idea because it had nothing to do with the group's mission. When they began detailing the proposed holiday ceremony and asked for volunteers, the salty woman locked eyes with Colleen's and motioned her head in that way that's universally understood to mean, *Let's blow this joint.*

The Psychotic Son

"Excuse me, ladies." Salty grunted. "I don't think I'll be employed when that event happens, and I have a few urgent matters waiting for me back at the office."

Colleen didn't have an explanation, and she assessed the potential consequences of a newbie bailing out early. As if the veteran advocate had read her mind, she turned around and said, "Best to catch me now, kid. Might be your last chance."

"Gotcha," Colleen whispered and followed her out, like a puppy, into the parking lot and to the woman's car.

Salty retrieved a pack of cigarettes and a lighter from the glove box and held the open end of the pack towards Colleen.

"No thanks." Colleen noticed the silver and turquoise ring that covered half of the woman's index finger. "That's gorgeous."

"A gift from my grandmother."

A cool breeze surprised Colleen, a nice reminder that summer wouldn't stay forever. It carried the scent of the freshly lit cigarette, a fragrance Colleen discreetly enjoyed.

Salty said as she extended her right hand, "I don't think we've ever properly met. Sally Skinner."

Colleen shook her hand. "Colleen Heenan."

"Now, that's a good Irish name if I've ever heard one."

"I have a bit of it running through my veins."

Then Sally got down to business. "I've gotten a few cases over the last couple months. An agg assault where he put a pistol in the victim's mouth, after one of his dirtbag friends beat the hell out of the guy. He's also suspected of shooting one of his own crew during that incident. Later on, some shitbird fired shots at a party, and that sounded like him, too. Had an agg robbery, too."

"It's the same suspect in all these incidents?"

"Not sure yet, but looks to be the same guy." She took a long drag and said, "The victim who was beat up thinks he ran track with him in middle school. He was spooked because he was certain the perp recognized him, too." Smoke poured out of her mouth along with her words. "The guy's backpedaling outta fear of retaliation."

"What middle school?"

"One in Alwin, which makes me think even more it's your guy." She sucked on her cigarette again.

Colleen's heart hammered in her chest, and the ground felt unsteady under her feet. "I don't know if I'm supposed to share this, but I have the name of the suspect in my cases."

Smoke crept slowly through Sally's lips. "You're good. Give it to me. I'll look into it and get back to you." She took a quick drag, exhaled and said, "As for the juggling act with two victims of the same perp, just do your best. Try to think of them as separate cases and forget it's the same shit stain on humanity doing them wrong. Serve them like you would if none of these coincidences existed."

"It's hard to do that, you know? I haven't had many cases yet that required much from me. They've been fairly cut and dried until now."

"I get it. It's messy. If you hear about any threats against them, or you get information from one victim that might benefit the other's safety or the investigation, *go to the detectives* on the cases. Get to know the sergeants and consult with them when you can, too."

"Okay." She felt her eyebrows draw together. "But I answer to the lieutenant."

Sally spoke like a gangster, only with a Texan accent. "You don't want to look like you're going over their heads. Even though your direct supervisor is a lieutenant, you gotta tread lightly."

"Okay." Colleen second guessed every conversation she'd had with Martinez.

"If you're always going to the lieutenant instead of directly to the investigators, they'll never trust you or share anything with you." She sucked on her cigarette and blew out a steady stream of smoke. "You're an outsider, a civilian. Bring them cookies or something. Something to ease the tension, but don't try too hard. You have to earn your way into their circle, and people like us will, at best, only get one foot inside, never two."

62

Because Kathleen was a teacher, it was hard to reach her during business hours, but Colleen hoped she'd had taken a few days off and was resting at home, considering the woman almost died. Nevertheless, she decided to wait until the end of the day to call. There was no good reason for it, only procrastination. Over the next couple of hours, she tried to clear Trudy's case from her mind by following up on Crime Victim Compensation claims and updating victims on the status of their cases.

As her workday came to a close, she reviewed the attempted murder report again, and her nerves agitated her stomach. The necessary withholding of truth was eating away at her, but she had to make the call. Finally, she dialed the number.

As the line rang, Colleen remembered horror stories about victim advocates calling domestic violence victims with good intentions, only to find out later the perp was listening in. As a woman's voice came over the line, Colleen envisioned the murderous teen holding a gun to her head. She confirmed she was indeed talking to Kathleen McDaniel, and then she introduced herself.

"My name is Colleen Heenan, and I'm a victim advocate with Alwin Police Department. If it's not safe to talk right now, please respond by saying, "*We're not interested. Don't call again.*"

"It's safe. I can speak freely."

Colleen released the death grip she had on the handset. "I'm so glad to hear that."

"What exactly is a victim advocate?"

"My job is to reach out to victims of crime, let them know about their rights, and share information about services. The criminal justice system can be a bit confusing, even frustrating, and I can be your contact person every step of the way."

Colleen thought she heard Kathleen sniff, and it was followed by a whisper, "Thank you."

She spent the next thirty-five minutes listening to Kathleen, offering support, doing some safety planning, and pretending she didn't know anything about her son's other crimes.

"I know it's getting late, but would it be all right if I came by with some information?"

Kathleen hesitated before answering. "That would be nice."

Twenty minutes later, Colleen pulled to a stop in front of Kathleen's house. The front lawn was cut, but it consisted mostly of weeds, with only a few small patches of St. Augustine grass. Unlike the neighbors' landscaping, this house had no hedges or flowers. The house paint was dull, and the front door was devoid of the status quo fall wreath. It reminded Colleen of the house she shared with her mom before her father ripped her out of Colleen's life. She thought about the family she'd never known, like her father's parents. What was it like to give birth to a murderer? Before she'd become a victim advocate, Colleen hadn't thought about this. Had Kathleen been aware her son was a killer? Colleen had never known her mom's parents, but they must have suffered terribly. She missed her mother, and she'd grieved fiercely, but she preferred not to ponder the fact that a murderer's blood flowed through her veins. The impact of her dad's atrocities slithered into everything and everyone around them. She felt like she owed the world an apology. Would Kathleen feel the same way?

Movement on the porch startled her out of her thoughts. A woman stood with the front door half open, watching Colleen, motioning her to come inside, and she picked up her pace.

The second Colleen crossed the threshold, Kathleen shut and locked the door and guided her toward a dining table off the kitchen, just as Maxine had when she'd visited her at her home.

"I thought you would be armed." Kathleen said as she removed a blue bandanna from around her neck, unveiling yellowed bruises.

"I'm not an officer. I'm a civilian employee."

"I didn't realize that. I'm not sure it's safe for you here if my son shows up."

"I thought about that before coming, but we'll be okay." Colleen hoped Kathleen hadn't detected the absence of confidence in her voice.

A boy was already seated at the table. Despite the purple half-circles under them, his eyes were inquisitive and fixed on Colleen.

Colleen heard the approval in Kathleen's voice as she said, "This is my son Matthew."

Matthew looked as exhausted as his mother.

"Hi, Matthew. I'm Colleen."

Colleen joined him at the table and offered information about services and Crime Victims' Compensation but kept it concise.

Kathleen didn't seem interested in services. "What are the charges again?"

"The report I received listed attempted murder as the charge."

"A felony, correct?"

"Yes, ma'am."

Victims tended to minimize crimes committed against them by family members or loved ones. Colleen anticipated an expression of regret that a young man's life would be ruined by such a serious charge.

Kathleen revealed no emotion. "And at seventeen, he's an adult in the judicial system, correct?"

"Yes, that's also correct."

Colleen prepared herself for the protests, for Kathleen to insist her son's behavior was out of character, that she'd provoked him, that he was a kid and prison wasn't the solution.

Instead, a tinge of anger peppered Kathleen's words. "You know, he was angry with me, enraged, for talking to a detective."

The statement stirred Colleen's curiosity. "I didn't know that."

Matthew interjected. "He's a psychopath." He said it with the certainty of a veteran forensic psychologist.

Kathleen said, "Matthew has read some books about serial killers."

"And psychopaths."

"Yes." Kathleen nodded. "Psychopaths."

Matthew stated his case. He emphasized each point with a knife hand cutting through the air in front of his chest. "He has no empathy. He lies all the time and doesn't care if he gets caught. He's manipulative." He'd stumbled over the last word, recovered and made his last point. "The detective needs to know that."

"That your brother's a psychopath?"

"Yes. It changes things. He's not just a rebellious teenager or a normal kind of juvenile delin…"

Kathleen finished for him. "Delinquent."

"Right. Delinquent." Matthew's diction was sharp.

Colleen said, "You were here when your brother hurt your mom, right?"

"Yeah."

Kathleen nudged him.

"I mean, yes, ma'am. I was here when he attacked my mom and tried to kill her. I called 9-1-1."

Colleen said, "Well, strangling someone is really serious, and the detective knows that."

"Well, he needs to know he's a psychopath, too."

"I'll tell him. I promise." Colleen wouldn't break a promise to a kid ever again.

Kathleen said, "I've read a little bit about this, too. Psychopathy. And I have to agree with Matthew. I know we're not professionals, but my son has just about every trait the books list about psychopathy."

"I believe you." Colleen made eye contact with the boy. "I believe you." Then turned to Kathleen. "You said he was angry because you talked to a detective?"

"He killed my dad."

Holy shit. What?

Kathleen's head snapped toward her son. "Matthew." She placed her hand over the one Matthew wasn't gnawing on.

Colleen tried to hide her shock. "When did he kill your dad?"

Kathleen began to answer, but Matthew beat her to it. "When I was a baby."

"We don't know that. The police said it was an accident or a suicide."

"My dad didn't kill himself."

Colleen felt unsteady, like the legs on her chair were different lengths, and the hairs on the back of her neck stood at attention.

Kathleen said, "Matthew, for now we need to focus on the present crime."

Colleen was out of her depth. Her mouth went dry, and she could feel her pulse against her scalp. She looked at the door and reminded herself that Kathleen had locked it. Surely, though, the psychotic son had a key.

"Matthew," Colleen said. The boy made intense eye contact with her. "I'm listening, and I'll pass on what you said to the detectives." Then, to Kathleen she said, "The detective assigned to your case is Detective Sutton. He's been in and out of the office.." she stammered. "He was out of town. Has he called you?"

"No. The detective I talked to was named Lawler. Do you know what that was about?"

Colleen noticed Matthew's face flush, and the boy chewed at the side of his thumb.

An image of Trudy surfaced in Colleen's mind, and she danced around the truth. "Lawler's a detective in the Youth Crimes Division, but he also handles crimes against children. Because it's Youth Crimes, I think the suspects are usually juveniles, but I'm not sure about that. I've only been with the department for a few months." It wasn't an answer, but it was the best Colleen could muster.

Matthew got to his feet. "I'm going to study."

Matthew had been so committed to giving information about his brother that his sudden departure didn't make sense. Colleen suspected he knew something about Trudy's case he was afraid to share, at least in front of his mother.

After he was out of the room, Kathleen said. "This has been so hard on him."

"I'm sure it has."

Kathleen continued. "Matthew's always been in his brother's shadow. A dark, ominous shadow. I pulled him from Alwin ISD and enrolled him where I teach in Plano. He deserved the chance to create his own first impressions instead of his brother's reputation doing it for him."

Colleen wanted to ask about that reputation, but she resisted, and simply nodded.

"Can I offer you something to drink? I'm getting myself some tea."

"Water would be great. Thank you."

"I'll fetch a bottle from the back fridge. We keep that locked."

"Please, I don't need it. That's too much trouble." *They keep the back fridge locked.*

"I'm going, anyway, for myself. It's no trouble."

Alone at the table, Colleen wondered what she'd do if the rapist, the *murderous* rapist, bolted through the front door. She noted the phone on the wall. Could she make it there in time to call for help? She placed her mobile on her lap and flipped it open. She could dial 9-1-1, but she'd have to give the address to the dispatcher, and she knew the rapist would be able to get to her before she got out the first number. She pressed the three numbers so that she'd only have to press the SEND key to connect. Even if she succeeded, it would be minutes before the cops arrived. She scanned the kitchen counters for a knife block or any weapon of opportunity, but she saw nothing. On the other hand, he could be hiding upstairs right now. She hadn't thought about that possibility. Kathleen could be protecting him. Maybe that's why Matthew was so on edge?

By the time Kathleen returned with a container of loose tea and two bottles of water, Colleen had seen herself murdered five different ways.

Kathleen washed a mug vigorously before pouring the bottled water into it and placing it in the microwave to heat.

"We don't keep any food here, and we keep the drinks locked in a fridge in the garage."

Colleen simply nodded, but the questions she had must have made themselves known.

"He, my oldest, has tampered with things in the past. It's safer this way."

That back of Colleen's neck tingled again.

"I have some bottled beer in the kitchen fridge, but that's probably not befitting official business."

Still at a loss for appropriate words, Colleen smiled and shrugged in agreement. *Say something.*

Kathleen asked, "So the charges, the attempted murder charge, that is. What's the punishment for that?"

"You know…" Colleen cleared her throat. "It's a range." She stumbled over the explanation. "A person with no priors could be eligible for probation. Your son is quite young, so—"

"No, that's not going to work."

Colleen couldn't get a good read on the woman. "I don't understand."

"He needs to go to prison long enough to die there."

Colleen noticed movement on the staircase and heard a thump. Someone was listening. Her heart felt five times bigger than it should, and it was going berserk.

Kathleen said, "I'm sure that's Matthew." But she inched toward the phone on the wall.

Colleen stood and leaned forward enough to get a look. She noticed a small pile of something at the top of the stairs. Clothes? Then a small, human-like face. The uncanny valley slithered through her, and she shuddered. Then she noticed the strings. A marionette.

Matthew's voice drifted down the stairs. "I *hate* these things!"

Another puppet landed in a heap next to the first.

"Excuse me," Kathleen said as she jogged to and up the stairs.

Colleen heard a muffled conversation, followed by an order. "Stay out of there. I mean it." Then hard footfalls and the slam of a door.

When Kathleen returned downstairs, Colleen noticed how gracefully the woman moved. Her long slip dress swayed with her gait. Her well-worn Birkenstock sandals disrupted the elegance but took nothing away from her femininity. She envisioned the woman dancing a waltz or the lead in *Swan Lake*. She seemed light and fresh until she reached the table and Colleen once again saw her face. There was no glow about her, no color in her cheeks, no sheen to her hair or life in her eyes.

Kathleen spoke quietly. "Matthew doesn't usually act like that. I'm sorry."

"Please, no need to apologize."

Kathleen stood by her chair and said, "Matthew's so intelligent and articulate. It's easy to forget he's still just a boy."

Kathleen returned to her seat at the head of the table. "He found me." She smoothed her dress. "Matthew did. After the attack. He called for help." She recounted the incident as if she hadn't heard the exchanges between Colleen and Matthew just moments ago.

"I saw that in the report. It must've been frightening for him. For both of you."

"His voice..." Kathleen fought back a sob. "He was terrified."

"The packet of information I'm leaving with you has some resources for both of you. Counseling can be really helpful."

"What we need most…" She wiped her eyes and straightened her posture. "Is for my son to go to prison, and I will do whatever I can to make that happen."

63

After cruising the perimeter of the block and confirming the coast was clear, the rapist's driver parked around the corner from the house he still considered his home, at least for now. Parked in front of it was a red pickup, and he watched a tall curly-haired woman walk from his front door to the vehicle and climb into the driver's seat.

The skeleton whispered, "Who's that?"

The rapist mocked him by also whispering. "I dunno, Bones. Never seen her before." Then in a regular voice he said, "She's probably a friend. Another teacher from school."

"What if she's a cop?"

"Why the hell would you think that?"

Bones shrugged. "Paranoia."

"She's not a cop. She'd have a gun if she was a cop."

Bones countered. "She could have it in her bag or something."

"Nah, she'd have a jacket on if she was a cop, hiding her gun under it."

The rapist had counted on his mother *not* calling the police after their scuffle. Perhaps he'd underestimated her. That would mean he had bigger problems than a bogus rape charge, but nothing he couldn't handle. He watched the red pickup pull away from the curb and out of sight.

"It's all good. Let's move." The rapist shifted in his seat to face his driver. "Hey, did your sister take care of me? You know?"

"You mean about the bullshit with that girl? Trudy or whatever?"

"Yeah."

Bones turned onto the rapist's street. "She and a couple of her friends set her straight." He pulled to a stop several houses down from the rapist's home and put the gear in park.

"Tell her I'll make it worth their while."

"Will do," the driver replied, but he sounded noncommittal and stared intently at his lap, running his fingertip over a loose thread at the hem of his shirt. Finally, he broke the silence. "What do you mean by making it worth their while?"

"The usual."

"Party with you?"

"Yeah. My mom should have one of those house-sitting gigs soon."

"A Special K party?"

"Maybe."

"Yo, that's my sister."

"I wouldn't mess with your kid sister, man."

"Tiny Trudy is *younger* than my sister."

"What's your problem?" He blurted out the challenge and then remembered he needed a driver now more than ever. "I'm just messing with you. Your sister's off limits." He held out his hand to shake on it.

"Dude, is that your mom?" Bones pointed to the house.

The rapist saw his mother glaring at him through the front window, with a cordless phone held to her ear.

"Go," he barked. "Now."

Bones put it in drive and stepped on the gas. "What's wrong, man? What's up with your mom?"

"She's pissed. That's all."

"Where you wanna go?"

"I don't know yet. Head east into Parker and then to Wylie."

"Wylie?" Bones asked with a confused smirk.

"I just need to think," the rapist snapped. He slid down in his seat. "Don't speed. Don't do anything to get pulled over."

Once they crossed into Wylie, the rapist said, "I better crash at your place."

"I don't know, man. I mean, it's okay with me, but my mom. It's her house, and she'll ask questions."

"Just tell her we're having the house fumigated or something." He needed to find some older associates.

"Can you drive me to Arlington's?"

"No way, I gotta get home."

"Seriously?"

"What about Mesquite? That's doable."

"Good idea, Bones. Gimme your phone."

64

Maxine, deadpan, sat across from the school principal. "You didn't return my call, Mr. Johnson. That's why I'm here."

"I assure you I planned to call you this afternoon or as soon as I had a few moments that wouldn't be interrupted. As I'm sure you can imagine, the first month of school is extraordinarily busy."

"The first month is nearly over, but it certainly has been extraordinary. Trudy is afraid to come to school."

"We looked at the video, and it doesn't appear that Trudy was threatened or even targeted."

"Then look again. Trudy doesn't lie."

"We could see there was a commotion, but we have conflicting details from students and witnesses."

"That delinquent tried to force my daughter to 'fight' her. Then, she and her little crew got on Trudy's bus. They didn't belong on that bus route. They did it to harass her and intimidate her."

"Can you provide any context for me? Did something happen between the girls?"

"No. Trudy doesn't even know them, but..." She took a breath before continuing. "There might be a connection."

"Can you elaborate?"

"Trudy told me that the girl who pushed her said something about Trudy lying or spreading lies. Something like that." Maxine didn't know how much she could or should say about the case. "I can't get into details, but a young man hurt Trudy. Badly. The police are investigating."

"I'm so sorry, Ms. Jackson."

"Thanks," she said, but she didn't want sympathy. "Look, the guy has a group of girls that are known to hang around his house. Some are his younger brother's age. Around the same age as the girls in that video."

"Does his brother go to this school?"

"I think he transferred to Plano ISD. His mom's a teacher there, and if I remember right, she transferred the boy there."

"That makes sense."

"Anyway…" Maxine gave the rapist's name and asked, "Do you know if the girl giving Trudy trouble runs in the same crowd?"

"I can't comment about other students, and it sounds like the suspect is in high school."

"This isn't a situation where a schoolyard bully called my daughter names. This is an assault committed by a student, and it took place on your campus, followed by harassment on the school bus, and I think the perpetrator is using his friends to terrorize my daughter, to retaliate against her for reporting to the police. That is a *crime*."

Despite her calm and controlled demeanor, the principal said, "I understand you're upset, Ms. Jackson."

"Of course, I'm upset, yet I'm not being unreasonable. I'm here for reassurance that my daughter's right to an education, without fear and intimidation, is fulfilled."

"I assure you we are committed to providing a safe environment."

Maxine felt as though they were spinning in circles, faster and faster.

"Isn't there a school resource officer here?"

"Yes, Officer Stevens."

"Why doesn't he charge the girl with assault or retaliation?"

"He reviewed the video and didn't see any assault take place. Only a disagreement."

"So, pushing and shoving a girl, and yanking on her hair isn't an assault?" she leaned toward his desk. "Since when?"

He folded his hands on his desk. "How can we help?"

"Protect Trudy. Expel that piece of trouble or send her to another school. Ideally, the other girls, too."

His expression provided his opinion, and after a tense silence, he said, "The best I can do is a stay-away agreement."

"What's that?" She folded her hands on his desk, mirroring him.

"It's a written agreement that the two students—the student in the video and Trudy— won't be in the same place at the same time while on school grounds."

"How does that work?"

"We'll look at their schedules and change them, if necessary, to prevent them from encountering each other in places like the lunchroom or library."

Maxine shut her eyes as if doing so would keep her tongue in check. She took a deep breath, which convinced civility to stay in the conversation.

"Her first year of middle school has already been complicated enough. She's dealing with too much uncertainty. Please don't change her schedule."

"I assure you we don't want any harm to come to Trudy. She's been a wonderful student, and we will do everything possible to maintain a safe environment for her."

Maxine knew that meant *no promises*.

#

Nausea crept around Maxine's stomach as she pulled out of the parking lot. School principals were so condescending. They talked so much but said nothing. This one had dodged responsibility with vague terms and canned responses.

"Everyone has a right to an education," she mimicked. "How the hell do you get an education when you're constantly looking over your shoulder?"

Her brain flipped through ideas for protecting Trudy, for putting a stop to it all, but her schemes were impractical, illegal, or both.

Anger burned in her chest. *Why did you go over there, Trudy? Right into the hungry wolf's den.*

She wanted to kill them all.

Only light drives out darkness.

"Does fire count as light?" She wanted to go home, make a half dozen Molotov cocktails and hurl them through the windows of wherever the cretin slept.

You don't even know what cretin *really means, and you don't know where he sleeps. You could end up hurting his mom and the younger son, and you'd go to prison.*

Maybe she'd show up just to warn his mother. Maybe the woman could talk some sense into her kids. Maybe that turd would be there, and she could look him in the eyes, let him know Trudy's mom isn't afraid.

The woman might call the cops.

She'd be gone long before they showed up to pretend they might do something.

But that detective might accuse you of messing with his half-assed investigation.

Maxine turned into the front driveway of her house with no memory of making the trip. Every muscle was flexed. Her jaw ached from being clenched. Her head hurt. She stayed in her car, rubbed her temples, and shook out her arms, and wondered if she'd run a red light or blown through a stop sign. In her anger and desire for vengeance, she could've caused a crash and hurt someone. *You could've killed someone.* She remained in the driver's seat and took a few breaths while scanning her surroundings. At the end of the block, she noticed a woman out for a walk, pushing a stroller. She had to have driven by them, but she didn't remember.

Maxine's rage transformed into tears of relief for not having run anyone over.

She whispered, "You better get it together and focus on what you can control."

That meant taking care of herself and Trudy. Her body felt agitated, like she'd had too much caffeine. Anger and anxiety rattled their cages and demanded their release.

Instead of using the front door, Maxine pressed the button on the garage door remote. The heavy bag hung alone, neglected. She hadn't had the energy for it until now.

65

Colleen closed her eyes and listened to the breeze flow across the trees. It was a *fake fall* day. Flukes that arrived every September, brief interruptions of the stubborn summer heat. She made a point to enjoy every one of them.

Colleen had grown to loathe eating lunch in the break room, with detectives and secretaries coming and going and the constant jabber from talking heads on a television that was always on. The fluorescent overhead lights in there created a dystopian atmosphere. When the temperature dipped below ninety, she'd taken a few lunch breaks in a nearby park, but the mom-groups with their toddlers reminded her of friends she never saw. They were busy raising babies and focused on their marriages.

She longed for shade, quiet, and solitude, and she could find it within walking distance of the station. She'd mulled it over for a few days, even driven past it twice before giving in. It seemed a bit macabre, but the cemetery offered what she wanted.

She sat on a Mexican blanket in what had become her favorite spot, under the shade of a cedar tree next to the final resting place of James N. Poindexter, a World War II pilot, whom she suspected had been killed in action.

After she'd finished a turkey and bacon sandwich, she pulled the weeks-old letter from her bag and talked to the marker. "I have someone in my life who is almost as inaccessible as you, sir."

The letter read like the others she'd received through the years. His environment didn't offer much variety, but his letters were nonetheless optimistic.

"Here's something new, Major Poindexter. William's taking college courses. Ironic. He had no interest in college before prison."

And as always, his letter offered an apology.

If I could, I'd go back and do things so much differently. I'd be there for you instead of trying to solve the problem for you. I was focused on my version of justice instead of helping you heal, and a million apologies will never be enough.

One punch had wiped away their dreams. They were teenagers' dreams, but they were made of hope of a bright future together. She knew of a few couples from high school who'd married young. She'd seen one recently from a distance at a burger place. They'd gotten hitched right after they'd graduated college. They'd had a newborn with them and seemed quite content. Fat, dumb, and happy. She'd caught herself smiling at the new family, feeling downright pleased by their apparent success, but she'd ducked out of sight before they spotted her. If they'd seen her, they'd have asked about her life, and people thought her life was depressing. To her, it was simply life. But people wanted to know *How's your husband* and *What do you do,* and she wasn't good at small talk. Their reactions to her candid answers had planted seeds of doubt. Maybe her life *was* depressing. Maybe her life *wasn't* normal. Would her life had been normal if she'd never met Steven, if William hadn't screwed everything up? Would she have a baby on her hip and an arm around his waist, while waiting in line to order cheeseburgers? Would they get together with other couples and their kids? Would she hang out with other moms, like the ones in the park?

Something tickled her waist.

She'd forgotten the text pager her lieutenant had issued.

What's your ETA?

She fumbled with the device and responded.

10 min.

OK.

She checked her watch. She'd spent more time inside her head than she'd realized, but she wasn't late. Something must have happened.

"Weather permitting, I'll see you tomorrow, Major."

66

Maxine was sitting at the kitchen table, staring at a phone book when Trudy burst into the house, ran to her room and slammed the door.

Maxine's wild emotions had been beaten into the heavy bag, and now she was left with fatigue. She took a few breaths and said a quick prayer before going to the girl.

She knocked gently on the bedroom door and announced her entry. Her hand felt like it weighed twenty pounds. She stepped inside the girl's bedroom and followed the cries to the closet. She found Trudy deep inside, curled into a fetal position on the floor, screaming into a pillow.

Trudy had always been gentle and tender-hearted, but she wasn't prone to crying. She'd certainly never seen the girl howl into a pillow.

Maxine lowered to her knees. The sounds of her daughter unleashing emotional agony snatched her breath. They were the cries she'd expect not from a young girl, but from a mother holding her murdered child. Pure despair. Maxine crawled into the closet and placed her hand on her daughter's hip.

"What happened, baby?" Her voice cracked. She fought tears so hard she felt like her throat would collapse, and Trudy continued sobbing and screaming. She was beyond being consoled. The bear was out of the cage. Maxine crawled in further, slid her hands under Trudy's body and lifted her into a sitting position. To her surprise, Trudy didn't resist. Then she pulled the girl to her, leaned back against the wall of the darkened closet, in the safe small space, with her arms embracing her daughter, and she breathed purposefully. She didn't ask questions. She didn't speak. She only breathed, deep inhales and long exhales, until Trudy's screams turned into sobs, and sobs turned into gasps and eventually into breaths that fell into rhythm with her own.

    Finally, Trudy spoke. "I want to be homeschooled."

    The thought of being a homeschool teacher made Maxine's head spin.

    "What triggered this, Trudy? What happened?"

    "Everyone knows," she cried. "He told everyone."

67

After consuming a surprising amount of tomato soup and grilled cheese, Trudy crawled into Maxine's bed and drifted to sleep. Maxine had consoled her daughter and made her comfort meal, yet her own anger burned as hot as it had hours ago. Reason prevailed against her desire to drive to the rapist's house, but she wasn't going to remain silent. Once she felt certain Trudy was sleeping soundly, Maxine grabbed the newest edition of the White Pages and found the rapist's home number. She repeated it enough to burn it into her brain. She grabbed the cordless phone, stepped onto the back patio and hit *67 before dialing the number.

A woman answered on the third ring. Maxine's tenor voice was icy but calm. "Listen to me. That bad seed, otherwise known as your son, and his catty groupies, and your little boy, better leave my girl alone. Or you all get to deal with me."

She ended the call without waiting for a reply, returned inside the house, and looked in on Trudy. The girl was still asleep, only now with her head on Maxine's pillow. Back in the kitchen, she poured herself a glass of pinot grigio and returned to the patio.

She sunk into the cushions of a large wicker chair, where she sat every morning with coffee and nearly every evening with a glass of wine, where she watched the birds on the feeders, read the newspaper, planned events, and thumbed through cookbooks. The moon was a sliver in the sky, and the darkness felt oppressive and looming. For months, she'd paced the perimeter of grief, but now she granted herself permission to step inside.

Trudy's unheeded cries for help.

Trudy's face shoved into a pillow, held down, muffled screams, the fight to breathe.

Her little body torn.

The terror she must have felt then.

The shame and fear she feels now.

The cutting, the loneliness, and isolation.

Maxine wept through her first glass of wine. Then, she returned her focus to now.

Trudy is alive.

Trudy's safe at home.

Trudy can heal.

Maxine was considering a second glass of wine when harsh scratches on the fence, followed by a thump, sent a jolt of adrenaline through her. In her peripheral vision, she saw something fall from the top of the fence to the grass below. She shot to her feet, and they cemented in place, and every muscle froze. All she could make out was the outline of the intruder, a subtle contrast of charcoal against midnight blue, but enough for her brain to identify it.

"Thank you, Jesus," she whispered.

The neighborhood cat was making its rounds and moseyed across the grass to her. Maxine slowed her breath while the marginally feral creature did figure eights around her ankles.

She was too focused on the cat to sense the other much larger but equally feral creature on the other side of the fence, watching her between the slats.

68

Kathleen looked at the phone as if it would come to life. The caller had blocked her number, but Kathleen knew who it was. The woman in the park. She wanted to respond to the voice. So many things she wanted to ask and to tell her.

What had he done?

Who were the groupies, and what had they done?

Matthew? What on earth did he have to do with anything?

What could she do to help? To prevent her offspring from hurting anyone else again?

The caller's tone had a jagged edge that should've scared her, but instead she felt a strange connection to the woman. She wanted to apologize to her for whatever her oldest had done and join forces to stop him from hurting anyone again, but the caller didn't give her a chance.

Still, there was someone out there who knew what she'd always known. *He's a bad seed.* Now, *that* was validating.

The woman had mentioned Mathew, though, and that had rattled her.

Matthew was sitting at the kitchen table working on a science assignment.

He must have felt her tension. "Mom? What's wrong?"

Kathleen stared at him while weighing her options. Then, she remembered how her own mom had tricked her older brother into confessing things by merely bluffing when he stepped through the doorway, ambushing him with utter bullshit. *The principal called* led to an excited utterance: "I skipped first period, but that's all, and I have an A in that class!" *The police called* once elicited a confession about having loitered with his friends in a shopping mall parking lot long after business hours had ended.

Matthew didn't get in trouble at school or anywhere else, but he was hiding something, so Kathleen employed her mother's tactic.

"What is it?" Matthew put down his pencil. "Mom, you're scaring me."

Kathleen placed her hands on the table and leaned forward.

"That call came from Trudy's mother."

The boy's face lost its color.

"What did you do, Matthew? You can tell me, or you can tell the cops."

69

Matthew stared at his mom, leaning on the table before him, pushing into his space. He'd read about how people and animals react to fear. He knew about fight-or-flight, but he was stuck in between. His mom's question froze his entire existence. He couldn't move. He couldn't talk. He couldn't focus.

Think. Think.

He'd never seen his mother like this before, at least not with him.

He felt like an elephant was pushing against his chest, making it impossible to breathe. His heart pounded between his scalp and his skull and inside his ears.

Just lie. Lie!

"I didn't do anything," he cried so loudly it startled her.

"Cut the crap, Matthew." The words hurt him. His mother never talked to him like that. She'd never had to. He was the good kid. Always the good one.

"What did I do?" His voice sounded babyish, like someone else had taken over his body. "I didn't do anything." But he knew his protests weren't going to convince his mother. They might even make it worse.

No matter what he said, horrible things would happen. The police would arrest him. He'd go to jail. His brother would kill his mom. Ideas, terrible ideas, buzzed frantically around his head like hornets stinging his brain.

"Take a breath," his mom ordered, her voice only slightly softer than before.

Matthew didn't even realize he was panting.

"Matthew, love, take a deep breath." His mother was no longer on the attack. She moved closer and sat down next to him. When Matthew tried to slow his breath, it rattled and caught in his throat, and then the tears gushed out of his eyes again.

"Matthew, whatever happened, we'll deal with it, okay?" His mother reached into his lap and separated his hands. He hadn't felt his thumb digging into his palm.

He couldn't think of a lie. The best he had come up with was *I didn't do anything*.

"Tell me, honey."

Matthew shook his head violently, "I don't wanna be here. I don't wanna be here." He was frantic, hoping that if he repeated that mantra enough times, he'd wake up in his bed in his mother's room and the nightmare would be over. "I don't wanna be here!"

Now his mother's voice sounded afraid. "Matthew. Honey. You've got to tell me."

"He'll kill me, Mom. He'll kill me." He didn't have to tell her who would kill him. She knew. Matthew rocked as he repeated the words. "He'll kill me. He'll kill me."

Three loud cracks snapped him out of his frenzy. The hornets vanished, and Mathew had only one thought, and that was about the cracking noises. They'd come out of nowhere.

His mother commanded, "Stop." *She* had made the noise. She'd clapped her hands to get his attention. It worked. She always knew what to do. Then, she put her hands on his shoulders and turned him toward her.

"Look at me." His mom's tone was calm and sure and strong. Her hands felt warm and secure on his shoulders. "He will *not* kill you." She was a protective bear now. "He will not lay a *finger* on you."

Matthew nodded his head in agreement. His eyes stung, not from tears but from not blinking.

His mom continued. "Something is going on, and I need to know what it is. The truth always surfaces. It might claw its way out slowly, but it'll come out." She grabbed the box of tissues from an end table and handed it to him. "I'd rather hear it from you than the police."

Matthew gave in. He wanted it over. "He wanted me to invite a couple friends over, and I invited Trudy. Only no one was here but him. I think." It was a gross image, but spitting out the truth felt like popping a huge zit.

"When was this?"

"The end of the school year. Last year."

"So, you invited Trudy over to do what?"

"To come to a party. To celebrate the end of school. I told her we'd have pizza." The words sounded so sick. He was the villain in this story.

His mother looked confused. "But we had a house-sitting job that weekend. Didn't we?"

"I know." He thought if he'd blurted it all out, it would get easier, but it wasn't. He felt evil.

"Did...did you forget?"

Again, Matthew considered lying. He could say he forgot, and then he might not get in trouble, and he wouldn't be a horrible person, and his mom would know he was still the good one. As he considered it, the easy lie she'd practically handed to him, he felt his stomach twist.

It won't work.

First of all, his mom was too good at detecting lies. Second, he might forget what he'd said later when the police interrogated him. They had ways of confusing people and tricking people into telling the truth. Even good liars would mess up, and he wasn't a good liar.

"No, I didn't forget. He wanted me to have some of my friends over for his friends to hang out with."

"But your friends are much younger than his. Isn't that a little weird?"

"I know, but they think he's cool. They feel popular or something when they get invited over."

His mother cocked her head, and Matthew could tell he'd slipped something important to her, but he didn't know what it was.

"They feel popular when they get invited over," his mom repeated. "So, this happens often?"

Shit.

"Only a few times."

His mother nodded, and Matthew could tell she wanted to hear more. "The first time was with Trudy. After that, I only called girls who were sluts."

His mother's mouth dropped open, and he tried to fix it. "I mean, girls who hang out with older boys, who smoke, and sneak out of the house to drink and have sex and stuff like that." Her face told him she understood, and Matthew added, "Not girls like Trudy."

"These girls are in sixth or seventh grade and doing..." She waved her hand around, "All this awful stuff?"

"Mom, you're a teacher. You know kids in sixth grade already do that stuff."

"It's a different world from the one I grew up in. I guess I haven't adjusted to it."

The pressure on Matthew's head and chest was less intense now, and he'd finally stopped crying.

"So, you invited girls over here knowing we'd be gone. Correct?"

"Yes, ma'am."

"And what happened to Trudy?"

The question caused heat to rush to Matthew's face. "I don't know," he whispered.

"What do you *think* happened to her? Obviously, it's something bad enough to have you really upset."

"I didn't know how to tell her not to come without hurting her feelings." He felt his chin tremble, and his throat got tight again.

His mom's tone remained even. "What do you think happened to her?"

"I didn't have her phone number or anything, and we weren't here, and I couldn't undo it."

"I understand that."

He could tell his mom was losing patience, and he started sweating.

"What do you think happened to Trudy?"

He whimpered and sounded like a baby again. "I think he raped her."

His mom's face tightened, and he could tell it was hard for her not to yell. "What makes you think that?" She cleared her throat. "Why do you think he raped her, Matthew?"

Matthew saw she had shoved her fists into her skirt, and her knuckles had turned white.

"He wanted me to invite her over again." His breath shook as he finished. "He said he wanted to go another round with her."

The familiar taste of lemon and pocket change flooded his mouth again, and he stumbled to the kitchen sink and threw up.

70

Kathleen sat on the sofa with a soft throw over her lap. She held out her arms. "Come here."

Matthew shook his head, as if he was no longer worthy of kindness.

"Come here now."

The boy acquiesced.

Kathleen embraced him and said, "You're not going to prison."

Matthew coughed, but Kathleen knew he was choking back a sob. She'd never seen him cry like this. She suspected he'd uncaged years of sadness.

"I love you. You got in over your head, okay? But you didn't harm anyone directly."

"Are you going to call the cops?"

"I'm going to call that detective who called the house. I have a duty to do that."

Matthew released a pathetic whimper. "Do I need a lawyer?"

"No, honey." She stroked his hair. "You didn't commit a crime, and you don't need a lawyer."

"But I feel so guilty. I feel like I *did* commit a crime because I think he hurt her bad and she was here because of me."

"Your brother hurt her, not you."

"You should've seen her face. She was so happy when I asked her to come over."

"I know, love."

"She's so small and nice. I didn't know how to tell her to stay away. I didn't want to hurt her feelings, but it would've been better."

Kathleen pulled the last three tissues from the box and patted Matthew's face. "We don't know what even happened, Matthew."

"I feel so bad, Mom. I feel like a horrible person. It hurts, like physically hurts."

"It's called a conscience. You have empathy." She kissed his head. "It hurts, but it's a good thing. It's what makes us human."

71

Colleen had received an email from the sergeant over Youth Crimes, requesting her attendance at his weekly meeting with the detectives in his division. The invitation had arrived shortly after Colleen had told Lawler about the rapist trying to kill his mother. In his email, the sergeant implied her attendance could improve communications between units. While the invite intrigued her, she anticipated questions from Lieutenant Martinez and possibly Sergeant Esquivel. After all, she understood her role as belonging to CAPERS. She'd sensed a competitive edge between the CAPERS and Youth Crimes divisions, and she didn't want the meeting to stir the pot. On the other hand, she'd worked almost in isolation since day one, and it was nice to be welcomed to the table, even if it came from a sergeant who'd never spoken a word to her before. Then, there was the Lawler factor to consider. She hadn't seen him since they'd crossed paths at the Child Advocacy Center. Colleen's insides started twitching. She was caught between excitement and reluctance.

She showed up several minutes early and entered the empty conference room. Eight chairs surrounded a long table, and each one presented risks. Both heads of the table she immediately ruled out. The chairs to the right of each head also felt problematic. She spotted a couple extra chairs against a wall and awkwardly lowered herself into one.

She checked the clock on the wall. Three minutes to go. She worked the edges of the French cuffs on her crisp white shirt, one of several items Aunt Ruth had bought her for the new job, and it was already damp under the pits. She made a note at the bottom of her legal pad:

buy men's antip...

She doodled around the note and then checked the clock again.

Just as she was second guessing the time and place of the meeting, two men burst into the room, like a couple of drunks.

When the younger one saw her, he grabbed his chest and shouted, "Holy shit! You scared me!"

The older man smirked and nodded a hello.

Colleen shrugged playfully.

The younger guy asked, "Why are you sitting over there like you're in trouble?"

"Just sizing up the crowd." Her attempt at banter sounded aloof, and she tried to recover. "I know people like their routines." She uncrossed her legs. "I didn't want to mess that up. You know, encroach on someone's territory." Now *she* sounded like the drunk. She crossed her legs again.

He plopped into a chair and pulled out the one next to him and said, "Come sit. There's plenty of room."

The older guy said, "Now, you're making things weird." He looked at Colleen and said, "He does that. He can't help it." He dropped a note pad onto the table across from the younger guy and sat down.

Colleen stood and accepted the seat the younger man had offered and hoped she wouldn't regret it.

Then Lawler entered, and Colleen worked over the gap between her two front teeth.

He looked at her and said, "Hey, Colleen."

The greeting almost knocked her out of her chair. His tone and body language might be described as friendly. Maybe they really were drunk.

She tried to hide her surprise and exude confidence. "Hello, Lawler."

He sat opposite her, leaving a chair in between him and the older guy.

The young man next to her said, "Everyone's here, so let's get started."

She blurted out, "You're Sergeant Perry?"

"Yes, ma'am. I am."

She felt her cheeks blush. "I've seen you in passing, and we've communicated by email, but I hadn't put your name to your face."

"You can't unsee it, either," the older guy said.

Perry smirked. "That's all right, Heenan. You're still getting your bearings."

"I feel like I should have them by now."

"Well, you seem like a natural. You handled those kids really well. The kids whose mom was murdered."

"You lied to me."

"And we appreciate you communicating that the suspect in our sexual assault of a child is a suspect in an assault against his mother."

Now, Colleen understood why Lawler was being so cordial. She kept her eyes on the sergeant. "I figured you'd know something like that."

Lawler spoke up. "You'd be surprised by how much we don't know about cases outside our division."

Colleen felt herself relax into her chair while she listened to the investigators review a few cases. Then, Sergeant Perry asked her to describe her role as a victim advocate, which she did, albeit briefly. Then she asked, "Did you know why I was hired?"

The three spoke at the same time. "Not really," and "Nah," and "Not a clue."

"Well, that explains some things." She liked these guys.

Perry asked, "Where did you train? Like, do you have a degree in victim advocacy or something like that?"

"Criminology, actually. I have a master's in criminology."

A cacophony of praise erupted between the three men, and Colleen wasn't sure if they were teasing her or impressed.

The older guy asked, "So is it *Dr.* Heenan?"

"No!" Colleen's hands waved involuntarily, like they were trying to erase the idea. "Not even close."

He shrugged in response and said, "You got closer than any of us goons got."

Then Perry opened the floor. "Any questions, comments, concerns?"

Colleen raised her hand.

With a half-smile, Perry said, "You don't have to do that. Just speak up."

She felt her cheeks turn red again. "I'm just trying to be respectful."

"Oh, don't do that." The older detective shook his head. "They don't deserve it."

"You three are the entire youth crimes division?"

"Yep." Perry quipped.

"Seems pretty small considering the number of reports I get with juvenile offenders."

Perry said, "Alwin's still a small town."

The older detective grunted. "It hasn't been a small town for a while now."

Perry countered. "A small city."

"Not for long," the older detective said.

Perry addressed Colleen. "He misses the old days." Then he asked the group, "Anything else?"

Colleen spoke up. "One more question."

"Hit me."

"You think Trudy would be able to get a protective order?"

Perry asked, "Did her mom request one?"

"No, and I haven't mentioned anything about it to her," Colleen said. "I'm just curious."

After a long pause, Sergeant Perry answered. "I don't think so. Protective orders usually involve domestic violence."

"I've heard they were available to rape victims, too."

The older detective said, "She'd have to testify, and I know the DA's folks don't like them to get on the stand at a hearing and then again at a trial, if this goes to trial."

"Why's that?"

"Whatever testimony she gives at the hearing is on record. Later at the trial, if she misspeaks or remembers a detail differently, the defense will try to discredit her."

Sergeant Perry said, "It's also a fishing expedition."

"What do you mean?"

"At a protective order hearing, the defense asks a lot of questions. They'll try to gather details that could help their case down the line. They'll also take her for a test drive as a witness, see what buttons they can push."

Colleen sat back in her chair.

Sergeant Perry continued. "Before any hearing could even be set, they'd have to serve him, and we don't know where the dirt bag is."

Detective Lawler offered another idea, "I'll contact the school resource officer. He can keep an eye on Trudy, watch her back. Maybe that will provide a little comfort to the girl and her mom."

"Thanks." Colleen had little confidence the plan would help, but it was something. "I promised a kid, the suspect's little brother, that I'd tell you something."

They looked at her like three curious monkeys, and she couldn't help but grin.

Sergeant Perry said, "We're all ears."

"The kid, Matthew is his name. He said his brother is a psychopath. His mom agrees."

"How old is this kid?" Perry asked.

"Twelve or thirteen, I think."

None of the detectives commented.

"His mom agrees. Evidently, they both have read up on it. They said he displays just about every trait, and the kid was adamant that you needed to know."

Lawler asked, "What are the traits?"

Colleen recited the list. "No empathy, incessant lying and no remorse when caught, manipulative. There's also criminal versatility. Oh, and the kid said his brother murdered his father, too."

The three exchanged looks, and Perry spoke up. "When was that?"

"Had to be over a decade ago."

"And the brother said something to Trudy. She wrote it in her statement. He said that what he'd done to her was in his nature."

Perry asked the older detective to run a call history for Kathleen McDaniel's address, then he turned to Colleen. "Can you join us every week, barring any crisis stuff you have to do?"

She scanned the faces of the three men and smiled. "Shucks, guys. Y'all know how to make a girl feel special."

Even though Colleen had been surrounded by people, she'd worked alone as an outsider, aside from her meetings with Martinez. Now, she felt like a member of a team. She had a big toe inside the circle.

72

"What if I told you that you were living with a psychopath? Would you believe me? Could you prove me wrong? Maybe some facts will help you decide." Matthew scanned the room, and by the look on the faces of his classmates, he was pretty sure he had their attention. At the word *psychopath*, he'd seen the whites of Ms. Houston's eyes.

"Psychopaths look like regular people most of the time. They can pretend to be normal, too. In fact, they can be *quite* charming and attractive."

Matthew held up a photo of Ted Bundy. In his other hand, he displayed the book he'd borrowed from his mother's nightstand. "They can wear a *Mask of Sanity*." He hadn't read much of it because it was surprisingly boring, but it was a good visual aid.

"Maybe they're not insane, but psychopaths aren't normal, either. Psychopaths lie, not my-dog-ate-my-homework kind of lies. They tell lies like 'I love you.' They tell lies like, '*I have a broken arm and need help.*'"

Matthew showed the class a large sketch he'd done of Ted Bundy with a cast on his arm. Every student focused on his artwork. Usually, at least one kid was picking at a scab or scribbling on the desktop, but not today.

"Psychopaths have no empathy, so they don't care if you're hurt or feeling sad. They might even be happy about it. They're also manipulative." He'd slowed down when saying that word, not for dramatic effect, but because he'd kept tripping over the syllables when he'd practiced his speech.

"They don't manipulate the way we do, when we say '*pleeease*,' to get a later curfew or play hooky." He pulled a face like he'd been caught red-handed and said, "Sorry Ms. Houston," and the kids laughed a little bit.

"No. Psychopaths manipulate to get what they want, no matter how bad it might hurt you. They do it to lure you into their trap. Another interesting fact is that a lot of psychopaths don't sleep much. They get bored easily, too. They don't feel fear like us, and they don't feel those butterflies in their stomach like normal people. They aren't team players. No, they're the opposite. They're backstabbers.

"Psychopaths have huge egos. They think they're better than everyone else and smarter than everyone else. They don't care about rules or laws, but they don't want to go to prison, so they're sneaky.

"Now, think of someone you know and compare the facts. I'll use my brother as an example. When I was younger, he hit me on the head with a ukulele."

The kids laughed at that, which was what he was going for. Getting hit with a ukulele was kind of funny. Getting whacked in the head with a fastball wasn't.

"He hit me so hard it made my hair turn white. I cried."

Matthew stopped and looked at several of his classmates, creating a dramatic pause before saying, "I was a kid! Gimme a break. Ukuleles sound real cute, but they hurt!"

Matthew waited for the energy to simmer down before he continued, in a somber voice. "I cried, and my brother laughed. I cried louder, and he laughed harder."

Ms. Houston looked serious. It was a mom look, like she wanted to give him a hug.

73

Matthew's hands trembled as he waited for the school resource officer to arrest him. He could see the thin, blue capillaries beneath his pale skin. He brought his hand to his teeth, unconsciously invoking a habit, but he'd chewed his nails to the quick. He expected his mother to walk in any minute. He was still only twelve years old, and he knew the officer couldn't interrogate him without a parent there. But he didn't know how helpful she could be. After all, she'd told him he didn't need a lawyer.

Officer Ridley had a shiny bald head and skin like black coffee. Matthew could tell he worked out, which made him seem young, but his mustache had gray hairs in it. Matthew didn't know Officer Ridley's age, but he was sure the man was old enough to be his dad, and Matthew often wished he was. Officer Ridley could kick the shit out of his brother.

Officer Ridley shut the door and then sat behind his desk. "I've never asked you before. Do you like to be called *Matthew* or *Matt*?"

He could hear his brother calling him *Matty*, and he felt his lip curl. "Matthew, please."

Matthew had watched enough *Hill Street Blues* to know not to say more than he had to.

"Matthew, is everything okay at home?"

How the hell was he supposed to answer that?

"It's okay to tell me if something's going on that isn't quite right, you know. You're safe here."

"My mom is a good mother. She takes good care of me, so yeah, I guess everything's okay at home."

"I get that idea. She seems like a good person."

"She's a great person."

"Has anything happened lately you might want to talk about?"

This didn't feel like interrogation. Officer Ridley was relaxed and talked to him like a teacher would or the school counselor. Officer Ridley was one of the good guys, and the more good guys who knew the truth, the better. He decided to rip off the band-aid.

"My brother's a psychopath, and he hurts people. He killed my dad and tried to kill my mom." Instantly, he felt lighter. He'd told the curly-headed lady at the house, but it hadn't felt like this. Probably because she wasn't a cop. She was just a messenger. This was different. For years, he'd been hauling a burden around like a backpack filled with bricks, and he'd finally set it down. He busted out laughing.

Officer Ridley sat in silence while Matthew laughed like a crazy person, and then he was crying and laughing at the same time, which was the weirdest thing he'd ever done.

"What's going on, Matthew? You all right?"

Matthew wiped the tears off his face with his tee shirt and leaned back in his chair. "It feels so good to say it, especially to a cop."

Maybe now, his brother would go to prison.

Officer Ridley leaned back in his chair. "Is that why your speeches are about serial killers and psychopaths? Because of your brother?"

Matthew sat up and shrugged. "I guess so."

"I think the topic has made someone uneasy. I got an anonymous *tip*, for lack of a better word."

"From Ms. Houston?" Matthew felt his nostrils flare, and just like that, Ms. Houston wasn't his favorite teacher anymore.

"No. It was anonymous, but I can tell you it didn't come from her. Ms. Houston says you're a very bright student who is respectful and considerate."

A wave of relief poured down Matthew's shoulders, and he wanted to apologize to Ms. Houston for thinking bad about her, even for a second. "She's my favorite teacher."

"I think she might be everyone's favorite."

"Probably. She's really cool."

Matthew knew Officer Ridley was trying to build rapport. That was one of the words he'd had to look up when he was reading books about serial killers. But Officer Ridley was doing it in a good way, not a tricky way.

"Matthew, you said your brother killed your dad. Are you sure about this?"

"I was a baby, but I'm pretty sure."

"I see. I'm sorry you lost your dad. I lost mine, too, when I was a little older than you."

"It sucks." Matthew said, and he felt his chin tremble, and he dropped his head. He didn't want to cry anymore, especially not in front of Officer Ridley.

"Yes, it does suck. It really does."

Officer Ridley didn't try to make it better, like most grown-ups did, and Matthew appreciated that.

Then Officer Ridley got back to business. "What about your mom? You said he tried to kill her?"

"He choked her until she passed out. She was on the kitchen floor, and I thought she was dead. I called 9-1-1."

"When did this happen, Matthew?"

"A few weeks ago, I think."

"Is your mom okay? I know she teaches here. Do you want me to get her?"

"Not really. I don't want to upset her."

"Okay." He nodded. "I understand."

Matthew believed he really did understand. "She's okay, though."

Officer Ridley sat tall in his chair and said, "You handled a frightening situation really well. You might have saved her life."

Matthew nodded.

"How old is your brother?"

"Seventeen. My mom says he's an adult in the legal system now."

"That's correct. Do you know if the police arrested him? Did he go to jail?"

"He took off like a coward. No one knows where he is. There's a detective on the case."

"Do you remember the detective's name?"

"Law? Something like *Law*. My brother said his name was ironic."

"Your brother came back after he attacked your mother?"

Matthew realized the order of events didn't make sense. "No. He didn't, but he knew a detective's name."

"You've been through a lot, Matthew. Our memories don't always fall in order." Ridley wrote a few words on his notepad. "Do you and your mom live in Plano?"

"No. Our house is in Alwin."

"And that's where he hurt your mom?"

"Yeah."

Officer Ridley's eyes shot up at him, and Matthew corrected himself. "Yes, sir."

Officer Ridley answered with a warm smile.

He could tell the cop was thinking. Maybe he was thinking about putting his brother in jail. "Can *you* arrest him, Officer Ridley? Please?"

"If there is a warrant for his arrest, and he showed up here, I could."

Matthew wondered how he could get his brother to the school.

"But it's not a Plano case, Matthew. It's Alwin's job to investigate and arrest him."

"But if he comes here, you'll arrest him?"

"If there's a warrant, yes. If there's not, I can tell him not to come here again because he isn't a student here. He has no reason to be here. And if he showed up again after that, I could arrest him."

Matthew picked at the raw spot next to his thumbnail and chewed on his lower lip.

Then Officer Ridley talked to him about safety, and he seemed to care. Matthew felt like he and his mom had someone on their team. Officer Ridley also promised to call the detective.

Fifteen minutes later, Matthew left Officer Ridley's office, standing a little taller, eager to tell his mom about his plan.

74

Matthew had waited all day to share his plan with his mom, and by the time the last bell sounded, he was about to explode with excitement and hope.

As soon as they got into the car, the words flew out of his mouth. "We have to get him to come to the school. If he comes to the school, Officer Ridley will arrest him."

His mother stiffened. "Matthew."

"He'll finally go to jail, Mom."

"Matthew, I know about your chat with Officer Ridley. I really didn't want people at work to know about your brother. It's the one place where I feel normal. I don't talk about him to anyone here. No one."

Matthew hadn't considered all the consequences before he blew the lid off the secret to Officer Ridley. His mother was right. School was the place where they could pretend he didn't exist, and Matthew had brought his brother inside the walls and poisoned the air. People would look at him and his mom and feel sorry for them, or stay away from them, and stop talking to them. Suddenly, Matthew worried that tomorrow, he'd sit alone at lunch, feel the torture of whispers in the classrooms and halls about him and his crazy brother, become more and more alone as people pulled away from him, like psychopaths were contagious.

His mom asked, "Do you know how embarrassing that would be? To have him show up at school and get arrested?" She sounded like she was about to cry. "Let the Alwin Police deal with this."

"Sorry, Mom." He picked at the bleeding crater by his thumbnail. "I'm sorry."

His mother gripped the steering wheel so hard her knuckles looked like they would pop through her skin. They'd always been a team, in this together, and he'd betrayed her.

"And why are you writing *speeches* about him?"

"I'm not."

"Don't *lie* to me." Her voice was almost a shout. "*How to Know If You're Living with a Psychopath.* That was your how-to speech."

"My informative speech." As soon as the correction passed his lips, he regretted it.

"The type is irrelevant, Matthew."

"How did you know about my speech?"

"Ms. Houston was worried about us. She was so decent about it, but Matthew, of course she'd tell me." She flashed him a look like he was an idiot. "You couldn't think of a different topic? Maybe one more appropriate for seventh grade?"

Matthew thought about his answer carefully before deciding to give it to her. "I couldn't, Mom. He's pretty much all I think about."

His brother lived in his head, clung to his every thought, and disturbed his sleep. He followed him around the hallways in school, and hovered over his shoulder when he studied and took tests. When kids asked why he went to school in Plano instead of Alwin where he lived, he gave muddy answers. Going to the same school where his mom taught would've made some sense if he was younger, but not now. Now, it made him look like a baby.

"Mom, I don't feel *normal* anywhere. When I said, 'he ruins everything,' I meant it. He doesn't have to *be* here to ruin school, too."

75

Another day reviewing reports of humans behaving badly was approaching its end. Then a call came from the salty Winston victim advocate. At first, Colleen was elated.

"Our guys arrested your perp."

"Yes!" Colleen jumped to her feet, discovering the limits of the phone cord.

"That's the good news, kid. Actually, it's mediocre news."

Colleen's heart dived into her gut. "What's the bad news?"

"Our guys requested the suspect be held without bond. The dumbshit judge, however, read *no bond,* as in *zero* dollars required, and dropped the turd into the punchbowl."

Colleen said, "Well, he should be sitting in the Alwin jail, right?"

Sally didn't answer.

Assuming she needed a reminder, Colleen tried jogging Sally's memory. "He's in the Collin County jail because of the existing warrant for the sexual assault he committed up here, right?" Then, she remembered. "Wait, there should be *two* warrants out of Alwin. He tried to kill his mom, too."

"No warrants."

No warrants. Colleen wanted to throw something.

"I'm sorry, kid."

"Thanks for warning me." Colleen's blood turned hot. She looked toward Martinez's office, gripping the spiraled phone cord hard enough to hurt. Martinez was gone for the day.

Sally asked, "You okay, kid?"

"Yeah. I guess so."

"I gotta share something else with you."

"Okay."

"Are you sitting down?"

She lowered herself into her chair. "It gets worse?"

"Not really. Just some context. It came from our guys who interviewed him."

"I'm sitting."

"I'm gonna read you something that came from a sergeant, okay?"

"Okay." The back of Colleen's neck already tingled.

"Our team's info about the suspect and his associates: They run the streets like a pack of jackals. They have no empathy. They don't think beyond fifteen minutes. They're a clan of psychopaths."

When Colleen's mind stopped racing, she said, "Somebody needs to do something."

"What do you mean?"

"This is bullshit. He's out. He's got no home, no family, no job, no car. He's a psychopath with nothing to lose. He's more dangerous than ever."

"And there's hundreds like him running around."

"I'm gonna call Lawler. I gotta go."

She hung up and dialed Lawler's number and got his voice mail. "Lawler, I wanted to let you know that the suspect in the sexual assault of a child, Trudy's case, was arrested by Winston PD." She didn't want to waste time with details about the idiot judge, so she simply stated, "He made bond, and because there was no warrant from Alwin PD, he was released. He's out."

Next, she picked up the phone to call Maxine, but slammed it down before dialing. The news needed to be delivered in person.

76

Colleen sat across from Maxine at the kitchen table and avoided staring as the bad news settled in. She perused the bright, immaculate space, the assortment of greenery throughout the living room. Pristine orchids here, impeccably pruned Bonsais there. A Peace Lily in one corner, a fern and water fountain in another. String of pearls succulents and Swedish ivy spilled over the windowsills. The air felt cool and clean. She made a mental note: *buy a house plant.*

When she'd digested the facts, Maxine spoke. "Let me see if I got this straight. We've got a judge who can't read, and a detective who can't be bothered with writing up a warrant?"

Colleen couldn't tell her about the attempted murder, or that would've topped the list. "I hope to have answers tomorrow." She hated delivering hazy replies. They made her sound like a politician.

Maxine softened, or perhaps surrendered to fatigue. "I'm tired." The words tripped up her throat. She wiped her eyes. "I'm just so tired."

"This has to be exhausting. I'm so sorry." Colleen didn't know anything better to say.

"You know how they say, '*you marry your father*'?"

Colleen pushed back against the horde of memories of her father.

It's not about me.

"I've heard that."

"Well, I didn't. I married an asshole, and now it's like I put a curse on my family." Maxine straightened her posture and rose from her chair. "I'm getting a glass of wine. Want one?"

Colleen's first instinct was to decline. This was a work call. She checked the funky cat clock on the kitchen wall and was surprised to see it was only 5:45 p.m. The sun began its departure earlier this time of year, making the hour feel much later than it was.

Maxine had noticed Colleen checking the clock. "You're not on duty, anymore. I'll grab an extra glass. We can go out back, change locations, shift subjects, so it's officially not work."

"Why not?" She was on call, but off the clock. A few sips of wine were better than the double-shot of whiskey she'd planned to pour at home.

Maxine's patio was as calming as the inside of the house. Colleen selected one of two large wicker chairs, resting between hibiscus plants. She listened as Maxine shared the condensed version of her story and how she'd moved to Alwin to distance herself from her history, mostly her tragic choice of a husband. She took Colleen further back, sharing how she'd studied martial arts, under her father's instruction. Then she moved forward in time again, to the irony of how she, a skilled fighter with a loving father, fell prey to an abuser. When Maxine had finished, Colleen saw her smile for the first time.

"That training…" Maxine said. "It feels like a lifetime ago, but I still have moves."

Colleen returned the smile. "Oh, yeah?"

"Maybe a couple." She chuckled. "BJJ was empowering, though. I even won a few medals." She finished her glass of wine and said, "But they didn't prevent my ex from intimidating me into submission."

Colleen knew next to nothing about martial arts. "I've never heard of BJJ."

"Brazilian Jiu Jitsu. You'll hear about it soon. The word's out, thanks to a guy named Royce Gracie." She rolled the stem of her empty glass between her fingers. "Trudy didn't want to learn any of that, though. She's tender-hearted. Meek and mild. Such an easy target. Maybe I shouldn't have given her a choice. You know, like some parents just *make* their kids do things, like piano lessons or tennis or whatever."

"I went to school with a kid who jumped off the roof of his house, once, hoping he'd break his arm and not have to practice piano anymore."

"Seriously?"

"Yeah."

"Did it work?"

"He broke an ankle, so not really."

They sat in silence for a few long seconds before Maxine spoke again. "Wanna hear something ironic?"

"Sure." Colleen raised the glass to her lips and let a tiny amount of wine trickle into her mouth, still feeling conflicted about having a drink in her hand, under the circumstances.

"It's got nothing to do with martial arts or this case."

Colleen shrugged. "That's alright with me."

"I've been asked to give a quote on a big shindig, a dinner thing. A catering job."

"How's that ironic?"

"It's for an association of *defense* attorneys. I'm not sure how I feel about that."

"Oh, I see." Colleen rubbed thumb along her chin as she contemplated Maxine's dilemma. "I bet it'll pay well."

"It would. That's the kicker." She grabbed the wine bottle and poured a second glass. "I'll have to meditate on that."

Colleen had barely touched her wine, and her conscience tugged at her to leave. She still had something to discuss with Maxine, though, so she killed the light mood by bringing up the subject. "Maxine, I want to talk to you a minute about your safety. Safety planning, just for the weekend."

Colleen offered some ideas. Most involved leaving the house, but Maxine refused to consider staying elsewhere, and her logic was solid.

"So, we hide out in a hotel or something all weekend. What do we do Monday if he's still in the wind? Tuesday? We can't stay away indefinitely."

"It might help you both sleep better, if only for a few days."

"That snake isn't running us out of our home." Maxine's mind was made up. "They just need to catch him. They just need to do their damn jobs."

77

As he'd done before, the rapist sat crossed-legged outside the mother's fence. He peered through the slats and wondered about the woman sipping wine with the troublemaker's mom. The lady didn't talk much, and there was no laughing. Perhaps she was more of an acquaintance than a friend. It had the air of a first visit, almost businesslike. The woman finished her glass of wine, and while he couldn't hear the exact words, they sounded gentle, and her body language said she needed to go. Lots of *thank yous* and follow-ups delayed her departure. He'd never understood the exercise in grace and excessive politeness. It seemed pointless.

When the unknown woman stepped into the house, he rolled onto his hip and got to his feet. He wandered half a block to meet his sidekick who waited in the car, his scraggly arm hanging out the driver's open window.

The rapist opened the passenger door, and Bones asked, "Who were you watching?"

"The mystery lady." He climbed in and shut the door. "It's the same chick we saw at my house the other day."

"No shit? You think it's a cop?"

"A cop wouldn't be drinking wine on the patio."

"Maybe she's a cop but they're friends or something, or she's off duty."

"She's not a cop," he snapped. "She'll be driving out of the neighborhood any minute. Red pickup. I want you to tail her."

"If she's a cop, then she'll spot a tail."

"I swear to God, if you say *she's a cop* one more time, I'll fuck you up." Evidently, Bones needed a reminder of what had led to the half-wit's demise.

"Dude, I'm on your side." He turned the key and started the engine.

"I admit it's not a coincidence that she was at my house and now she's here." The rapist used the big brother tone. "But she isn't a police officer or detective or anyone like that."

"What do you think she's doing?"

"Maybe she's a social worker or something. She feels like a helper."

"Huh?"

"Just tail her. I'll figure out who she is and decide if she's trouble."

78

Kathleen stood outside Matthew's bedroom door. They'd had enough time to themselves, enough for her to fix her attitude and consider a few facts, like the fact that Matthew was still only twelve years old, not yet capable of thinking through the consequences beyond the ones he'd hoped for. She'd had time to consider, again, how unfair it was for Matthew to co-exist with an older brother who hid broken glass in sandwiches and tried to burn the house down with them in it, with enough plausible deniability to avoid consequences. And trying to strangle her to death. What had *that* done to Matthew? When she thought about the danger these living arrangements had posed to Matthew, the guilt was suffocating.

She knocked on his door and heard his socked feet approach. He turned the lock and opened the door.

She wasted no time. "I'm sorry, Matthew. I shouldn't have gotten upset with you about your speech and for telling Officer Ridley about…what's going on here."

He nodded, but his eyes remained on the floor.

"I think you were just trying to help."

He nodded and said, "Someone has to do something, Mom. Someone has to help us."

The gas can and the paint returned to her mind, but that window of opportunity had closed. Her offspring was wanted now, and she doubted he'd ever sleep in the house again. But she felt certain he would lurk, possibly strike in the night. He was their boogeyman now.

An hour later, they'd made peace over pizza. They sat across from each other at the dining table with one remaining slice of pepperoni in the pizza box between them.

Kathleen asked, "When did you know something was wrong with him?"

"I don't know when for sure. I remember when he hit me in the head with that baseball, the way he acted about it was…just wrong. I was too young to know something was really messed up with him, but I knew that something wasn't right. I don't know if that makes sense."

"It does." Kathleen picked at a piece of crust on her plate, and she felt her throat tighten as she remembered how little Matthew was when the baseball incident happened. It was probably the first assault of many. She'd believed it was an accident because that's what she wanted to believe. "When did you become convinced he was…what he is?"

"When I saw a show that had some F.B.I. profilers talking about it."

"When did you see that?"

"Frankie and I watched it at his house. They have all the cable channels."

"Frankie knows about your brother?"

"Pretty much."

"Frankie's a good friend, huh?"

"Mom, he's pretty much my only friend, but yeah, he's a good one. A great one."

Kathleen saw him eye the last piece of pizza. "Go ahead. It'll just go to waste if you don't."

Matthew smiled and whispered, "Thanks," as he slid the last piece out of the box and onto his plate. "After that, I read a book called *Whoever*

Fights Monsters, which is about serial killers and an FBI profiler who tracked them."

"How did you get a hold of that one?"

"The public library." He said as if everyone knew that book was there. "Well, I went with Frankie, and he checked it out." He took a bite of pizza and chewed with purpose before saying, "Oh, then we got *Murderers Among Us*, too."

Kathleen nodded, pretending this was normal reading for a young boy. "*Murderers Among Us*." She pictured the two boys, barely able to see over the counter, checking out a murder book. "How old were you?"

"I dunno." He shrugged. "Maybe ten or eleven."

Kathleen struggled to hide her astonishment. She wanted him to keep talking, and if he knew she was "freaking out," he'd clam up.

"When did you know something had to be done?"

"Now, *that* I remember well." He nodded his head when he said "*that*," just like his father used to. He sounded much older than twelve. Kathleen kept the tears at bay because they'd only stop the conversation, and she was fascinated by Matthew's intuition and insight. She wanted to hear more, to see what he had seen, what she'd refused to see.

He continued. "I knew something had to be done the day I saw he could write with both hands."

\#

It had happened over the summer. Matthew had come downstairs on his way out of the house. His brother was sitting at the dining table, not something he normally did. Matthew had noticed a sketch pad in front of him, and his brother was fixated on whatever it was he was drawing. It sure as hell wasn't art.

Matthew tried to pretend his brother wasn't there, but of course he couldn't pull that off.

"Matty, c'mere for a second." He summoned him without looking up, his pencil moving wildly against the paper.

As Matthew approached, he got a look at what his brother was doing. He was drawing something fucked up. It was a close-up of woman, screaming in agony, her face all contorted. A naked woman and a naked tree behind her, with a noose hanging from a branch, and a big full moon in the background.

Matthew let a scenario play in his head like a scene from a movie. He saw himself lifting a wooden bat from his side, swinging it over his right shoulder and bringing it down against his brother's head, cracking his skull, blood splattering across the table and his hideous drawing. Matthew's stomach muscles tightened, and he was clenching his jaw, standing over his brother's shoulder fantasizing about bringing him to an end.

"Stop breathing so loud. It's vexing." And as his brother had said one of his new words, he moved the pencil from his right hand to his left, and continued sketching with ease.

That was the last straw. It was nothing to his brother, but it meant everything to Matthew. At that moment, he realized the rules didn't apply to his brother and never would, that he'd never get in trouble for anything. He'd always get away with it. As long as his brother was breathing, he'd go back and forth between torturing people and convincing others he was normal, just passing the pencil from one hand to the other. The only way to stop him was death or prison.

79

The rapist scaled the fence scrupulously but swiftly. There was no leverage on the backside, but he was lean and strong, and the rounded tops of the pickets offered dependable grips. He dropped onto the soft grass inside the feeble barrier. The clouds enhanced the darkness, but his eyes adjusted easily. He meandered to the middle of the substantial back lawn, paused between two monstrous live oaks, and scanned the sky. He examined the trees' bent arms and crooked fingers grasping at each other under the waxing crescent moon. The scene was apropos of his favorite season, that of Halloween and Dia de los Muertos.

Tonight, he wanted to get the lay of the land, to gain an understanding of the unknown woman's home and her nighttime habits. Warm light bled through sheer curtains over French doors, leading to what he assumed was a living room. He noticed a structure adjacent to the attached garage. Maybe a greenhouse or a shed. He took only two paces toward the mystery before an explosion halted his steps. The blast was followed by a familiar, vicious sound, and a black mass shot out of the structure and charged him.

The animal's motion triggered two flood lights that both blinded and exposed the rapist. He spun and ran and sprang onto the fence. The interior backer rails made his escape easier than the entry, but before he could throw himself over the top, the dog snagged his heel. Teeth penetrated his sneaker and tore at his skin underneath. He sacrificed a shoe and a sock, but it did little to appease the beast.

Bleeding, the rapist hobbled against the searing pain to the end of the alleyway, and the dog's ferocity continued until he reached the point where the alleyway intersected the street.

I'm going to kill that fucking dog.

He turned left and saw Bones' car parked several houses ahead. Even under the cover of darkness, a limp would attract attention, so he ignored the pain and maintained an even stride.

I'm going to kill that fucking dog.

80

One minute, Sam was licking his chops at Colleen's feet as she prepared his dinner. The next, he was charging through the pet door into the garage. She heard the slam of the second pet door into the shed followed by a merciless bark, nothing like the normal warning he gave passersby. When she heard snarls, she grabbed the cordless phone and moved toward the French doors, killing the lights on the way, and peeked between a sliver of space between the curtain and the door frame. The floodlights lit up the back lawn but stopped at the trunks of the live oaks. In the darkness beyond, her loving lab Sam had transformed into a bloodthirsty animal hell bent on tearing to bits whatever threat had neared the property.

She could only make out shadows and silhouettes. Massive branches. The fence line. Sam's raised hackles, no longer a dog but a monster. She watched his silhouette move along the length of the fence. Colleen saw no cats or critters taunting him from above. She saw no movement other than her faithful protector's. Every bark propelled him forward. At the property's edge, Sam continued with his baleful barking for several seconds. Then he stopped, turned toward the house and wagged his tail as if expecting to see Colleen come out to praise him.

Before she could register the change in his mood, he darted to the opposite end of the fence, snatched something from the ground, and pranced toward the house with something clenched in his jaws. At the sound of the pet door in the shed, she braced herself for what he would present her when he crashed through the pet door in the kitchen. Still holding the phone, she hoisted herself onto the kitchen counter, putting as much distance as she could between her and whatever Sam had clutched between his teeth. He charged through the pet door, blinking furiously and wagging his tail so hard it rippled through his body.

She gasped. "Is that a shoe?"

Sam's tail beat against the cabinets as he walked the short distance to her. She lifted her feet and sat cross legged on the counter, unable to get any further away from the object.

"Drop it, Sam."

He complied. She stared at the bloodied sneaker and dialed 9-1-1.

81

    Colleen sat on the sofa with the twelve-gauge shotgun across her lap. She'd retrieved it from under the bed immediately after the two patrol officers had left. It was a double barrel, just like the one Elmer E. Fudd used to hunt Bugs Bunny. Loading it would've been easy if she'd had any ammo. The officers had looked around the property and they'd taken a verbal statement of what had happened. It was probably a burglar, or maybe a drunk who had the wrong house. Either way, it was a mistake unlikely to be repeated, thanks to the fiercely protective dog. Colleen had told them about her job, the case, and the dumbshit judge who'd turned the psychopath loose. They responded by exchanging glances, looking unsure what to do with her information, and probably assumed she was exaggerating. Colleen had been on the job long enough to know that people in crisis indeed tended to exaggerate, but that most cops didn't know shit about predators. She had to admit it was improbable that the suspect knew who she was or cared enough to show up. It wasn't impossible, though, and that's what would keep her up all night.

    She looked at Nathan, sitting in an easy chair directly across from her. "Thank you for coming. I didn't want to worry Aunt Ruth and Martha, and you're pretty much my only friend."

    "Of course." A grin surfaced through his serious countenance. "Of course I'm your only friend." His eyes moved between hers and the shotgun across her lap.

    "Is this your new safety blanket?"

    She didn't answer.

He sat with her while she drank another double shot of Jameson and told him more about the case than she probably should have.

After hearing Colleen's opinion about the suspect, Nathan said, "I'm not leaving."

She started to protest.

"You're drunk. I'll sleep on the couch."

She nodded. "Okay. Fine."

"Just leave the shotgun with me."

"It's not even loaded."

"Rule number one." He held up his finger and said, "Every gun is loaded.

82

"Is this how it works? *Months*. Months since the rape, and Lawler didn't write up a damned warrant?"

"No, Colleen." Martinez spoke softly. "It is not how it works."

"We *talked* about that case in one of their weekly meetings. What's the point of those meetings if they're not going to do shit with the info?" She felt betrayed. "And the attempted murder? What happened with that?"

"You really want to know?" His question sounded like a challenge, or a warning.

"Yes, I do."

"Cool your jets, and I'll tell you."

Colleen could keep her mouth shut, but she wasn't cooling off.

"The attempted murder got assigned a little later than normal, due to Sergeant Esquivel's absence."

"I thought *you* were assigning cases when she was out."

"I was, and I *did*, but before the detective could get a look, his wife had their baby, so he was out for a week."

"Okay, that explains only two weeks of a delay." Colleen shook her head.

"That case isn't an attempted murder, and the conversation about that caused additional delays, but that's another story."

"I've got time to hear a story."

"What happened was an assault. A misdemeanor assault."

"It landed on my desk as an attempted murder."

"Charges can change. You have to prove intent to have an attempted murder."

"Strangling someone until they're unconscious? Isn't that at least an *aggravated* assault?"

"That requires serious bodily injury."

"Or a deadly weapon. His hands aren't a deadly weapon?"

"The DA doesn't think so."

Colleen felt her face heat up, which meant it had flushed red, along with her neck, so there was no point in trying to hide her anger. "You—"

Martinez interrupted her with a snap of his fingers. "*You* nothin'. The DA kicks those back. We have to reduce the charge to a misdemeanor family violence assault, and then file it."

"You know how relieved she was to hear it was a felony?" Colleen expected her face to burst into flames any second.

"You already contacted her?"

"Of course. The case was included in a big pile of reports, but I considered it a priority unlike some—"

"Watch it, Heenan."

The conversation reminded her of two boxers sparring. Dodge, jab, block, deflect.

She wanted to kick Martinez's desk. "Has anyone up here, other than me, even *talked* to the victim? Kathleen McDaniel?"

"I'm sure someone has. I'll find out."

"Her son tried to kill her. I don't care what the DA thinks."

"The DA doesn't care what you think, either."

Colleen resisted a knee-jerk response of *no shit*.

"We're still pursuing the case, Heenan."

"Meanwhile, he's free to terrorize the town."

"We'll get him."

"I'd bet my salary that's who was in my yard last night."

He dragged his hand over his mustache. "We don't know that."

"Winston PD has the bloody shoe he left behind. We'll know some day." She held up her hands, "Do they need to catch this guy for you again?"

"You need to take a breath, kid." Martinez warned. "You still have a lot to learn. You're a *puppy*. Lawler is new to investigations. He screwed up."

"But you're not new. You're counting down the days until you retire." She zeroed in on the board. "Eleven days." She wished she could snatch the words and shove them back into her mouth.

"I've been on this job since you were shitting your britches. Twenty-five years. You've been here, what? A few months? Don't make assumptions about me, kid."

Colleen slumped in her chair. A thousand thoughts and emotions scurried around her head, but she mustered the sense to apologize. "Sorry. I was out of line."

Without missing a beat, he said, "Apology accepted. The day is almost over. Go tidy up your desk and go home before you say something that gets your ass fired."

Colleen felt frozen to the chair.

"Go, Heenan."

Colleen returned to her cubicle to grab her things before leaving. Unsure if she'd be back at all, she slipped the two photos on her desktop into her work bag. As she began to step away, her phone rang. It was a Winston PD number, and she couldn't resist. When she answered, she heard the voice of Sally, the salty victim advocate.

"I got a report with your name on it. Literally. Your name is listed as the complainant."

"Yep." She heard defeat in her voice.

"You okay?"

"Kinda pissed off, but I'm all right."

"You think it's that perp, don't you?"

Colleen did, of course, but she hesitated to share that theory. "What makes you say that?"

"You told the responding officer."

Colleen hardly remembered the conversation with the cops. "It probably isn't him, but, yeah, that's who was on my mind."

"Do you feel safe at your place?"

"Safe enough. I don't think he'll come back after the greeting he received."

A raspy laugh came over the line. "Your dog sounds like a real badass."

Colleen couldn't help but smile. "That was a side of him I hadn't seen before." In her peripheral vision, she noticed Martinez closing his office door.

"I can put a special watch on your house, so patrol keeps a closer eye on your street."

The idea provided Colleen some comfort.

"Can I do anything else for you?" Sally seemed genuinely concerned.

Colleen eyed the lieutenant's closed door and lowered her voice. "Put in a good word for me whenever you decide to retire. I think I might get fired."

"Already?" she cackled.

"I ran my mouth to the lieutenant, but I was singing Winston PD's praises." She tittered.

"Believe me, I understand your anger. But you're not telling them anything they don't already know, and getting your ass canned won't help anyone."

"Understood." She let out a heavy sigh.

"I *am* about to announce my retirement. Behave yourself, and apply for my position."

"Really?"

"I'll even put in a good word for you, but you won't get hired if you get fired there."

"I'll miss you when you're gone." Colleen hardly knew the woman, but she meant it.

"I'm retiring, not dying."

"I realize that, but you won't be around. Who's going to keep me in line?"

"You'd like it here, kid, and you'd fit in. You remind me of me, thirty years ago."

Colleen considered Sally's advice as she drove home. When she pulled into her driveway, she lacked the usual comfort of coming home for the day. Dark fell early now, which exacerbated her unease. Nathan tried to persuade her to go stay with Aunt Ruth until the rapist was arrested, but Colleen wanted to stand her ground. Plus, Winston officers were paying closer attention to her house, at least that's what she was told.

Sicario sat in the glow of the porch light. He needed a crown and a scepter to complement his look. He rubbed against her legs as she unlocked the front door. She heard Sam's tail pounding against the entryway wall, and her gut and shoulders relaxed. When she opened the door, Sicario slipped inside and into the front dining room and explored his provider's home.

"This should be interesting," Colleen said to Sam as she greeted him with a rub behind his ears.

She dropped her work bag onto the sofa, and Sicario promptly examined it.

Hours later, after she'd fed the animals and herself, she checked the locks on the windows and doors, covered the pet doors, and felt safe enough to take a shower. When she emerged from the bathroom, she found Sicario perched at the foot of the bed.

"What's gotten into you?" She avoided making eye contact, for the creature's murderous nature still unnerved her. The cat lowered to its belly, laying claim to his spot. Sam remained lying by the bedroom doorway, his eyes shifting between Sicario and his human, as if anticipating a protest. Colleen slipped into bed, careful not to disturb the feline, and grabbed a pen and notepad.

A letter to William was overdue.

83

The rapist noticed a fortunate change in patterns. Trudy's mother didn't stay on the patio as late as she used to. She did, however, spend a lot of time in the kitchen long after her neighbors had darkened their houses and nestled into their beds. The bright interior lights of the woman's kitchen and living room invited him to observe her habits and the details of her domain.

He knew where she kept the knives, where the phone was, and how easy it would be to keep her away from them. He knew that Trudy slept in her mother's room every night, the farthest room from the kitchen. He also noticed that on some evenings, a cat pawed at the door. Not all nights, but enough for the woman to have hung a little bell from the back door handle to alert her when the animal wanted inside. Her ignorance, her naivete was utterly amusing. She'd made it so easy for him. He'd have total domination over them both and then snuff out their miserable lives.

Act two would be more complicated.

His mother had changed the locks, so he'd have to rely on his charm to gain entry. He planned to apologize and pretend he was afraid of going to prison, and that he was remorseful for hurting his dear mommy. Then, he'd declare he needed help. Triggering Kathleen's empathy was the key. If that failed, he'd coerce her with the gun.

When it was time to end them, the rapist knew Kathleen would put up a fight, and Matthew would call for help. Shooting at least one of them might be the only option, and the noise could attract attention. He'd have to scramble for his belongings, just the essentials, and waste no time gathering anything of value that was easy to carry and sell. And the car. He'd take the car and head south for act three.

That one was purely on principle. He wanted to kill that fucking dog and the meddler. How he would love to take his time punishing her, but he'd have to keep moving.

He needed to strike on a Friday night and finish by 3:00 a.m. on Saturday. By Monday or Tuesday, his mom and his brother's absences would generate alarm, and it wouldn't be long before their bodies were discovered. All hell was going to break loose, but by then, he'd be in Matamoros, swimming in tequila and whores. Maybe he'd marry one of them to get citizenship. The opportunities in Mexico were endless. Reviewing the details energized him, and he could hardly sit still.

Through the slats, he watched the light go off in the mother's bedroom. That meant Trudy was going to sleep. He saw the woman move through the living room, closing the blinds over the windows as she passed. This would've been an excellent night to execute his plan if the moon wasn't so bright. He practiced his sad face.

84

Most mothers would wring their hands with worry over a missing son, not await in terror for his return, or pray for his death. For most moms, a son's death would trigger devastating grief, not overwhelming relief.

Since the incident, Kathleen and Matthew were separated only during school hours, and even then they remained in the same building. Matthew insisted on staying at home with Kathleen. He refused to be sent to Frankie's house, even though they were on edge at home. He was protective of his mother, a saddening role reversal, and an unfair, heavy burden. They startled easily, spoke little, and slept lightly. Every time they heard a car approach, a leaf brush against the window, or the house settle, they stiffened, listened, and locked eyes as they assessed the noise and determined if it was benign, natural, or if it was the fiend attempting to strike. The television muffled potential warnings, so they read, sometimes to each other.

They'd rediscovered Shel Silverstein. They read aloud from *Where the Sidewalk Ends* and *A Light in the Attic*, using different accents and overdone gestures. The words from the comedic poems comforted them like a soft warm blanket. They both agreed, however, that the boy in *The Giving Tree* reminded them too much of their missing family member. A taker. A parasite. They promptly returned to poems about "Sleeping Sardines" and mustache swings.

Her offspring was in the wind, but she knew he'd show up at some point.

A couple of weeks earlier, Detective Lawler and a crime scene technician had collected her offspring's bedding. It seemed pointless for a sexual assault committed last summer, but the detective said it was possible they'd find evidence. She'd promised to call 9-1-1 if he showed up, and the detective assured Matthew that he wasn't in any trouble and praised him for doing the right thing by telling his mother what had happened. Kathleen had used a credit card to pay for new locks and a cheap alarm system. That allowed her to sleep, but she had recurring nightmares about coming home to find the house on fire with Matthew trapped inside. In some of the nightmares, her offspring had started the blaze. In others, she had.

After her oldest's bedroom was released, Kathleen considered taking his mattress to the dumpster, but that would require touching it. She couldn't look at it without feeling her skin crawl. There was no way she'd lay hands on it. But she did take scissors to the marionettes' strings. Each snip a catharsis. Bodies of men and women, young and old lay lifeless on the bed and scattered about the floor. After ninety-six snips, his room resembled a miniature Jonestown.

As Kathleen returned downstairs, the doorbell rang. Matthew, who'd been dozing on the couch, bolted upright and locked eyes with her. With a look of terror, Matthew shook his head and whispered, "No."

Kathleen descended the last few stairs and moved to the front window. There, she peered between the curtains and saw a bicycle on the front sidewalk, propped up on its kick stand.

Kathleen motioned Matthew to her side, and the boy moved toward her like his feet were encased in concrete blocks. Kathleen snapped and signaled him to pick up the pace.

Once Matthew was at her side, she asked, "Do you recognize that bike?"

"They're going to see us," he whispered sharply.

His anxiety was wearing on Kathleen's patience. "The lights are on outside, not inside, not behind me anyway. Whoever is out there can't see us." She felt her frustration creep into her tone. "You don't have to move the curtain to see, either. Just look and tell me if you recognize the bike."

The doorbell rang again.

Matthew glanced through the window and said, "That belongs to one of his girlfriends."

"What is she, ten?" Kathleen moved to the front door to look through the peephole.

Matthew pulled on her arm in protest, but she yanked herself free and scolded him with a frown. "How dangerous can a kid on a bicycle be?"

"He could be out there, Mom! She could be a decoy."

Kathleen viewed a scrawny teenage girl with a mass of blond braids held together by a scrunchy. She remembered the girl, but she didn't remember her riding around on a bike.

"Who's there?" she asked with authority.

The girl focused on the peep hole and said, "My name's Stacy. I'm a friend of your son. I just want to talk to him."

"He's not here, Stacy, and I don't know when he'll be back."

"Then, *you* talk to me." Her voice carried an urgency. "Please."

"It's not a great time, Stacy. What do you need?"

She shouted, "I need to know what's going on!"

Kathleen thought the kid might fall to the ground and throw a fit. The last thing she wanted was more gossip among the neighbors. She rested her forehead against the smooth wood above the peep hole and kept an unblinking eye on the distraught young girl on her porch.

"I'm sorry. I'm sorry I yelled." The girl shifted from one foot to the other while gnawing on her finger.

"Are you alone?"

"Yes, ma'am." Stacy looked over her shoulder and up and down the dark street. "Completely alone." Kathleen watched the girl in the glass circle wipe tears from her cheeks.

Kathleen left the chain secure but unlocked the deadbolt. Matthew gasped and scurried toward the kitchen phone even though Kathleen had no intention of opening the door just yet. She clutched the knob firmly and pressed her body against the door. If he was indeed out there, she'd just given him a good opportunity to attempt entry. She anticipated pressure against her palm, counterclockwise movement of the doorknob, at which point, she'd throw the deadbolt and tell Matthew to call for help. Yet the doorknob remained still in her grip.

Kathleen told Matthew loudly enough for their visitor's ears, "You dial 9-1-1 if she's not alone. They're waiting for us to call." That last bit felt a bit over the top.

Kathleen cracked open the door, and Stacy seemed alarmed by her vigilance. She looked sixteen or seventeen but had the presence of a much younger girl.

"I'm not a bad person," the girl blurted.

"It's not you that causes me concern."

"I'm sorry to bother you, but if you could give me a few minutes." The girl was on the verge of tears.

"Come inside, Stacy."

Matthew shouted in disbelief, and Kathleen closed the door and removed the chain. She glanced over her shoulder at her son, who had the phone in his hand and said, "I've already dialed 9 and a 1."

Kathleen opened the door swiftly, gently pulled Stacy inside, and immediately shut the door and barricaded the three of them inside her sanctuary.

"What's going on?" Stacy's voice was thin and trembling, "Are you okay, ma'am?"

Her large round eyes reminded Kathleen of an anime character. "You don't know, do you?"

"Know what?" Her eyes darted to Matthew who stood frozen in the kitchen with the phone in his hand.

The words gushed out of Matthew's mouth. "For starters, your boyfriend tried to kill my mom." Matthew hadn't registered the disparity between the girl's appearance and her intellect.

"I don't understand." Stacy scanned the room as if an answer would leap from one of the walls. She acted like she hadn't heard what Matthew had said. Kathleen wondered if the statement was too difficult for the weary kid to believe.

The girl muttered, "He said he loved me, and then it was like he vanished."

Matthew chuckled. "He said he loved you?"

"Yeah, he said I made him want to be a better man."

Matthew spoke with a matter-of-fact tone. "That's a line he stole out of a song or movie."

Stacy defended herself. "Why would he do that?"

"Because he's a liar, and a rapist, and a killer."

"Take it easy, Matthew." Kathleen realized this poor girl had taken the bait and been duped. She seemed utterly lost. Kathleen turned to her and said, "My son, your boyfriend, that is…" She minimized reality. "He isn't well."

"Is he in the hospital?"

Kathleen surmised the girl was developmentally delayed. And all at once, she felt muscles tense in the back of her throat. "Oh dear God."

Kathleen remembered the girl's bike was right out front, and she felt like a dozen spiders crawled up the back of her neck. "Stacy, it's probably not safe for you to be here, with your bike right out front. I've no doubt he's passing by, watching the house."

Matthew added, "So are the police, and I hope they run into each other."

"What if he's been kidnapped or worse?" Stacy still didn't grasp the situation.

Matthew finally seemed to get it, and he offered compassion. "He's not hurt, Stacy. He just left. He does that."

"He said he loved me, so why would he leave and not call me or anything? You don't do that to people you love."

Kathleen and Matthew traded looks of pity.

"Can I leave him a note or something?"

"Sure, hon," Kathleen's voice was gentle.

Matthew said, "I'll get you a notepad and pen."

"Stacy, can I call your mom or dad? It's kind of late to be riding your bike. Don't you think?"

"My dad passed a long time ago. My mom's at work now."

"I'm sorry." Matthew's anxious demeanor had shifted to one of empathy. "I understand how hard it is not to have a dad around."

"I know. He talks about that a lot, how he misses your dad."

Matthew slapped his hand over his mouth and shot Kathleen a look indicating he couldn't take it anymore, a feeling Kathleen shared. The thought of her offspring feigning sadness over her husband's death made Kathleen so angry she could spit nails.

Stacy seemed clueless to the tension. "I don't live far. I ride all the time. I'll be fine."

"You have our number, right?"

"I only have the number to his mobile phone."

"His mobile phone? Are you sure?"

"He said you gave it to him for his birthday."

"He did, huh?"

"Uh-huh. The Nokia. It's nice."

Kathleen scribbled the home phone number onto a piece of scratch paper and handed it to the girl. "Call me when you get home, please."

The girl gave her a puzzled look.

"Stacy, I'm a mom. I need to know you made it home safely."

85

Colleen made it through another week with her attitude in check, and Martinez had taken action. Two warrants were active for the rapist. Martinez even pushed the DA's office to put the attack on Kathleen before a grand jury as an aggravated assault although he fell short of persuading them. While he didn't suspect the rapist had been the intruder, he reached out to Winston police and asked them to keep the special watch on Colleen's house.

Martinez had summoned Colleen to a final meeting.

He asked, "Will you be there today?"

"Of course." Then she thought better of it. "If that's appropriate, I will be."

"I'd like for you to be there, Heenan." His tone said he'd forgiven her. He sounded almost fatherly, and she wondered what kind of dad he was. Probably a decent one, maybe a little overprotective. Who could blame him?

He stroked his thick mustache. "Twenty-five years end with a crappy white cake and a cheap plaque."

"Having regrets?"

"I'm conflicted, but it's time." He shrugged. "Now, back to business." He drummed his fingers on his desk. "Any questions for me before it's too late?"

"Actually, yes. Do you know who I'll be reporting to?"

"I do." He cleared his throat. "He wasn't crazy about it when the department added a victim advocate position, so be careful."

Colleen ran her tongue over the gap between her teeth.

"He's a little rigid. He's a good investigator who made sergeant and went to patrol. He'll be acting lieutenant over investigations, so he'll be your direct supervisor until something permanent happens."

Martinez must have noticed her apprehension because he offered some reassurance. "As long as you leave Sassy-pants at home, you'll work out a routine with him. You'll be fine."

"Sassy-pants?"

"You know what I mean."

She did.

"Look, the real party is afterward, at Bethany Tavern. You should come by after work."

"Does this mean I get to put one foot into the circle?"

He winked. "Maybe."

86

Colleen parked outside Bethany Tavern and watched about a dozen men approach the entrance and disappear inside. Many had significant others with them, and they all seemed friendly with each other, a tight-knit group of which she wasn't and never would be a part. She grabbed the bottle of Jameson and the card she'd picked up for Martinez and exited her truck. She slipped inside the bar and found a table that held a few other gifts, mostly bottles of booze. Maybe she'd get points for that. She scanned the faces at the tables spread across the worn dark carpet. She recognized none of them and wanted to turn around and leave.

Out of sheer politeness, she waded into a sea of loud music and louder cops until she found Martinez. She delivered a hug, a few awkward words, and finally a *thank you for everything, sir.*

Within minutes, she was back in her truck and heading south on Central Expressway. Twenty minutes later, she was home, packing an overnight bag for herself and food for Sam. She put enough cat food outside to last a couple of days, and secured the pet doors, checked the window latches, and threw the deadbolts before heading to Aunt Ruth and Martha's to live among the rich for the next forty-eight hours.

She had almost made it to their street before noticing the tail. Instead of turning into their neighborhood, she made a U-Turn, and the car following her did, as well, so she headed toward Winston's police department. As she turned on Akers Avenue, with the police station less than a block away, the car whipped around her and sped off. She couldn't make out any details, but there appeared to be two males inside.

She took a tour through the east and west sides of the city, watching her rear-view mirror, before heading to her destination. She called Ruth on the way and let her know.

"Don't park in the drive," Ruth ordered. "Park in the garage."

When Colleen arrived at the huge home, Ruth was waiting for her on the front porch. She opened the door to the three-car garage and motioned her inside.

#

After picking at her dinner, Colleen had curled up in her favorite chair, finished a double shot of a high-end Irish whiskey, and placed the empty glass on a coaster. Sam observed her and then returned to his nap.

Aunt Ruth's face revealed displeasure. "I didn't expect this job to be dangerous."

Colleen stared at the dog at her feet. "Me, either."

"You're safe here." Her tone became tender. "I'm going to tidy up."

Colleen and Martha exchanged glances. Aunt Ruth cleaned to cope.

Martha sat in her usual spot in an overstuffed chair opposite Colleen. Both extended their legs and rested their feet on the ottoman between them.

Martha said, "She lost your mom. You *must* outlive your Aunt Ruth." She nodded toward Colleen's empty glass. "If you want another, help yourself."

"I've been indulging in that too much." She poked her belly and said, "It's softer than it was a year ago. Once upon a time, I could bounce a quarter off it."

"There are better ways to cope with stress, dear."

"I need to get back to walking Sam, maybe take my mountain bike out to the lake like I used to." She could hear the weariness in her voice.

"You're doing good work, Colleen."

You lied to me.

"What the hell do I do, anyway? I give people handouts of information. I deliver bad news. I'm helpless to help. Powerless. I can know where a suspect is, but I can't arrest him. I can't get any of these guys, these detectives, to do it, either." She stood up, grabbed her empty glass and walked to the wet bar. "I knew that asshole would take off. I warned the investigator."

She reenacted the conversation out loud. "Detective Lawler, you think he might take off? Oh, no, Colleen. He doesn't have anywhere to go." Even though she heard herself slurring her words, she dropped a fat ice cube into her glass and poured a generous amount over it. "How stupid can a person be? Now, I can't even go home. That piece of shit invaded my..." Colleen's throat tightened, and she didn't want to cry. Not here.

"They will find him, dear." Martha's eyes oozed compassion. "You said Winston has a task force looking for the young man, right?"

"Yes. They seem to care about catching him." She walked to the back patio windows and peered between the linen curtains. Sam joined her and made whisper noises. "Their victim advocate put a special watch on my house. Yours, too."

"Good." Martha's voice was warm and reassuring. "And you can stay here for as long as you want."

"Thank you. I'm not sure what I'd do without you two." She stroked Sam's ears and turned to face Martha again.

"We love you." Martha blew a kiss. "You, too, Sammy." At the sound of his name, his tail beat against Colleen's thigh. "As for your feelings of futility, you're doing more than you think. You're a good navigator."

Colleen made a conciliatory shrug. She hadn't thought of her role that way before.

"You're fighting for them." Martha added, "How might things have been different for you if you and your mom had had a victim advocate?"

Conversations with Martha were never superficial, but that topic cut too deep. As Colleen returned to her chair, she countered. "I listen. That's about all I can do without getting reprimanded."

"Never underestimate the value of being heard."

Colleen plopped down into her chair and rubbed the back of her neck.

Martha continued her soothing pep talk. "People need to be heard. It might sound trite, but it's powerful medicine, being heard."

"I can see that." Colleen tempered her attitude. "If only because I know what it's like to *not* be heard." She brought the whiskey to her lips but didn't allow any to pass.

Martha shifted her weight and returned her feet to the floor. "These cases, they're similar to your life."

"Kind of."

Martha glanced toward the kitchen, where Ruth continued to clean. Then, she leaned forward and lowered her voice. "A father killed the mother of young children. A young man raped a girl and, so far, has gotten away with it. These are *kind of* similar to your life?"

Colleen swirled the whiskey around the ice in her glass.

"How does one not spill into the other, dear?"

"I compartmentalize, I guess."

Martha blinked dramatically. "Have you ever sought professional help?"

"Therapy?" She coughed and smiled.

"Yes. Something you've undoubtedly recommended to the people you help."

"I'm not a victim."

"You were indeed a victim. And what you're at risk of now is vicarious trauma." She nodded firmly. "You are swimming in human suffering."

"Maybe I'm not ready to kick over all those stones."

"Afraid of what lies underneath?"

"Maybe." She smelled the whiskey, respecting the need to slow down. "I'm not sure I can do therapy and do this job."

"I think you have to. Otherwise, your core will disintegrate. You need to strengthen your core, just as in physical training. Therapy can help with that."

Aunt Ruth finally emerged from the kitchen and took her place on the sofa.

"Actually, I'm thinking of leaving."

Aunt Ruth looked at her like she was crazy. "You're three sheets to the wind. You're not going anywhere."

"Not here."

Aunt Ruth asked, "Your job?"

"Yep." Colleen took a sip.

Her aunt seemed surprised but pleased. "What are your plans?"

"I've put in for the position here in Winston."

Martha chuckled. "Same job, different place."

\#

Colleen had teetered on the edge of sleep for a few hours before giving up. Being on the second story provided some comfort, but the unfamiliar house noises sabotaged any chance of her feeling at ease. She started each time the air conditioner kicked on, and every time it kicked off, the silence amplified ordinary noises. Passing cars were few in number, but she listened intently until they were gone. A car door slammed shut, and her heartbeat doubled its speed and intensity.

Her senses were heightened, as was her imagination. Had the rapist followed her here? Was he outside, staring up at the bedroom window? Was he probing the boundaries of her little, vulnerable house? Would he hurt the cat? The fact that she had a cat tugged at the side of her mouth. She couldn't wait for the return of peaceful mornings, sipping coffee in her new space and cool evenings. North Central Texas had a small window of opportunity to enjoy perfect weather, and she wanted to relish every minute before it abandoned her. This case was stealing those moments from her.

She made a mental note: *buy one of those cat perches for the shed and a chimenea for the patio.*

Colleen slipped out of bed and moved to the window of the guest bedroom, overlooking the back lawn. She wished Martha had some flood lights. With the cloud cover, all Colleen could see was a quarter-acre of shadows and darkness. Black branches and leaves brushed against an indigo backdrop. Her eyes strained as they searched for shapes, features or lines that cut through the shadows. When she focused on spaces she knew, she was able to make out the edges of a few objects.

The pergola.

The garden shed.

The fence.

A man?

87

Matthew was snoring on the sofa.

Kathleen opened the journal she'd retrieved from her hiding place under the floorboards in her closet. She called it her *Book of Worsts*. Whenever she felt guilty about the thoughts she had about her offspring, all she had to do was read a few entries.

The kindergarten teacher requested a meeting with me today. Peter had bitten another girl. According to the teacher, he was unprovoked, and he'd bitten down hard enough to break the girl's skin. When she cried out and told him it hurt, he smiled at her, without a hint of remorse. None at all. The teacher suggested counseling and provided referrals.

She flipped a few pages and arrived at the next year.

1st grade isn't offering much hope. During a school event to raise awareness about special needs, Peter convinced a girl with Downs Syndrome that the boys would play with her if she dropped her drawers. He told the girl it would "work like magic." She did it, of course, and he laughed at her for being "such a retard."

Several entries later she'd written about the travails of second grade.

Another parent-teacher meeting. A student told the teacher that Peter had been bullying a girl in their class. The students were supposed to be lined up and silent before lunch, and the teacher had to step out of the classroom. The kids were left alone for a few minutes, and Peter crushed the poor girl against the wall while telling her she was worthless and should kill herself because everyone hated her. He refused to apologize and failed to see what he'd done wrong. He implied that what he'd said to the girl was the truth and that the truth sometimes hurts, and perhaps he should be praised for being honest.

The next day, the student who'd "snitched on him" found a dead rat in her backpack, like something out of a damned gangster movie. Peter denied knowing anything about that, of course. He said, "It was merely a coincidence." What 2nd grader speaks like that or acts like that?

The school counselor has suggested that Peter is grieving the death of his father. She said he's acting out. The therapist I've paid gobs of money makes the same claim. But he doesn't improve. When does he stop "acting out," for God's sake?!

She remembered setting aside time for Peter, just for the two of them. The therapist had suggested "meeting Peter where he was" and doing things he liked to do. The boy needed constant stimulation and grew bored within minutes with any activity he chose, and bored with her, too. She tried active listening and speaking affirming statements. She demonstrated empathy, as she always did, but he seemed immune to it. She did everything the professionals suggested to connect with him, but there was always a distance between them, between Peter and everyone.

She paged ahead to another entry.

The school counselor expressed concerns about Peter's ability to "gaslight" his classmates. A 3rd grader gas lighting?

A few pages later detailed fourth grade. That year, he demonstrated his improved manipulation tactics on a long-term substitute who'd come in while the regular teacher was out on maternity leave.

The school counselor called to check on me. She asked how my treatments were going and if there was anything the school could do to help. Peter had convinced his substitute I had cancer and was at death's door. He'd kept the charade going for several days, relishing the attention the substitute gave him.

In fifth grade his lies took a wicked turn.

Peter told his teacher that his father killed himself because he couldn't tolerate my infidelity.

In sixth grade, he went public with his cruelty.

Peter brought a dead kitten to school for show-and-tell.

In junior high, he had a blank slate on which to scribble a myriad of new lies.

Thankfully, a school counselor saw through Peter's bullshit. He'd been tardy to one of his classes a lot, and he'd blamed me. He told his teacher I'd been in prison for killing his father, and that I was recently paroled and having difficulty adjusting to "life on the outside."

When Peter had arrived home that evening, she'd confronted him and lost her composure. She remembered the exchange so vividly her throat burned with sadness and rage.

"*You* murdered your father. *My husband.*" She'd never spoken that truth aloud.

"You're being dramatic, Mommy. Have you quit smoking again?"

He'd taken a step closer, into her space. He sniffed the air around her like a dog, posturing to make himself appear menacing, but he was still too young to intimidate her.

She took a step toward him, and stood tall to emphasize the disparity in their heights. "There's no statute of limitations on murder."

"Oh please. I was, like, five years old. Gimme a break."

He leaned against the kitchen island, and she remembered so clearly how his face had shown no emotion. He'd revealed no feeling whatsoever about his father's death. He hadn't responded to the accusation like a normal person would. Even a teen would've shouted in protest.

"There is something terribly wrong with you." It had taken so much effort to maintain a calm facade, but her anger had peppered each word.

"What? Because I don't freak out about shit?" He'd scoffed. "Look at you." He'd waved his hand at her smugly. He'd always been so smug. "Why would I want to be like that?"

"You don't get it." She had laughed out of exasperation. "You don't get it that you don't get it."

"Oh, I get it all right."

"You don't even know what I'm talking about. When we talk of feeling joy or we express empathy or compassion for another person, it's like you're hearing a language completely foreign to you. You have no idea what we're experiencing. It used to sadden me, but you don't understand that, either."

He'd shoved a piece of gum in his mouth and chewed like a horse.

"Your only emotion is anger, which normally represents something else, like fear or hurt, but for you, it's actually a pure emotion. A reaction to not getting whatever you demand or desire. Even your demeanor now..." She'd opened her hands in front of him, a gesture of desiring peace. "So glib. You're incognizant of how oblivious you are of the human experience. Absent in you is the very thing that *makes* us human." She'd noticed a subtle change in him. "Are you confused? You're blinking at what would be considered a normal frequency."

"I'll tell you this," he'd retorted. "If this house caught fire, would you rather be with a crying mess, someone who's shitting his pants in fear, or with me? A guy who can keep it together and get us out?"

"Would you get us out or just yourself?"

"Depends." He'd shrugged. "Today? Nah."

Unloading a heaping pile of reality on him had been cathartic, but back then she was still naive enough to believe her words, or anything, might motivate him to change.

Peter. So much hope in that name. His father's name. An apostle of Jesus. Kathleen flipped to the last entry in her notebook, which took up several pages. It was her obituary and her wishes about who would take care of Matthew.

88

Maxine looked in on Trudy and relief washed over her. Her little girl was sleeping soundly in her own bed for the first time in many weeks. She forgave herself for using an over-the-counter sleep aid to get her there.

She started her nighttime ritual, a sweep of the house, confirming locks were thrown, and blinds were closed. As she flipped off the kitchen light switch, she heard the bark of a neighbor's dog, followed by the jingle of the bell on the back door. Earlier, the air felt electric and smelled of coming rain. She guessed it was her turn to provide shelter for the furry community pet that kept vermin away from every home on the block.

She cracked open the door enough for the cat to enter, but she saw not orange and white fur but a black boot. Her instincts signaled her to fight, to throw her weight against the door, but the action trailed too far behind the thought, and the human on the patio had predicted her move, and his boot stopped the door from closing. Maxine kept her body pressed against it, but the intruder had the advantage.

"Let me in," he whispered.

"No, no, no!" she hissed. She cursed for being so stupid, and scanned every space within arm's length for a weapon. Her chef knives were far out of reach.

The predator revealed a pistol and hushed her. "I'll spare you or kill you. It makes no difference to me."

Her focus zoomed in on the weapon, not the predator wielding it. She stepped back slowly, as directed.

"On your knees."

His voice was unnervingly calm, like he was ordering a cup of coffee. He'd done this before. Gripped by fear, she couldn't move.

"I gave you fair warning. Like I told you, it makes no difference to me." He shoved her down to the kitchen floor.

White hot pain shot into her tail bone. A potted plant fell to the floor.

Don't wake the girl. Don't hurt my baby.

In the dimness, she watched his shadow tuck the pistol between the small of his back and the waistband on his loose jeans.

He's young.

Even from the floor, she could see he wasn't even six feet tall, and his clothes fit too big. Maybe wet he weighed 150 pounds. Was it possible that without the weapon, he was nothing but an underfed punk?

Appeal to his humanity?

Light from the moon seeped between the cracks in the curtains and slits between the blinds. She noticed his eyes. They were piercing, unfeeling and empty. There was no humanity to appeal to. That left her only one choice.

This is my house.

You know what to do. Breathe.

Her fear turned inside out and wild anger flooded her body.

This is my house.

Wait and breathe.

She figured the punk had sized her up as another weary woman, living alone, a stray cat her only company. He probably thought that on her back she was weak and vulnerable, but she knew that on her back, she could inflict a world of pain. She could end him.

She lay on one hip, knees bent, her hands gripping the front of her dress. He stared down at her and cackled as he kicked her legs apart, rolling her onto her back. His form blocked out the light. She could only see his silhouette, but she heard the rustling of his clothing, the opening of a zipper. She noticed his head turn toward the living room, like he was scanning his surroundings. When his gaze stalled in the direction of Trudy's bedroom, Maxine's heart beat against her chest like an enraged animal.

Stay away from my baby girl. Focus on me.

"Please don't." Adrenaline and anger raged within her, but she produced a pathetic whimper. "Don't rape me."

"Rape is a harsh term. Don't you think?" He cocked his head. "I prefer *fuck*."

I'm going to kill you.

He lowered himself between her knees.

Perfect. Come into my guard, you piece of shit.

She lay still, encouraging her anger, resisting fear, praying for Trudy to stay asleep.

He mistook her stillness for compliance. "Not as stupid as I thought."

Forcefully, as if to invoke fear and display his power, he jerked her dress up to her waist and he grabbed her face, a move to demean her.

In an instant, Maxine unleashed years of training.

She threw her legs around his waist, locked her ankles behind his back, swept her hands between his arms, and hooked her right arm under his left, pinching his triceps inside the fold of her elbow.

He feigned laughter. "That's cute." Still acting like he was in charge.

She smacked her left hand against the back of his head and pulled him closer.

"Oh, you like it rough, huh?" His forced laugh couldn't cover his shaken confidence.

From there, she predicted his every move. He resisted and tried to put space between them. She let go of his head, and knowing he'd try to punch her with his free hand, she grabbed it with her free hand and shoved it down toward her belly. Immediately, she secured it in place with her right hand, still hooked under his arm, and she held on like everything decent and good in the world depended on it.

Keep your ankles locked. Darkness gives you the advantage. You can do this with your eyes closed. You've done it a thousand times. A thousand times.

He tried to pull back, again, which created enough room to rock her hips and shift her legs higher up his body.

Textbook. Keep your ankles locked. Keep your right hand clamped to his wrist. Breathe.

Now, her right leg was clamped against his ribs, just underneath his left armpit, and she slammed her left thigh against the outside of his right shoulder. His right arm flailed over his head, useless to him, but priceless to her. She pinned his right shoulder between her inner thigh and his throat so that it pressed hard against his carotid artery, preventing the blood from flowing to his brain.

She grabbed the back of his head again with her left hand and shifted her hips swiftly and hooked her left foot under her right knee to tighten the grip.

He grunted and struggled to speak. "Well, this is interesting." And then he said, "Now, I *have* to kill you."

"Hush your mouth." She whispered. "Don't you wake up my girl."

"She's next, you know." His tone was guttural, his words garbled. He was losing steam.

She was panting but invigorated by adrenaline. "Hush." She whispered and then spewed her words. "Wait. Just wait."

Her heart thrashed against her chest and throbbed inside her skull. She could feel him flapping his right arm in desperation.

Probably trying to reach that gun. He knows he's in trouble now. She tightened the squeeze and snatched his focus away from the gun and toward the need for air and freedom from the vice she'd created with her legs.

The triangle choke, down to the gritty details, came naturally. The submission move had earned her several gold medals.

Keep the left foot flexed, so it stays hooked under your right knee.

Breathe.

Turn out the right foot a bit, and bend the right knee some more. Pull his head down, and he goes to sleep.

Breathe and squeeze.

Years ago, she'd experienced the other side when she refused to tap. She'd marveled at the two black curtains behind her eyes, drawing closed. It was happening to him now. The curtains were closing. He could no longer form the words he needed, to beg her to stop.

Breathe and squeeze.

Finally, he went heavy and limp. Still, she held tight and listened, but she could hear nothing except the pounding of her heart. No breath. When she felt certain the intruder was a member of the departed, she remained in position, eased her grips in case she was wrong and needed to return to the fight.

"Hey," she whispered and felt for a pulse. "Hey." She jostled her hips.

She listened again. No evidence of life.

Nothing.

She unhooked her left foot from behind her right knee.

He collapsed onto her, and she scurried out from under his dead body.

Suddenly, panic rushed her from scalp to her toes. The muscles in her legs quaked, and her hands trembled, and her thoughts went to war.

It was self-defense. Call the police.

Then what?

Trudy. Is Trudy awake? She can't find out someone broke in. She can't take any more. She'll never have peace.

Maxine crawled to the edge of the kitchen tile floor and toward the hallway, looking back at the dead body like it might be resurrected. She peered toward Trudy's room. The door was shut, and no light filtered below it. She worked herself upright. Her legs were on fire, and her feet heavy as bricks as she eased her way to the girl's room. She opened the door a few inches to check on her, to make sure she wasn't frozen in fear under the covers or hiding in the closet. Trudy was in her bed sleeping like she hadn't slept in months. Maxine closed the door without making a sound and returned to her problem on the kitchen floor.

Call the police.

The freezer. The garage freezer is empty.

Call the police.

The duffel bag lay on the floor just beyond his limp legs, next to the gun that had slipped from his waistband.

Still unconvinced he wouldn't spring back to life, she kicked at his feet. She stepped closer and kicked him in the ribs hard. *No way he could be faking it after that.* She crouched over him and felt his pockets. A knife. A wallet. An expired driver's license revealed the identity of her attacker. Peter McDaniel. The monster who raped Trudy.

Call the police. It's a no-brainer self-defense situation.

Deborah Dobbs

But the freezer is empty.

She looked at her chef knife set on the kitchen counter.

You've butchered animals before.

89

Colleen sat across from Maxine at the kitchen table, clutching a half-drained cup of coffee. Once again, she'd wanted to be there in person. She silently debated about whether it was wise to share any of details of the case that didn't directly involve Maxine and Trudy. Maxine seemed strangely peaceful yet not fully present, and her gaze hadn't left the table. Colleen genuinely liked the woman, was worried about her, and even though she'd been there for thirty minutes, she didn't want to leave. She made light, albeit forced, conversation.

"Did you decide to cater the dinner for the defense attorneys' association?"

Maxine nodded slowly and drew in an exceptionally long breath. "I wasn't sure what to make, but I think I've figured it out, so...yes." She paused and returned to the here and now. "Yes, I'm going to do it."

"What's on the menu?"

She fiddled with a place mat. "Something I've never done before."

She didn't elaborate, and Colleen didn't press for details. Instead, she said, "I wish I could've done more for you and Trudy."

Maxine looked up and spoke with that firm voice Colleen had grown to admire. "You were the only person who was there for us every time, any time we needed you. You listened to us. You believed Trudy. If you hadn't followed us into the parking lot that night we first met, who knows where we'd be now?"

Colleen closed her eyes, embarrassed by memories of the inept desk officer.

Maxine finished her thought. "You did what you could to put him where he belonged, behind bars, and to let the justice system do its job. Whatever that is."

"I've learned there's not much I can do." She looked around the kitchen, where she knew the horrific events had happened, just days earlier. She felt her face heat up, and her eyes stung.

Maxine replied through a clenched jaw. "I've learned an important lesson, too. You can be patient, follow the rules, bite your tongue, and trust the process, only to end up unheard and alone with a little girl who will never be the same. I guess that's why they call it the *criminal* justice system."

Colleen resisted the urge to suggest there was a silver lining. "She can recover, but you're right. She'll never be the same."

Maxine's tone lightened. "I got her set up with one of those counselors at that child advocacy place."

Finally, Colleen thought. "From what I hear, it's a great operation."

"And maybe she'll sleep better knowing he can't hurt her anymore." Maxine's shoulders softened, and Colleen detected a load of guilt bearing down on them.

"I wish they had called me that night. I wish I could've been here for you both."

"They were in detective mode, but they were pretty decent about it all. One of the cops was great with Trudy. He stayed with her the entire time, and I could tell she felt safe with him."

"She slept through it all?"

"That girl will sleep through a hailstorm, once she finally drifts off." Maxine laughed in disbelief. "Plus, I'd given her a sleep aid. Even so, I can't believe the sirens didn't wake her. She stirred just before the medical examiner got here. The cop kept her from seeing any of that mess." Maxine paused and looked hard into Colleen's eyes. "Do you think what I did was wrong?"

"I'm not a lawyer, but the guy broke into *your* home, had a firearm, attacked you, and said he would kill you. He had the means to do it, to kill you both right then and there. How could anyone think it wasn't self-defense?"

"I didn't mean legally. I meant morally. You know, he was still a kid."

Colleen folded her hands on the table. "I'm not sure if I'm supposed to tell you this, but I'm going to."

Maxine leaned forward. "It'll stay with me."

"Detectives talked to the perpetrator's mother. She believes Peter, her son, killed his father, her husband."

Maxine slumped back into her chair. "When?" she whispered.

"When he was only five years old."

Maxine's jaw dropped and her eyebrows shot up towards her hairline.

"On record, it was determined to be self-inflicted, like a weird accident or possible suicide, but she thinks the boy shot him."

She noticed the hairs on Maxine's arms come to life.

"She spent her life protecting her youngest son from her oldest."

Maxine looked horrified. "What a miserable way to live."

"There's more." Colleen paused to sip her coffee while she considered how much more to tell. "He's also suspected of murdering someone in Winston and committing other violent crimes there." She allowed the information to settle before continuing. "We suspect he had intentions to come after me, too."

Maxine looked confused.

"Someone jumped my fence. My dog ran him off, but not after ripping off one of his shoes, and his mom confirmed it was his size and said it looked familiar."

Colleen watched the severity and versatility of Peter's violence settle into Maxine's mind. It was the first time Colleen had witnessed her speechless. Colleen weighed her words carefully before continuing. She remembered the parents of the arsonist, the sorrow on their faces. And the man who killed the mother of the blue-eyed girls, how his dad regretted his very existence. She thought about her father and how death was the only end to his violence. She recalled how she felt when Steven, her own perpetrator, was killed. Shocked, yes, but relieved he couldn't hurt anyone else.

Colleen chose candor. "There are some people who have insatiable appetites for inflicting pain. They have no regard for life and no remorse for taking it. When they want to get from here to there, and you're in between, they're as likely to kill you as they are to ask you to move. I don't believe people like that can be rehabilitated, and no, I don't think you were morally wrong. I wholeheartedly believe that you've prevented a lot more suffering and saved lives by removing that parasite from the planet."

Maxine still looked diminished.

"He would've killed you, Maxine. You *and* Trudy. You survived, and you kept Trudy safe."

90

As Colleen drove away, Maxine gave a final wave goodbye and then returned inside. She heard the bell jingle on the back door, and her chest tightened, and blood rushed to her ears. "It's the cat." She reassured herself. "Just the cat."

Trudy emerged from her room, sleepy eyed. "What's wrong, Mom?"

"Nothing, baby. I just need some sleep."

"I feel like I could sleep for days." Trudy sounded like an old woman, and Maxine couldn't help but chuckle.

As she walked toward the back door, Maxine said, "We'll have a lazy weekend, okay?"

"Okay." Trudy shuffled into the kitchen, opened the pantry and grabbed a bag of chips.

Questioning Trudy's choice, Maxine checked the clock. One could argue it was time for brunch. "Put those in a bowl, missy."

"I will," she moaned.

"And get something with more substance in your belly, too." Maxine reached the back door and cracked it open. "Hey, cat. Where you been?"

The cat rubbed against her legs, and Maxine's mobile phone vibrated in her back pocket. She checked the display. It revealed a number she'd recited and remembered. *Kathleen McDaniel.*

"I'm going to take this on the patio, Trudy."

Trudy was busy piling as many chips as possible into the largest bowl she could find.

Maxine closed the door behind her and answered tentatively. "Hello."

All she could hear on the other end was soft crying.

"I'm sorry you're hurting," Maxine said.

"No." The word punched through the whimpers.

Then she heard two more words repeated like a mantra, whispered between faint cries.

What was she saying?

Wait you?

Hate you?

Maxine's heart sank. She closed her eyes and listened intently until the words sharpened. Suddenly, the woman's message was clear.

"Thank you."

91

December.

Colleen didn't believe for a second that the sugar and eggs would absorb the flour, no matter how much elbow grease she added. For the third time, she read the instructions on the back of the chocolate chips bag. *So much flour.*

Tomorrow she'd begin her new gig as Winston Police Department's Victim Assistance Program Director. The title was fancy, but the role wasn't much different from the one she'd held briefly at Alwin, except she'd work for a nonprofit instead of the municipal government. Sally Skinner had put in a good word for her, which probably landed her the position. Colleen planned to arrive with two batches of Christmas cookies, sugar and chocolate chip, neither of which she'd ever baked from scratch. She didn't bake, period. Until now, she'd always been a salivating spectator, an impatient taster. The holiday season and the excitement of the new job provided the motivation she needed to give it a try.

The smell of sugar and butter lured memories out of their hiding places. Licking chocolate cake batter from a wooden mixing spoon, the one with a charred spot from resting too long against a hot saucepan. Standing by her mother's side at the avocado kitchen counter. Mom wearing a winter snowman apron in July because it was the only one she had. Her first taste of raw cookie dough. Chocolate chip. Her father stomping into the house from God knows where, his sour stench slicing through the magnificent fragrance that had been drifting from the oven to her nose and into her entire being. *The man ruined everything.* Colleen remembered his demands that her mother "cook 'em to a crisp," and her mother pulling a couple out of the oven early while they were still soft and gooey like normal people preferred. The rest emerged twelve minutes later, blackened on the bottom, rock hard, and bitter, the sweetness having burned away.

According to her father, a minute less would give him "the salmonella." So fearful he was. She could see that now. Terrified of what his life would look like if he didn't wield complete control over everyone and everything, if he wasn't the puppet master. Her mother was fearful, as well, but her reasons were practical. She believed her husband when he said he'd kill her and leave Colleen motherless if she ever tried to leave, to reclaim her life and do better by her daughter. He'd proven he meant it.

There was no help for them back then. Sometimes the neighbors called the police when her father's rage reached a decibel every resident on the block could hear. The officers came, wrote things down, and abandoned them, left them alone with the ill-tempered man who needed to sleep it off. Sometimes Colleen's mother rushed her across the street, a place she mistook as safe, where another predator lived, only Steven was smarter. He preferred younger victims who were vulnerable and easily deceived. Colleen was the ideal offering.

She thought about her role now and what a difference a victim advocate might have made for them. Aunt Ruth had tried to lend a hand, but Colleen sensed her mother felt defeated and ashamed whenever she looked to her big sister for help. Perhaps a victim advocate might have been more encouraging. Someone who would offer hope, show her mother a path to freedom, and navigate her along the way. Someone who listened, who allowed her to be heard. If an advocate had entered their lives, would her mother be standing by her side now, sneaking a taste of cookie dough? Would she brush Colleen's wild curls away from her eyes and kiss her forehead?

Nothing could've prepared her for the work, how the cases would unlock the closets in her mind, poke at the dormant memories inside, and drag them out of hibernation and into the spotlight. Nothing readied her for how lonely life would become. At Alwin PD, she'd been an outsider, but she hadn't *wanted* more than one foot inside their circle. At the end of every day, she longed for solitude, even if loneliness came with it. When she was in graduate school, a professor once implored students to resist unhealthy coping strategies, like drinking. At the time, Colleen couldn't imagine finding comfort in a bottle. She wouldn't have believed that one day she'd turn to whiskey and wine to draw a curtain over the faces of anguish. To numb the feeling of helplessness. To silence the blue-eyed girl.

You lied to me.

A healthy person might pursue another line of work.

But Colleen was all in now. She'd found her calling.

THE END

From the Author

This story was inspired by several events and the people who either caused or were affected by them.

First on the list are the inept investigators in a small police department, who sat on an investigation instead of upholding their oath, and permitted a rapist to continue preying on victims. For *months* the investigators failed to act, despite having DNA evidence. Because of their inaction, the perpetrator not only raped but also murdered two more women.

The department's victim advocate resigned after the travesty. She spoke publicly about her grief over the mishandling of the case and the lives taken because of it.

Evidently, they didn't learn from their mistakes. Within a year, the same department failed to act against another violent young man accused of rape. Again, a suspect was allowed to terrorize people in North Central Texas, and his violence was prolific and versatile.

Fortunately, a nearby police department maintained higher standards. Thanks to the Intelligence Unit of the Plano Police Department, the psychopath was captured. Plano and surrounding communities owe great thanks to Lieutenant Doug Deaton (retired), Detectives Joe Claggett and Greg Ulmer.

Once detained, the offender showed no remorse and spoke coldly about his violence. Although he was convicted of many violent crimes and sent to prison, by 2025 he will be released to walk among us. He received a light sentence. He was an adult in the criminal justice system, but he was young, after all. A sympathetic judge threw out his confession because while fighting detectives, he'd bruised his wrist and complained about it during the interview. The judge decided the young psychopath had needed medical attention and, as a result, the jury would never hear the recording of him bragging about his crimes.

On one occasion, I crossed paths with the offender's mother. She was a single mom, and she seemed pleasant and kind, but so tired and weary. She had health issues and other kids to care for. She'd moved at least once because of her son's criminal activities. I felt badly for the woman, and I wondered what it was like to live with someone who was so violent and apathetic.

Another influence on the story came from a social encounter I had with the parents of twin boys (from the same town), who could check all the boxes of Robert Hare's Psychopathy Checklist. One was, as my dad used to say, "dumber than hammered owl shit." The other, however, was highly intelligent, and he knew how far he could go without legal trouble. He also was a star athlete, so school officials and coaches tolerated his harassment of other students. He made up for it on the scoreboard. His parents were in tears as they described the physical, emotional, and financial chaos their sons created in their lives. The twins seemed to delight in it.

While this story was *inspired* by real events, the characters (the humans, that is) are fictional, as are the crimes the fictional psychotic son committed.

Sam was real. He was my wonderful, loyal companion for thirteen years. Sicario the cat is real and utterly terrifying.

Acknowledgements

If you're like me, then you usually skip the acknowledgements section. I'm going to keep mine brief, with hopes of enticing you to read them because this novel didn't land in your hands without the help of many people.

My *thank yous* fall in chronological order:

To my mom, a voracious reader, who always encouraged me to pursue writing. She covertly read one of the first drafts of *The Psychotic Son* after I'd left it behind on her kitchen table. If she hadn't liked it, she never would have said a thing about it. But she *did* like it; She said, "I couldn't put it down," in addition to nasty things about the villain, which he deserved, and heartfelt compassion for Matthew (originally a female). Her enthusiasm for this project had so much value because she not only is an avid reader, but she has nearly three decades' experience as a victim advocate. Thank you, Mom, for always believing in me.

To Mr. Cotton, my Senior English teacher, for encouraging me to pursue writing. You fanned the flame in me to write.

To my husband Wayne, for being my champion long before we married, and for ensuring any police procedural or firearms content is accurate. This series started only because of you.

To all my beta readers, your support kept me from quitting. To my first beta reader Rebecca Fischer, your vigor, sticky notes, and scribble scrabble…all of it mattered. You boosted my morale.

To my dear friend Beka Almen, for serving as my informal editor. You catch consistency errors and typos like nobody's business. Thank you for returning again and again to my drafts!

To my daughter Faith, your love of the triangle choke created the perfect ending for the sack of evil in this story. Thank you for making sure I wrote it correctly.

To Jerry Todd, for bringing your *best-seller* cover art to my first novel!

To Dan Larsen, my first editor, who discouraged me from softening the story, even after my manuscript traumatized a literary agent. Your faith in *The Psychotic Son* helped me find it a home.

Thank you, Micah Campbell of Anatolian Press, for *not* being traumatized by my manuscript, for believing in indie authors, for helping us, who love the craft, get our work into the world, for giving us a chance, and for making this journey less lonely. Thank you for seeing the potential in *The Psychotic Son* and for working with me to strengthen the story when it would have been easier to turn me away.

To my fellow authors of Anatolian Press and *Autumn Tales*, I love our community. Thank you for your support.

To Mike Schlista's Facebook group "Psychological Thriller Readers," thanks to you, I've learned a lot about the psychological thriller market and my TBR list is outrageous. I both look forward to and fear your reviews of *The Psychotic Son*. I'll be holding my breath, without realizing it of course, anxiously awaiting your comments.

Thank you – *you*, still reading. Thank you for purchasing my debut novel. I hope you'll continue with me on this wild journey!

CHAPTER ONE

Officer Garrett Corcoran had to work New Year's Eve, and he didn't want to. Since the fuckers made him work, he'd formed an action plan: snag a DUI. New Year's Eve was amateur drunk night, and amateur drunks made terrible drivers, so he would find one fast and take his time making the arrest, impounding the car, and processing the drunk at the station. He could stretch one arrest over the entire shift.

It wasn't that Corcoran didn't love his job. Hell, he had the best job on the planet. He just didn't want to spend his night at work because he had too many questions about how his wife would be spending hers. Annette was uncharacteristically understanding when he'd announced he had to work on their second New Year's Eve together. Because she hadn't shown a hint of disappointment, an already wary Corcoran secretly continued trying to get his shift covered, with hopes of surprising his wife, although *ambushing* was a better word. He figured her reaction would either support the nagging suspicion she was having an affair or assuage his concerns.

Speculating or fantasizing would only drive him nuts. The turn of the new year would involve neither celebration nor answers, and Corcoran returned his focus to hunting drunks. In a marked squad car, he headed west on Main Street into an area with a couple of popular bars.

Winston, Texas had some good citizens, but it had some unruly and dysfunctional ones, as well. It suffered a high rate of suicide and domestic violence and an impressive amount of organized crime within its sizable Asian community. A number of Winston residents had insatiable appetites for meth and cocaine, so the drug trafficking business was good, too.

Driving westbound upon the first intersection near a redneck watering hole, Corcoran looked down the street and spotted a bunch of cars swerving and jerking around like they were trying to avoid something.

There's my drunk. I'll go sack him.

As he accelerated to get up there, he saw an average-sized female running eastbound through the traffic. The cars were swerving to avoid *her*, not a drunk driver.

Still a good block away, he could hear the woman screaming as she charged through traffic looking crazed with fear. He pegged this as a damsel-in-distress situation and liked the idea of ending his shift as a hero.

He grabbed the radio mic and checked out with Dispatch. "I got a female running in traffic."

He let Dispatch know he'd be on an 85, an investigative stop, and gave his location.

The woman continued sprinting down the middle of the street directly toward his vehicle. He stopped the car, put it in park, and turned on the overhead lights. Before he could step out of the vehicle, she was within a few feet, still running full speed, and then, like a wild-eyed cat, she leaped onto the hood of his car and scurried to the windshield. She slapped her left palm against the windshield and kept her right hand behind her back. With piercing hazel eyes, she glared at him through the glass.

"Easy, now!" Corcoran ordered. "Show me your hand."

"Gimme a ride! You got the power!"

This wasn't a damsel in distress. He pulled his pistol and oriented it on her through the windshield and demanded, "Show me your hand!"

She leaned in, with her eyes locked on Corcoran's, and pressed her grimy forehead against the glass, and chanted with an eerie detachment. "She's hungry. Gimme the gun. You got the power. Gimme a ride. Gimme the gun. You got the power. You got the power."

Holy shit!

He realized he was dealing with a nutcase. He updated Dispatch, using the department's radio code because he couldn't straight-up announce he was dealing with a nutcase.

He spoke evenly into the mic. "This is a Signal 10." Then he told them he needed assistance, and he needed it quickly. "Give me a cover unit, Code 3."

Corcoran returned the mic to its clip and secured his gun in its holster on his strong side, his left. Then he slid out of the car, leaving the door open, and stepped to the side of it, keeping his eyes on the woman. She moved along the hood to face him, like a predator fixed on her prey.

Corcoran firmly but calmly told her, "Get off my car."

His size had earned him the nickname *Monster*. His dimensions, accompanied by his deep voice, usually produced the desired results from a suspect.

His presence made no impact on this one. The woman swayed back and forth on the hood of his squad car, never breaking her stare. "Gimme a ride. Gimme a ride. You got the power."

"Oh me." He heard the horn of a passing car. From another, a male hollered something he couldn't make out. He could hear shrieking laughter coming from women across the street. The warm air encouraged all kinds of booger-eaters to come out, and they were getting rowdy.

He remembered he'd left his baton in his car. He gave a quick glance back at the car door, which was still wide open.

Mistake.

The woman pounced from the hood to the pavement and slipped between him and the door. The headlights of the passing vehicles melded with the flashing colors from his overheads, creating a confusing strobe light effect. As she tried to climb into the driver's side, he grabbed her shoulders from behind, thinking he could fling her away from the car with little effort, but she spun around and launched into a fury of kicking, screaming, hitting, and scratching. She had a terrifying amount of strength, and he knew he was in trouble.

He didn't want to hit her, and for about fifteen seconds, which feels like forever in a fight, she continued her frenzy of swiping and clawing his face and head, tearing at his uniform, kicking his thighs and shins, and she showed no sign of tiring. He tried to palm-thrust her in the chest, but she deflected his hand like a cat batting away a toy. She was getting the better of him, screaming all the while, and he was almost in a cover-up mode when suddenly she stopped. She just stopped. He heard her panting and thought she'd run out of gas, or maybe she was taking a break.

Oh no.

She wasn't gassed. She wasn't taking a break. She had a gun in her hand, and it was a gun he knew well, his Colt Government Model 1911 .45 ACP. She'd taken it from his holster, and he hadn't even felt it. He hadn't felt a thing. She pointed his firearm at him. Chest high, then face high, and she pressed the trigger.

Made in the USA
Las Vegas, NV
31 July 2024